According to pretty much everyone, Lavario sucks at being a werewolf. He'd rather go shopping than run around in the forest eating campers. Besides, he loves people. That's exactly what got him exiled from the Isangelous pack and will most likely get him killed.

Now dwelling amongst the Varcolac, a wolf pack that detests humans almost as much as he loves them, Lavario lives at the mercy of his daughter Kijo, who has continually refused to challenge him despite mounting pressure.

Together, they have enough power to stop the scheming Mazgan from seizing control of the bloodservant trade and killing off humanity. But Kijo's association with her father has eroded the good will of her packmates. They have begun to see his faults in her as well. They believe she, like her father, wants to coddle humanity rather than conquer them.

Mazgan seizes on this opportunity and plans one last embarrassment for Lavario: the abduction of his bloodservant Tovin. This will prove, once and for all, that Lavario thinks far too highly of his pets.

An explosive confrontation between Mazgan, Lavario, and Kijo looms. The outcome will decide the fate of humanity and the future of the Varcolac and Isangelous.

Published by
NineStar Press
PO Box 91792
Albuquerque, New Mexico, 87199
www.ninestarpress.com

Warning: This book contains sexually explicit content, which is only suitable for mature readers, violence, and death of children.

Print ISBN # 978-1-945952-67-8
Cover by Natasha Snow
Edited by Cora Walker

THE WORST WEREWOLF

The Immutable Moon, Book 1

Jacqueline Rohrbach

DEDICATION

To my husband. This book is what you get for saying, "Write whatever you want!"

ACKNOWLEDGMENTS

Mike Mattison, thank for your help and support. You suffered through the early drafts and helped me make a story out of a tragic mess. Anna Kaling, thank you for being an awesome beta reader. Your comments really helped me see the manuscript's weak spots! L.M. Langley, I might have gone nuts without your pep talks. Thanks!

Susan Pratt, Shaffer and Amy Claridge, Dan and Matt, and Michael Hanscom and Prairie Brown: thank you all for being awesome, supportive friends. Big shout out to Shaffer and Amy for letting me pay them in baked goods. Also, thanks for not calling me a total idiot when I needed my fingers for math-based games. You at least waited until I left.

Thank you, Mom and Dad. I know you thought I was crazy when I started this project.

Big thanks to NineStar Press for taking me on as an author. Very excited to work with you all, and I appreciate the opportunity to do so!

PROLOGUE: YOU'RE NOT THE BOSS OF ME, MOON

I enjoy eating people the most when the moon is in its crescent stage. Those strangled utterances, those blood-soaked-urine-stench denials where you turn to me and say, "But the moon isn't full." It's your fault. You're far too enamored of the mystical powers we give rock. Half, full, quarter. The cycles are only shadows.

I get it, though. You're attached to what you think we ought to be. The hopelessly cursed writhing about on the floor, clawing and heaving out of our skins until monsters bend and twist upward from the wreckage, howling before we zoom off to go kill what we love most in the world.

You were told so many things that it's going to be disappointing to hear about how awesome being a werewolf is. It's nearly impossible to kill me, I have a fabulous head of hair, and I never met a problem I couldn't eat. The transition from man to wolf is painless, like slipping on a much beloved sweater before running off to kill something.

Misconceptions abound.

We're not big skulkers in our everyday lives. We even go to conferences wearing T-shirts that say, "Blame Bigfoot." Sort of an inside joke. And I resent the notion I—or any of my kind—seek out promiscuous teenagers like some punitive abstinence-only education. Pure and simple, I'm an opportunist. Teenagers out in the woods alone and having sex are distracted, isolated, and vulnerable. Plus, you get two for the same amount of effort it would normally take to get one. All in all a low-risk, high-reward proposition.

You'll find most werewolves are similarly pragmatic feeders. What we are doesn't demand we eat virgins, evildoers, do-gooders, loved ones, or any particular classification of people. What we are doesn't even require that we kill. It simply requires that we feed.

That's not to say that we don't have limits. Most of us won't target children unless we're desperate. It's also not to say that we don't ever have motivations. Everything else takes a backseat to the necessity of it all. I might prefer to eat bad people, but I'll eat whatever is convenient when I'm hungry enough.

Here is where we prefer the version of events we sold to you. Hapless victims of moon and circumstance who slipped and fell on your throats only to wake the next morning with some dreading sense of *what have I done* are far more sympathetic than monsters who made the choice to kill.

* * *

I'm a Moondog.

The Isangelous and the Varcolac, the self-described trueborn werewolf packs, see the similarities between Moondogs and them as the trivial stretch of space where dirt touches sky. Technically, it's there. That's all there is to say about it.

My kind will never be authentic werewolves like margarine will never be real butter. We've got the magic, we've got the hair, we've got the teeth. Somehow, though, we don't have enough of it for our trueborn kin, who catch us and cull us the same way humans thin out unwieldy deer populations. And for the same reason.

Food is limited. Moondogs hunt, we kill, we eat. Usually.

Our reasons are as varied as we are. Scattered, often nomadic, my kind are a breed stuck in the miscellaneous folder. One pack might kill because it makes good, practical sense. Another because they enjoy it. There are even a few packs who keep their humans around as pets the way the trueborn do. Bloodservants they call them.

My pack calls the bloodservant system slavery. Freedom is important to us, even yours to a certain extent. Killing you rather than enslaving you is a courtesy. Eating you is practical. Bodies talk, and not all of us want to be storytellers.

* * *

Telling someone you're a werewolf is pretty much a commitment to eat him later. Many of us confess anyway, mostly newcomers and sadists. No matter the reason, no matter how innocuous or vile the intent, those conversations have a certain trajectory to them.

My therapist thinks the werewolf is something I created, my way of dealing with a trauma he's going to uncover after enough tell-me-about-your-mother sessions. Eventually I'm going to eat him. People have a difficult time accepting the randomness of it. One day you're a court-appointed therapist so sure that the person sitting across from you is confused, possibly insane. Then, your car breaks down on an isolated road, and the poor, deluded man you've been helping along appears with some very bad news. His monster is quite literal.

And that's the truth of it. There is no karma, no overarching system of justice. My street address is at the intersection of time and opportunity. If you and I are there, and I'm hungry... I'll eat you. Because that's what predators do.

* * *

Don't stab me with your silverware. It won't hurt me. I'm still going to kill you. Now it's going to be painful.

* * *

Vampires exist. They're not the suave, sophisticated monsters of lore people love to hate and desire. Created to destroy humanity, they are a biological weapon manufactured with one mandate—feed. One can become hundreds in days. Millions after. The disease they carry takes the rest.

Wolves had a natural immunity. Surviving victims of the undead found themselves subject to a magical experiment of merging beast DNA with human. An oopsy daisy with the same blood hunger was born.

I've eaten so many nerds who could not accept it, who could not let go of their precious, precious lore. It's worse than the moon thing. Honestly, I seek them out in bookstores. I linger by the comic book section, knowing one always comes along at some point.

"Oh," my know-it-all nerd will say, "I don't like that one because the werewolves are not realistic."

"Absolutely," I'll say back, and before I know it, we're talking about it over coffee. He's ripping apart the absurdity of comic-book werewolves while I'm memorizing the scent so I can rip him apart later. At some point I'll ask, "What about werewolves who drink blood?"

Those delicious little geeks and dweebs can't help but argue. "That's vampires!" If I persist—and I often do—most leave, huffily looking over their shoulders as if to tell everyone else in proximity, *The nerve of this guy.* Telling them I don't have to eat them is a must in the final seconds. I *could* just drink their blood, leaving them dizzy, confused, and unharmed. But they insisted a werewolf who does this could not exist. Who am I to argue?

* * *

Tovin didn't remember this when I asked him about it, but that's how I first met him. There he was...this green-eye, shy-smile masterpiece I was going to make a Happy Meal—fuck, and then eat. There I was at the table saying to the universe, "The usual, please." Then, somewhere in the middle of the routine, he became unusual and said, "It could happen. Why not? Maybe they have a salt deficiency."

It was so adorably specific.

* * *

This started out as a love letter if you can believe it. Anyone will tell you I'm prone to this sort of thing—off track, side-tracked, drifting along until finally arriving back at the same point, only to get off track again. Somewhere in the middle of writing my letter, it occurred to me that it wasn't who I am. Despite all those times I placed my nose against his head to sniffle up his familiar dander, I ended right back at the beginning, as a werewolf who likes to kill people in those small moments when they think they're safe.

I didn't eat him, if you're worried about that. Those normal things that would have tipped me over the edge—snoring, farting, arguing, moralizing—somehow became endearing with Tovin. Small changes, more like accommodations, came over me until I big-spooned him like a chump. Now that he's gone, I look back on our love like I look at peanut butter and banana sandwiches. It was moment where the universe bent its will and allowed something to be awesome despite everything working against it. *Yeah,* it said, *I'm going to let this just be.*

Of course, it couldn't last. I could go on for days listing people I ate and then told him I didn't. Before you think too poorly of me, keep in mind that the lies I told were no more egregious than the questions he didn't ask. Really, though, I want whomever you might be to find my green-eyed, shy-smile exception so you can tell him what I can't.

Tell him the moon is full.

PART ONE

THE BLOODSERVANT

CHAPTER ONE: LIVE ACTION ROLE PLAY

The speech began with a "Did you know that?" and expanded like the infinite universe. Garvey felt the collective agitation of the people around him who were waylaid by the speaker. Their polite recognition of the man's existence somehow turned into a half-hour explanation of medieval shoe making. *Don't worry,* Garvey wanted to tell the captive audience, *I'm going to kill him for you.* Well, more for himself. But they would benefit in the long run.

"Are you stalking someone?" Mazgan towered above Garvey because he was too good to sit on cheap lawn furniture. He twisted his head in the general direction Garvey was looking. He wouldn't see anything too obvious. Colt—the great shoe orator—was way off in the distance.

Garvey hesitated. "Well—"

"Stop. I need you focused."

Focused for what? All Mazgan ever did was talk. Besides, as a modern werewolf, Garvey knew how to multitask. He could hunt and listen at the same time. The uppity, self-aggrandizing Alpha Guardian from the Varcolac pack would nag until Garvey was servile and attentive. He put on his best show of being meek and said, "Yes, Alpha Guardian." The title fumbled out of his mouth. Moondogs like Garvey didn't buy into honorifics. Saying them now tasted like treason.

"As you know..." Mazgan began the usual speech, a protracted, theatrical time sink Garvey had heard at least a hundred times by now. Blah, blah, blah. Go to the door between worlds and get vampires.

The Door wasn't very impressive. Always far more practical than whimsical, wolves were not much for show. It was exactly as advertised. A large motherfucking door. The frame of it was dragon bone—cut clean, symmetrical like any other frame. But the actual doorway hid in a casing of wood. Despite its drab appearance, it had a power almost anyone could feel. Garvey wanted to experience it again.

At first, the plan felt like a grand adventure that was most definitely going to happen. Mazgan even had him go on a practice run. Then disappointments began to heap up afterward—one on top of the other— as the alpha delayed. *Perfect moment,* he kept saying, *we must wait.*

There were only moments in Garvey's mind. And they were what one made of them.

Dwelling on such things wouldn't feed him. Either Mazgan would eventually get around to sending him after the vampires or he wouldn't. Afterward, they'd either use the vampires to kill humans or not. Until then, listening to the scheme was more drudgery than thrill. Garvey let his senses drift back out to the crowd, back to the hunt, when he was sure Mazgan was too caught up in the I'm-so-great moment of his speech to notice.

Humans were everywhere. They hobbled along in their makeshift period costumes. Even the fake vampires and werewolves in attendance were trapped in a time where lords, ladies, and peasants all inhabited the same space, ate meat on a stick, and mangled Old English.

Mazgan was miserable around them. Getting him to see the utility of the venue was a long, violent process. There were lingering marks across Garvey's back where the Alpha Guardian's claws tore into his flesh. But here they were. As Garvey watched a green-faced woman whack away at something on the ground with a foam club, he couldn't help but feel that all the pain had been worth it. Live action role-playing—or LARPing as the humans called it—was hilarious.

"Can you get access to one of the portals to the Door?"

The last bit made Garvey snap to attention. Once Mazgan started his speech, he rarely asked questions. For once, maybe they *were* going to do something. "Yes, I can." Mazgan raised an eyebrow higher and higher until Garvey addressed him properly. "Yes, I can, Alpha Guardian. There's one in the Boo Hag library."

"You mean the Isangelous." Mazgan raised his eyebrow at Garvey's use of the common pejorative for the Isangelous pack. Such insults were off limits to wolves of Garvey's status. Happily, Mazgan moved on without a violent reminder. "They'll let you in there? You are certain of this?"

Garvey nodded. Mazgan couldn't make him tag on an honorific title to a head gesture. The other wolf gave him a narrow-eyed, skeptical look. A natural-born screw-up and a Moondog, a pack of other screw-ups, castoffs, and exiles, Garvey understood he wasn't exactly known for his efficacy. A guarantee from him wouldn't mean much. Time to change topics. "When do you want me to go?"

"Soon." The dismissive tone didn't do much for Garvey's hopes. "You are going to get Lavario's bloodservant next week?"

Garvey repressed a sigh. "Yes, Alpha Guardian. Next week."

"That needs to go poorly."

"How poorly, Alpha Guardian? Like, kill the guy?" Garvey did not want to do that. There was no reason for it as far as he could tell. Plus, the guy was smoking hot. Garvey planned on having himself a taste of that. This would be impossible if Tovin, the bloodservant, were to die. Or if he got rejected at distribution, which was pretty much the same thing.

Eyes narrowed, nostrils flared. After a long pause, Mazgan smoothed down his hair, already slicked back with a heavy oily product, and snapped his teeth shut like a bear trap. "Do as you are told."

The welts on Garvey's back itched. He looked to his left, then right. There were so many people around he doubted Mazgan would try anything. "Kill him, Alpha Guardian?" Garvey asked again. He'd pay for it. But that was later.

"It can go that far, but does not need to." Mazgan finally said after a long, seethe-filled pause.

Garvey thought about it right up until he saw a vein pop. "Damaged goods it is, Alpha Guardian."

"Excellent." Mazgan clapped his hands together. "And Garvey."

"What?" The Mazgan paused again. Seriously. "What, Alpha Guardian?"

"Make sure everyone knows it was you who caused all the fuss."

Garvey chuckled. "I promise the boy will have my scent all over him."

* * *

White plastic tables occupied by hucksters selling a variety of nonsensical goods—enchantments, cures to enchantments, and various pin-on ears—outlined the field area where the gathering took place. A human female with a red and yellow glittery star taped to her forehead breezed past and shouted, "Flameball!" A male fell the ground where he convulsed and screamed until an ally, some whelp wearing a makeshift cape, shouted, "Extinguish!"

Occasionally, it occurred to Garvey that he looked ridiculous. It hit home now as he adjusted his fake werewolf ears, these grotesquely long and pointed things made of plastic and sadness. But he'd made himself a promise to feed on Colt. Few other werewolves were so dedicated to a particular outcome—unlucky humans bumbling their way into hungry mouths were plentiful enough that it wasn't necessary to latch on to one. But stalking his food enriched his life. Garvey learned to ski, fish, knit, paint, and dance all during the chase. LARPing was the latest on the list.

"Garvey. *Garvey.*" Contingency A, some human he might kill instead of Colt, poked him in the side to get his attention. The two other sour humans in the group had given up trying to engage him a long time ago and just sat there trading cards with each other.

"Yes?"

"What about your princess?"

He had a princess? He'd told so many lies he couldn't remember. "She died."

"By the Light!" Contingency A made the sign of a cross against his chest, saying a small prayer for the made-up woman. The young man role-played an undead priest of some sort, which meant he was always giving blessings, saying ancient rites, and then running off to do something for the light as part of a redemption quest to regain his mortality. "Are you going to turn her?"

"Can't. She's dead."

"Are you going to avenge her death?"

"Nah."

"Well. Okay." The agreeable fellow didn't say anything else after that.

As far as Garvey was concerned, Contingency A's circle was nothing more than a depressing talkative shrub—behind which he hid—covered in velveteen, faux leather, and long, baggy shirts tied at the waist to simulate tunics. Shrubs with what had to be the most soul-crushing fantasies he'd ever heard. One battled to regain mortality, another searched for the vampire who had killed a first cousin of all things, and then just some poor idiot who got bitten by a werewolf and spent the rest of his time searching for a cure.

Garvey's team was the bottom of the barrel. Colt was at another table with the cool kids, who had real metal swords, real leather accessories, leggings, and tunics. Real tasty. They were knights, wizards, and mighty orcs. Garvey watched Colt with growing hunger. It had been far too long since he fed. The processed food smell coming from of the lawn furniture was appetizing at this point.

"Can I borrow a dollar fifty?"

Contingency A gave him a you-must-be-joking look. "What for?"

"The vending machine. I want some Cheetos."

"No way."

Cheap prick.

Colt was still talking. From where he sat, Garvey could barely make out the man's wagging jaw. He could hear and smell him perfectly, which didn't exactly feel like a perk of werewolf membership at the moment.

Soon, hopefully, Colt's little group would go out to play out a magic battle. Pew pew. Magic missiles and such.

When the troupe finally left, it took what little bit of self-control Garvey had left not to follow them immediately. Five minutes. Ten minutes. Fifteen. Thirty. That was probably good enough. "Excuse me for a moment, boys. Nature calls."

The trail wasn't difficult to pick up. By now Garvey knew Colt's scent as well as he knew his own. And his habits. After about an hour of LARPing, the group said their good-byes—long bouts of *verilys*, *doths*, and *fare thee wells* that Garvey gritted his teeth through—and Colt went to smoke.

To hunt was to wait, albeit with impatience and concern as Colt's cigarette got shorter. Time constricted with each huff, puff, wheeze. There were too many people around to make a move—mostly young men and women relieving themselves, or farting now that they thought they were alone. There were a few, off in the distance, fucking. One human peed on the bush right next to him. The man was far too drunk and caught up in a song to notice. Sharp, flat, and then off-key. Garbled and slurred to the point where all the words just melded together, the song was barely recognizable as such.

Maestro finally moved on. Garvey and Colt were alone at last. "I hear you're the man to talk to about medieval shoemaking," Garvey asked him.

Colt did an excessive amount of double takes before hastily putting out his cigarette on the tree trunk. "Sorry. What? Who's there?"

"Just me." Garvey stepped out from the shadows and gave him a little wave. The man visibility relaxed when he saw Garvey. Dress for the job you want, as the old saying went. Outer appearances were calculated to send the signal that everything was fine, just fine. To humans, he was a man in his midtwenties with brown eyes; strong features; dark, shoulder-length wavy hair; and a lopsided grin where one tooth poked out playfully. He looked affable, even somewhat dopey, and wholly harmless. "Hi, there."

"Yes, greetings." Nonthreat established Colt immediately went to putting on airs. "I am the man you seek. I am the top expert on medieval footwear." Garvey nodded with encouragement, as if he believed that was a thing. "Mark Birch, Joseph Colvin, and Annabela Veneto all come to me for my advice."

Garvey could only imagine the legions of people who wanted to know how shoes were made. "Well, fantastic then. I'd hate to ask for information from someone those people didn't chat with. Tell me all about it. My character is a shoe guy."

"A cobbler." Colt corrected him. "No wonder you hang out with James. You don't even know the proper names."

James was probably Contingency A—good to know. "I thought cobblers only repaired shoes?"

"A common misconception. Did you know that..."

Here it was. Colt would be good and distracted for a while, leaving Garvey to give the area one final scan. There were a few couples off in the distance going at it. Garvey could hear their moans, some fake and some real. It seemed like they'd be caught up for a bit at least.

It was important not to give someone time to react. Abracadabra-ing the prey to sleep was usually the safest bet, which was why most wolves who hunted preferred this method. Spineless amateurs in Garvey's view. Much like having an affair, the thrill of the hunt was bound up in the risk of getting caught. Also similar to an affair, the thought of getting caught was generally more appealing than the reality of it. Caution was necessary. Garvey waited until the man closed his eyes, took in his last deep breath before he began what he probably thought would be a masterful lecture. "Did you know that..."

He swept the man's leg, Cobra Dojo style. As Colt went down, Garvey added his own body's weight to ensure that hitting the rock below would, at the very least, render him unconscious. Bam. Dead. No fuss, no muss. Features that were already cramped closed together whirlpooled toward the center, awash in blood, gore, and dirt.

Technically, he only needed the blood. Garvey drank as quickly as he could until the clawing hunger receded. The moon *was* the easiest way to track the cycle. Humans got that partly right at least. Not much else.

Garvey looted the man's body for murder swag. Only five dollars? Colt was lamer than he thought. Garvey pocketed it and then fished his backpack from the tree above. It had been sitting there for months now—a change of clothes, some sanitary wipes, and he was good to go.

Cheery after feeding, Garvey made his way back to his own little LARPing group with a spring in his step and a dead man's blood in his heart. He'd probably have to endure a few more weeks of dress-up princess rescue in order to avoid suspicions, which made him a little less jubilant, but eventually, they'd all go their own ways naturally.

Today was a good day, a productive day. He'd done some sinister plotting and taken care of his monthly feeding.

One more stop. Two dollars for a bag of Cheetos? Unbelievable.

CHAPTER TWO: WORRISOME GLOATING

Mazgan gave Kijo a succinct ultimatum: decide if she wanted to rip Lavario apart or if she wanted to be ripped apart alongside him. Mazgan was done protecting her from challenges. He was through making excuses. Her unwillingness to side against Lavario with the rest of the Varcolac pack was unforgivable. Indifference was complicity. Complicity was guilt. Soon, the guilty would be punished.

Mazgan's chest puffed up but he softened his voice a bit after the tirade. "I know he became your father when he made you wolf, but there was a reason for his exile from the Isangelous pack. I tried to make him welcome here amongst the Varcolac, but he refuses to abandon his Boo Hag ways."

Boo Hag was a pejorative term the other packs used for Isangelous wolves, given because they waited until nighttime to feed, creeping in like the beasts of lore to siphon blood while humans slept. Calling Lavario by that name pegged him as weak, sentimental, privileged. Amongst the Varcolac, strength was an end in and of itself. They sparred for rank, for possession, for sport. Boo Hags fought for nothing. Their leaders were born. Their possessions given. Their altercations mere tussles, done more for fun than any practical purpose.

Mazgan stressed the point. "Your father stands in the way of our progress. He is caught up in the old ways of the Isangelous. He's tried to teach you the same."

"Yes, he is very old-fashioned, Alpha Guardian," Kijo agreed. As her maker, Lavario had tried to pass down his legacy. He'd also made it clear Kijo was Varcolac. Because of him, she'd never be Isangelous.

Her anger simmered. Perhaps her father had once been a guardian of another pack, but his power was undeniable. He belonged here. The fact he'd risen to the rank of second by defeating all other wolves in single combat proved it.

Mazgan reached out to touch the side of her face. "I know it hurts you to hear such things about your father. You must understand I'm only here to protect you."

"Of course, Alpha Guardian," she responded with as much gratitude as she could muster. It might have been a bit too dry if the sudden twist of his lips was anything to go by. Rather than deal with an argument over proper decorum, Kijo rushed to placate her alpha's bruised ego. "Such is your duty as my superior."

Eyes brimming with overwrought sweetness, he grabbed her upper arm and pulled her toward him. Possessively, he bound her in his embrace. "My beloved one. All I've ever wanted was to have you with me."

Mazgan wore a ceremonial sword, a blunted decorative token with no use other than to dangle at his side. She felt certain he'd like her to do the same. Kijo kept her face expressionless, her tone neutral. "Yes, I know, Alpha Guardian."

"Then you must know how much it breaks my heart to tell you this. But if you won't submit, you'll be destroyed alongside Lavario."

"Naturally."

"It does not have to be that way." One of his massive, clumsy hands brushed a loose strand of hair back from her face. "You will see how weak he is before too long. Remember, my beloved, your association with him is tangled in the minds of your brothers and sisters. They need you to choose the pack. You *must*."

"Understood, Alpha Guardian."

Pleased, he stepped back. "Good. Your father's new servant..."

The suspense. Kijo did her best to mask her impatience with the way he tried to protract the moment. She flipped her hand up in the air, suggesting he should get on with it. "What about him, Alpha Guardian?"

Suddenly, he turned serious. His teeth protruded. "I have arranged an accident for him. It will be the perfect opportunity for you to distance yourself from Lavario. It will be the last one I give you."

* * *

"I watered your plants." Kijo told her father the same lie whenever she entered his chamber. He gave her the chore to help her see beauty in the world. She failed to do it because she was Varcolac, above such things.

Although he knew she lied, he did his steps in their dance. "Excellent, did you enjoy the roses? The lovely orchids?"

"No," she said simply.

He gave her an appreciative chuckle. He loved how she got right to the point.

Normally, this was her favorite part of the day. She'd sit on the chair beside Lavario's and they'd discuss politics. Though her father gave up on trying to influence the pack directly, he loaned her his sharp mind whenever she needed it. Today, he needed hers as well.

"Mazgan told me I have to choose. You or the pack. Challenges are coming."

Lavario didn't seem particularly worried. "Nonsense," he said. "Have they decided to attack me all at once? Or at least five of them at one time?"

Ritual surrounding challenges mandated one-on-one combat, a tradition her father thought helpfully stupid. "No. Challenges are the same as they've always been. Single combat."

"Well, then. My shows are on."

He settled back down in his chair. The television screen in front of him flashed with images. Engrossed by the human drama, her father leaned back and propped his feet up on a cushion.

Lavario didn't just enjoy a Boo Hag lifestyle; he flaunted it. His expensive clothes, his lavish apartment, his human pets, his plants. All of it proudly on display. Worse, he'd used pack rules to obtain it all, twisting their might-makes-right mentality to his own desires as though he didn't have a care in the world. Mostly, he didn't. Ancient, he'd lived through a long line of challengers—dogs barking at his door as he called them.

Kijo knew she was not like the rest. She stood in front of the TV to get his attention. "This is different, Father."

He gave her a dismissive hand wave similar to the one she'd given Mazgan. *Bored but listening*, it said.

"He wants *me* to challenge you. He said he was going to humiliate me through you, something to do with your bloodservant and that would be my last chance to side against you."

"And if you don't challenge me, what does he have?" Her father snorted. "That blunt sword he lugs around with him?"

"My family. He'll take them from me."

Finally, her father stopped his show. To him, the pack meant very little. He'd come to it as an exile from the Isangelous and lived here as an outsider. No matter what he did, they hated him. Wherever he went, they turned their backs. However much he advocated for their interests, they treated him with measured disdain. He would never be one of them. But she was. And she loved them.

"I will call Yuri about Tovin."

"Forget the human. You do not even know him. Most likely he's stupid, dull as all your other pets have been."

"His features spare him from the necessity of being interesting."

Kijo gritted her teeth, irritated for having to repeat common sense. Had her father been a lesser wolf, she would have walked away. "Forget the boy, Father."

Lavario dialed numbers on his phone. "I will talk with Yuri. I am sure she would not plot against me with Mazgan, him of all wolves. Try not to worry, my daughter."

Frustrated, Kijo left. Lavario would do what he wanted. Part of her admired the Varcolac fearlessness, the measured confidence that allowed him to believe no one could stop him from getting whatever he wanted. Uneasiness within her fretted it was arrogance, stubbornness. As Mazgan said, Lavario was stuck in his ways.

Kijo went to her father's garden, noting with a wry twist of her lip how well maintained the area was. Perhaps it should have bothered her. Instead, Kijo momentarily ached for her childhood, for tiny hands her father once placed a simple daisy into. It felt so wondrously delicate then, its petals smooth. Her adult eyes saw things much differently. Tiny, delicate blossoms sunbathed. Fragrances she couldn't identify crawled up her nose. There was a pointless sweetness to all of it. She left with the same mentality she had before going there. She had no more use for flowers.

CHAPTER THREE: MOONDOGS

No streetlights. Narrow roads. Cramped buildings. In the dusk light, the shadows of the apartment buildings pointed like helpful fingers to the secret nooks and crannies where a predator like him might hide. Garvey took note. "This neighborhood would be a good place to hunt," he concluded.

Phil, the alpha of Garvey's Moondog pack, nodded briefly and continued to fidget in the passenger seat of Garvey's truck. Nervous as always, the chronic worrier checked and double-checked around for some sign they were being watched. Eventually, he got around to asking, "Why am I here?"

Garvey dodged the question. Instead, he bragged, "Stole Yuri's phone."

He held it up to show Phil. Outdated, it was a blue flipper that could only receive calls and voice messages. Judging by her call history, she wasn't going to miss it anytime soon—three in the last week, all of them from Lavario. Geesh. He pressed the speaker button so they could both listen to the exiled guardian's laconic requests for Yuri to get in touch. The last one was a simple command, "Call." And then silence.

"Ah, darling Kijo told daddy," Garvey laughed. "Poor heartbroken Mazgan."

Phil's features looked buggish and swattable. Whenever he was in a panic, which he was now, his tick eyes, mantis nose, and slug mouth jittered around enough to remind Garvey of what it was like to lift up a rock and watch whatever was under scamper for cover. Good guy, though.

"Shit, you stole the phone of an Isangelous wolf? Were you followed?"

"Does Kijo in the black sedan behind us count as followed?"

Phil jumped in his seat, hitting his head on the roof of the car.

"Ha!" Garvey laughed at him a bit before sobering. They were False Moons in the eyes of the two great packs, no better than talking dogs. No true wolf would follow them. "No one cares what we do, Phil. Relax, you don't even know why you're here."

Unamused, Phil rubbed his bald spot hard enough to summon a genie. "With you, secrets are *never* a good thing."

Fair point.

What Garvey needed to say couldn't be sprung on someone. For a polite amount of time, he made small talk. Family first. Nieces, nephews, extended family who would hopefully die before too long. Pack politics went on for a bit until some guy in orange biker shorts slung a used condom on the hood of the car. Then they talked about the rough neighborhood. The two of them chatted and grinned a good hour before Garvey thought he'd done enough.

Time to pull the Band-Aid off this mess.

"Mazgan wants me to bring back vampires. He's going to use them to kill off free-range humans and take over the distribution of bloodservants. First, he wants me to get rid of Lavario. I assume it's related."

Phil looked like a child who'd been thrown into the deep end straight from the kiddie pool. Garvey clicked the door-lock button so he couldn't skedaddle. The man floundered for a bit. Once he tried the doors, his head whipped around like an owl addicted to meth. Seeing no escape, he blurted, "Vampires are extinct!"

That was the current story. Manufactured by powerful magic to kill humanity, vampires were no more than a pestilence designed to hunger, feed, and destroy. Werewolves were created to combat the threat but ended up being a different version of the same problem.

"Nope," Garvey assured him. "They're alive, smelly, and gross."

"Thanks for letting me know! Any other bad news, asshole?"

"Yes, actually. I've been stalking Lavario's bloodservant this entire time." He pointed at the blond-haired man helping an elderly woman with her groceries.

"What the actual fuck, Garvey?" Phil tried the door again.

"I know, right? Look at the little do-gooder out there doing good. What a sweet little treat. Now he's holding a kitten. Where did he get a kitten? This shit is brutal." Garvey tossed his hands up in the air, slamming them back on the wheel for emphasis. "Too bad I'm probably going to kill him."

Phil stared forward as though counting the number of days he had to live. "Is he...is that the guy you're going to extract tonight?" Garvey confirmed. Phil stammered out another reply. "And you're going to kill him? That's bad, Garvey. Why—"

"Because it's part of whatever stupid scheme Maz—"

"No, *why* are you telling me all of this?"

Garvey took a deep breath. "Because I'm doing this, Phil. With or without your permission, I'm getting the vampires, and I'm probably going to get this guy killed. The true wolves are going to cull from our pack next round. I saw the spreadsheet. Our time is due."

Experts on werewolves, exactly the type of people Garvey liked to eat, would have been shocked to hear him talk that way to his alpha. But Moondogs were an independent breed. They saw the true wolves' frills of ritual and supplication as a colossal bummer. Like, one day they all got bored of being awesome, powerful monsters and said *how can we make this totally suck*?

Respectfully enough for a Moondog, Garvey prodded his leader for a response. "Well?"

"Oh." Phil replied. He was pale. "They'll find out it was you, Garvey. You know they will."

"Yeah...but if the two of them are warring..."

"Right. But, uh. We need people to live. Food source and all."

Best he could, Garvey communicated that being chased down and executed also hurt survival odds. The true wolf packs' idea of population control was quite severe. "I don't intend to kill *all* people. Just enough to make waves."

Garvey's alpha blinked a few times, processing it all. Although he didn't look like much—a balding man with the world's most unfortunate features heaped on his face—he was a calculating wolf, a schemer. Perhaps Phil was only in charge because he had a computer and could run a business for a front, but his opinion mattered.

He eventually concluded. "Why not? If they're going to kill us all anyway."

Garvey was more relieved than he would ever admit. "Glad we're on the same page."

The two of them sat there for a bit. Sirens blared. A mother called her child a food-gobbling piss pot. The father agreed. Others argued over turf—tapping their chests and posturing the way people imagined werewolves did. There were drugs. There were fights. There were cars going way too fast for a residential area. Off to the side, but somehow at the center of it all in Garvey's vision, the blond-haired guy sat on the front steps reading, only pausing when one of the nearby kids showed him something brown and lumpy. Probably a rock. Garvey felt himself frown at the child's outstretched hand as his mark's lips lifted in a smile.

Soon, the guy checked his watch and went inside.

Date night. "Time for me to make a love connection. How do I look?"

"Like a total asshole."

"Perfect."

Chapter Four: Time For A Change

Pep talk time.

This was the start of a new Tovin, as someone who did things. Risks would be taken. Gone were the days of watching from the sidelines as other people did things that the universe never punished them for. He would not hold other people's belongings while they went on the ride of life. He would not hold their hair back while they puked. He would try some sushi from the food truck. Okay, too far. He would try sushi.

Most important, he'd show Miller—his on-and-off-again boyfriend who was getting married to some lady—that he wasn't the world's dullest idiot. He wasn't an idiot at all. *Fuck Miller.*

There were a series of musical taps at the door. Tovin reminded himself not to run and answer it with doglike eagerness, as his ex had called it.

One last look at his reflection. He leaned in close, lifting his lips to make sure he didn't have anything as embarrassing as a piece of broccoli stuck between his teeth. Nope. Good. The collar of his button-up shirt was straight; his tie looked formal but playful in a loose half-Windsor; all the wrinkles from his pants and shirt had been pressed. Everything checked out.

Tovin opened the door and said, "Hi!" to the tall man on the other side of it.

"Hello. Hi!" His date matched his energy with some humor.

Despite all the catfishing tales Tovin heard about online dating, his suitor looked exactly like his profile picture: well-muscled; teasing brown eyes; long chestnut hair; and strong features. Unlike most men who lived in rural Washington, he had an air of sophistication intermixed with good humor that Tovin found very appealing. Hopefully, he wasn't some kind of psycho. "It's nice to meet you at last, Mr. Garvey."

"Just Garvey. Now I can wink at you IRL."

Tovin gave him a confused look.

"In real life."

"Oh! Of course."

There was a bloated silence Tovin wasn't sure how to fill. As it expanded, Garvey's lip twitched upward. "This is when you invite me inside and offer me a drink."

"Oh. Right." Tovin stood aside to let him enter. Garvey immediately flopped down on the couch, which buckled and squeaked, and gave the type of easy attractive smile Tovin practiced a billion times before the man arrived. Self-consciously, Tovin lugged his own lips upward in what he hoped counted as a close-enough response. "Do you want orange juice, milk, or water?"

"Water." Although the man seemed befuddled by his list of options, he said thanks politely enough as Tovin poured. He swirled the cup around afterward, looking at the floaters. A filter was on Tovin's to-buy list. "What's the plan for tonight?"

"Bar trivia. I thought we'd go down to the Oak on Third."

"What about parasailing?" Garvey lifted up one of the brochures on Tovin's coffee table. "That looks like fun."

Tovin flushed. He'd forgotten it was even there. "I've thought about going, but that's in Seattle."

"And spelunking." Garvey held up another pamphlet as he continued to inspect all of Tovin's stuff. There were various advertisements strewn about the table to sift through, all of them offering some form of adventure at minimal risk. "You don't seem the type. You break up or something? Gonna show the fellow what a good time you are?"

Tovin bristled a bit at the tone, the accuracy of the assessment, and the long look his date gave him. He knew he wasn't some muscle-bound strongman, but he was fit, lean, somewhat muscular. Surely that qualified him to jump down into a hole—less athletic people than him did it. "I work out. Besides, there is a rope." Maybe. Tovin looked at the picture again to be certain.

Garvey gave him a hopping chuckle that tested the frame of Tovin's couch. "Yes, there is a rope, sweet treat."

"At any rate, all of that is somewhere other than here. This town has bar trivia or cow tipping."

"I could think of another option." Garvey tapped the cushion next to him. When Tovin didn't respond, Garvey jumped to his feet with spry vigor. "Well, bar trivia it is, then."

* * *

There were two women in the bar. One of them looked virginal enough to sacrifice to a kraken in her white dress covered in tiny, pink flowers, while the other looked like she was about to Hulk right through the flimsy fabric of her dress. Tovin appreciated their beauty.

Tuft boys—Tovin called them this due to their ragged, patchy facial hair—gathered around hopeful that one of the strange women would pay them some attention. Simultaneously annoyed and grateful, Tovin was unhappy the two ladies were so close score-wise in bar trivia but pleased they'd be the subject of water-cooler conversations instead of him and his date. *Hey,* they'd say, *did you see that hot Asian chick and the redhead last night?* A few would claim to have slept with them. Only after a few weeks of bragging and shared fantasies would they even remember that Tovin was there at all.

"You swing both ways?" Garvey smiled when Tovin jumped, caught in the act of staring.

"No. No. They're just unusual for around here."

"That they are." There was something about the way he said it that made Tovin pause. He couldn't tell if Garvey was annoyed or amused by the two women from the way he looked over at them with a raised eyebrow and a twisted smile.

The quizmaster went on to the next question, which diverted Tovin's focus away from Garvey's strange reaction and the out-of-place feel of the ladies. Time to maintain his no-loss streak.

Garvey was no help in that area. If Tovin were being honest with himself, his date skated by on his good looks and great body. Superficial though it made him feel, the attraction persisted despite all the confused looks and the occasional, *Who even needs to know something like that?*

Tovin got it right. So did the ladies.

"You're good at this." Garvey raised his vodka shot glass up until Tovin rammed his plastic water bottle up against it. Garvey had been drinking heavily ever since they got there. Curiously, he wasn't drunk. At least he didn't seem to be—no slurring, no staggering, no sweating, no random bursts of anger, melancholy, or silliness. Clear-eyed, he studied the room as though he couldn't quite believe he'd ended up there.

"Thanks."

"You're going to get your prize for sure."

"The ice cream here is great." The bar gave the winner of the contest a free ice cream sundae.

"No." Garvey said and squeezed Tovin's inner thigh. "Your prize, sweet treat."

"Oh." Tovin flushed but managed a shaky smile. It finally occurred to him that this might be the *other thing* Garvey alluded to in the apartment. Part of him was sad that he missed out on that hint earlier. Another part was glad. Now he was going to have ice cream *and* sex. "Right. *Right.*"

CHAPTER FIVE: BLOODHOUNDS

Behind Yuri, a van idled. Inside, a group of sedated humans were loaded and ready to be dropped off at the distribution point. She had expected to be gone by now. Instead, she was stuck waiting for Garvey, who was only part of the extraction team because Eresna—Yuri's leader and alpha of the Isangelous—coddled the False Moon wolf. She and the other high-ranking wolves enjoyed him the way kings and queens of medieval times enjoyed jesters.

Everyone got a kick out of Garvey's antics, though no one had to pay for them the way she did. Bloodhounds worked as a team. All members were accountable for the screw-ups of one. Although the pack gave a lot of leeway for mistakes or unforeseen circumstances, there was no room for foolish errors, carelessness. Such strictness was necessary given the value of bloodservants. Werewolves from the two true packs depended on them for survival.

And this wasn't just any bloodservant. No, it was a guardian's. Worse, Yuri had personally brought Tovin to Lavario's attention. For her, trouble kept coming. She'd bonded with Tovin as a child, and considered herself a mother to the boy. Eresna would take far more than her job if she learned of such involvement. Yuri was beyond stressed.

"It was a mistake to let him take Tovin," she said to Nadine.

Her friend didn't sound concerned and barely opened her eyes when she retorted, "You can't rush an artist, Yur. Garvey's only a few minutes behind schedule. 'Sides, we weren't Tovin's type, and I don't think we could have lured the guy by putting a dildo under a giant box."

"Very amusing," Yuri muttered.

Nadine stuck out her tongue, leaving it that way until Yuri finally stuck hers out, too.

Quick as it came, the moment of humor passed. Yuri tapped her little pink clutch that matched the flowers on her dress against her thigh. Persistently windy, central Washington was her least favorite place to hunt. Nearby cotton from the Aspen trees stuck to her hair, her lips, her clothing, consistently forcing her to use the lint roller. And spit. Very crass.

Nadine and the wind got along well enough.

Boisterous, with big blue eyes that winked with good humor, her friend was more overtly wolf-like than her. Hair that was its own entity sprang from her scalp and fell far below her waist in a massive braid. Bits and pieces of it unfettered themselves and curled fire around her cheeks and neck. She looked—and often acted—wild.

Yuri, in contrast, was a confined space. Her dark hair was always smoothed down to a perfect bob. Her clothes were always pressed and tidy, nails painted, makeup cleanly applied. She was a vision of middle-class modesty, a tiny, unassuming, delicate, beautiful lure perfectly tied to attract the attention of the fishes.

"Chill, boss wolf," Nadine offered her usual advice.

"You look like a strawberry sprouting white mold."

"I would have gone for 'vagina.' But then I always do."

An aggravated sigh was the only acknowledgement Yuri gave her friend's raunchy joke. Nadine smiled, showing off a full mouth of razor-sharp teeth. Transforming so close to humans was forbidden. Nadine loved to skate the line.

Local law enforcement was either bought or one of their own. Yuri still paced—or power walked, depending on her anxiety level—down the length of the road to check for interlopers.

As she walked, Yuri ran through the plan to comfort herself. Procedure, comforting procedure.

One. Find potential bloodservants through the internet.

Two. Vet potentials. People who could vanish for any number of reasons were the best. Drug dealers. They had a lot of drug dealers.

Three. Stalk them, learn their habits.

Four. Collect them.

Five. Transport them.

Six. Distribute them.

Yuri went through it about seventeen times before Nadine interrupted her, stuttering words like Rain Man. "One missing. Definitely, definitely one missing."

Yuri ignored the jab. She tried to communicate her suspicions with certainty rather than with the concern she felt. "Garvey should be back by now with Tovin."

"Uh-huh." Disinterested, her friend shrugged. The top half of her blouse bobbed awkwardly with the gesture. Nadine, who disliked wearing dresses, had hiked the skirts all the way up around her waist to play with the scraggly threads unraveling from the seam.

Fancy clothes never survived Nadine for very long. She'd torn her dress to shreds. Pieces of the fabric frayed out in bits of floral pattern around her bust and torso. Her makeup looked like it was painted on by a child who was told to do her best to stay within the lines. There were a few nights Yuri wouldn't have been surprised if Nadine got out of the car and ran into the forest never to be seen again. Tonight was one of them.

Suddenly worried about her own appearance, Yuri smoothed her dress down. It made her feel like a higher-ranking wolf when everything was in its place.

"What could he possibly be doing?" she demanded.

In response, Nadine licked the tip of her incisor the way she always did when she found something amusing.

"Put those things away." She pointed at the fangs, then at the woman's lower body. "What if a human sees?"

"We can turn into giant wolves. I'm sure we'd think of something."

Yuri glared at the other wolf, knowing her persistence was petty. If a human did stumble upon them, they had bigger problems than Nadine's teeth and exposed vagina. Behind them was a van full of kidnapping victims. Still, Yuri persisted.

With a sigh and a roll of her eyes, Nadine opened her mouth wide and sucked the fangs back with exaggerated care, like a kid showing her mother that it had taken her medicine. Yuri didn't acknowledge the defiance underlying it. Instead, she looked at her watch, agitation growing as each minute passed. "We should check on them."

"Uh-huh." She licked her tooth again, amused. This time the gesture cut through Yuri's anxiety.

"You know something."

She shifted her weight. The thin metal of the car hood buckled. "No."

"That wasn't a question. You know something."

When it became obvious that Yuri wasn't going to let up, Nadine heaved another great sigh. "Garvey is taking him to the woods for some..." she made a sign for sex and followed up with a tilted smile.

"*What?*" Yuri was going to lose her mind. Concern for Tovin quickly turned into concern for herself. This was Lavario's bloodservant. Aside from Eresna, the wolf guardian Yuri served, Lavario was the last werewolf in all the five worlds she wanted to piss off. What was his was his.

Images played out in her head. Garvey having sex with Tovin, Lavario finding out and being furious, or someone other than Lavario finding out and him being embarrassed as well as furious. After all of it, Yuri would be at the end of the line as the wolf in charge of the extraction. "No."

Nadine shrugged as though she didn't understand what the big deal was. "Relax. It'll be fine. Garvey has done this before. Besides, that kid could use a good screw. *Ice cream*." She gave a little shake of her head. "What a nerd."

"No." Yuri repeated. "We need to find them. Now."

CHAPTER SIX: TOVIN'S REALLY BAD DAY

City people came to the forest with heads full of Whitmanesque romantic notions. Most didn't discover themselves there. Rather, they were found by search and rescue, cold and shivering from disenchantment. And sometimes pneumonia.

Garvey seemed to fall into that camp. At least he sounded that way when he said, "The forest is magical, right?"

Carpenter ants bit his arms and legs, rocks dug into his butt cheeks, pine needles stung the palms of his hands, and droplets of deer poo splattered around the area gave the air a musky odor. The forest sucked. It was about as nonmagical as a place could get, the very definition of earthy. But his date's ass was spellbinding, so Tovin remained agreeable. "Sure," he said, "this is great."

Tovin wasn't dumb, only horny. He'd heard countless stories about people having sex in the woods that all turned out okay. Kids in high school talked about little else, each locker room story was the start of a cautionary tale that ended in sexual conquest, not anything terrible. Even adults did it. His coworkers met women out here. All of them were fine. Just fine.

"...and that's why I'm here." Tovin was done explaining himself to Garvey.

Garvey turned. "So you're here because you finally decided to take a risk and treat yourself?"

"Yes."

Garvey chuckled. "Oh dear."

Nervous, Tovin fiddled with the edge of the blanket and sipped at overly sweet wine as his companion fussed to secure the backpack he brought with him. Garvey insisted on lugging the junk with them to, as he said, *do it right*. A blanket, some cheap wine, a few candles. Tovin wasn't exactly dazzled. His date was as cheap as he was weird.

Once settled, Garvey was right down to business—taking off his shirt, his shoes, and undoing the top button of his pants. "Too much too soon?" He didn't wait for a response, only browsed through Tovin's facial features. "Pants it is. To be clear, we did come to the forest to screw, yeah?"

Tovin nodded.

"Fantastic, then. Let's get on with it."

Given the precipitous nature of the man's undressing, Tovin expected a rough, demanding mouth upon his, taking what it wanted. Screwing, basically. Instead, Garvey traced the lines of Tovin's face with soft kisses. He used the back of his hand to tenderly follow the same path. Noses bumped. Brown eyes continually met his as if asking, *Is this okay? Do you like this?*

Tentative, Tovin reached out to touch the nest of hair at the nape of Garvey's neck, drawing away when the man arched his eyebrow at the gesture. "Sorry." Tovin mumbled to his lap.

"I'm sorry, too, sweet treat. I want you to touch it, just not like that. It's not going to kill you." Garvey presented his head, shook it slightly so that the hair tussled and realigned itself around his crown.

Tovin stammered out a quick reply, "No, it's made of keratin. Keratin would not kill you. Unless it's in horns. Or nails. Then, I guess it could." Inwardly, Tovin sighed at himself when Garvey tilted his head and once again raised his eyebrow. "Sorry, I'm a little nervous."

"Noted," Garvey quipped. "Touch my glorious mane of nonlethal keratin, then. It's the best type of keratin, I say."

Tovin was in the process of reaching for the second time—faster, slightly more confident—when two howls interrupted. He jumped at the noise, once again pulling back his fingers. He withdrew to the edge of the blanket. "What was that?"

Garvey smiled his same swagger smile, the right side of his mouth curving so that one lone incisor poked out of his lips. "Feral dogs." He bent again to kiss at the corners of Tovin's mouth. "And just when I thought you were going to make your move at last. You are so much work."

"Feral dogs? What are they doing?"

"Being feral dogs. Hunting. Don't worry. They're not hunting you, sweet treat." A reassuring hand traced the length of Tovin's jaw. "They probably got scent of a rabbit, a squirrel...a something."

"How do you know? They sound close."

Garvey's eyes darkened. "I know," he paused slightly to bring Tovin's mouth level with his, "because you've already been caught."

This time the lips against his were compelling. Garvey's tongue traced the edge of Tovin's mouth. "Now, I'm pawing at your door here. Are you going to let me in or not?" The tone was amiable enough, teasing. His eyes conveyed a contradictory message. The remaining brown edges around the dark center of the pupil seemed to pulse.

Tovin opened his mouth and, for a few minutes, felt the bliss that beforehand had simply been theoretical to him, an imagery construct of how sex in the woods with a handsome stranger was supposed to go. Cold, windy, uncomfortable, and buggy, the forest could still be a place of magic.

Magic and feral dogs. They howled again. They sounded closer. Tovin was distressed. Garvey was simply annoyed. "The children of the night. What persistent mood killers they are. Hold up here a tick, sweet treat. I'm going to go check it out."

Tovin grabbed at his hand. "We can go somewhere else."

"What? You don't want me to go off into the forest?" The dogs howled again. "Don't talk to my sweet treat that way," Garvey shouted back.

Tovin started to consider the possibility that his date might be insane. "Please. Let's move to a different location."

"I like that you're worried for me. Adorable. But I'll be back. You stay here and enjoy the stars." He swatted at his arm. "And the bugs."

Funny how a quick change in circumstance altered the world. Before, the darkness felt like a friend, a coconspirator who'd taken Tovin and his lover to a secret location. The darkness ended up taking Garvey, making him vanish like some slight-of-hand magician. Outside the small circle of light the candles provided, there were only hints of movement. And the howling. "They're only dogs," he said to himself. "Only dogs."

Leaving was an option. Tovin considered it. Stars were in full view, the air colder for it. Off in the distance guttural whines, yelps, snarls cut through the night, making the cold seem somehow colder. The option became even more tempting as the minutes added up, yet somehow leaving seemed unjustifiably ungallant. *What if he is being eaten?* Tovin didn't know what he'd do if that were the case. He wasn't about to go searching for his would-be lover and his fine collection of structural fibrous proteins. Cheap wine plus some heavy petting did not add up to that much debt.

Waiting was the least he could do.

It wasn't too much longer as it turned out. Garvey stumbled out of the woods and gave Tovin a sheepish expression. A small grimace spread across his face as he sat on the blanket. "Sweet treat, I have something I must confess. I'm afraid it will upset you some." He pouted slightly. "So...chatted with our noisy friends. They say the fun is over. More splitting, less lickety."

Tovin smiled at him. "We've been overruled by dogs?"

"Sort-of wolves.

Tovin laughed slightly. "*Sort-of* wolves? On what grounds do they object?"

"Well, long story short. You're supposed to be drugged by now and on your way to a distribution center where you will be catalogued and then sent on your way to your werewolf overlord to be his bloodservant." Always smiling in one form or another, Garvey looked at Tovin's face expectantly. "At any rate, they're terribly vexed by me not following the script."

Tovin laughed again, feeling his first easy smile trip its way to his face. The man's mannerisms and humor were so strange, yet Tovin was starting to become comfortable with Garvey. "First feral dogs, then wolves, now werewolf overlords. Whatever. Explain to them that you have promises to keep." He lifted his mouth to Garvey, who cupped his chin before placing one small kiss on the corner. Tovin's blood responded, redirecting itself to the appropriate areas of the body.

Garvey did not continue the kiss. He remained distant. "I tried, sweet treat. I did. But they're very insistent. And none of us are werewolf overlords I'm afraid. Just bloodhounds."

"None of us?" Tovin started to pull away, ignoring the rest. With Garvey, there always seemed to be a great deal to ignore.

"Yes. Us." Tovin said nothing but could feel his facial muscles swerving head-on into a grin he was pretty was a gross overcorrection.

"You're a werewolf now?"

"I was a werewolf before. I assume I'll be one later. At least I'm not a vampire, huh? That would be awkward."

"Right. That's fantastic. Good. Good for you." Tovin said and started to rise from the blanket. Garvey forced him down, somewhat gently, with one hand. "This is not funny. I want to leave." Tovin started to get up again and again was forced back to the blanket, a process repeated five times until Garvey simply kept one hand pressed against Tovin's chest, pinning him. Tovin continued to twist around on the blanket, trying to rise. Garvey clucked his tongue and shook his head at the efforts.

"This is not funny. Let me go."

Garvey laughed. "It is a little. To me. Probably not to you." His face grew semi-serious. "I'm not joking, though. I am a werewolf. You're going to be a bloodservant to a werewolf overlord. Overall, pretty bad day."

"You're an asshole."

"I'm an asshole werewolf."

"You're a *crazy* asshole."

"I'm a crazy asshole *werewolf*. Really, you can add as much as you want in front of it. The end of the sentence is the same. Werewolf, sweet treat."

Tovin did his best to keep his voice level to sound menacing with some edge of command. He forced himself to look directly into the brown eyes. "Let. Me Go."

"Nope." Brown eyes looked back, unwavering and good-humored.

"Fine." Then, Tovin said words he would come to regret. "If you're a werewolf, show me. Be a werewolf."

Garvey showed him.

CHAPTER SEVEN: UNFRIENDLY STATISTICS

Mazgan's orders called for injury. Not death necessarily. At least that's what Garvey told himself. Whatever harm befell Tovin out in the woods tonight, Garvey didn't want to dish it out himself, so he took Tovin's shoes, glasses, and shirt and let him run wild and directionless into the forest. It was dickish to grab so much from someone already fighting unfriendly odds. His pack brothers and sisters would sneer, say, *Be a better wolf. Make it fair. Hunt.* A better wolf he was not. "I should have grabbed his pants," he told himself with regret.

Garvey watched Tovin for a bit to make sure his ice-cream-sundae-winning trivia guru didn't suddenly develop a practical skillset. Nope. He'd already tripped five or six times. Eventually, to make sure Tovin was injured enough to be rejected at distribution, Garvey would need to follow him, maybe even do some werewolf growl, howl, and prowl bullshit. For now, Garvey twirled the glasses frames in one paw and did something he rarely did. He thought about consequences.

He didn't want Tovin to die. He *liked* this dopey kid. It was an odd, unexpected realization. Clueless as Tovin was, there was something sweet about him that Garvey wanted to keep in the world. It tugged at a part of his heart he didn't know existed. "Cut it out," he reprimanded himself, "gonna kill a lot cuter men when you've got the vampires." He heard Tovin fall again. "More coordinated men, too."

He kept fretting, a feeling he attributed to his nerves. This was further than he'd ever gone during an extraction hunt. Even he feared what Eresna might to do him if he damaged one of her precious bloodservants. Fond of mischief but never over the line, he'd always reined in his shenanigans after a few harsh words and some snarling. Yuri would expect the same tonight. She'd said as much when she snarled her order to bring the kid back to the van. But she'd be wrong.

Off in the distance, not too distant, Garvey heard a yelp and a thump.

He'll be fine, Garvey told himself. Or not. He prepared himself for that, too.

* * *

Tovin had heard all the horror stories about online dating. People who were far less attractive than their profile picture, people who lied about their jobs, people obsessed with their exes to the point of being stalkers. His date turned out to be a werewolf.

And a jerk. *Race you to the road.* That was the last thing Tovin heard from Garvey before things went sour. Now Tovin was running. Only he was doing a terrible job of it.

First, he went deeper into the woods. That was understandable, since where he lived was about 80 percent forest. Statistical odds were not in his favor there. But then he fell. Kept falling. As it turned out, the forest was a mess of things to trip over: branches, roots, rocks, and holes. In his idealized version of events, these things were blurry and shapeless as he sprinted past them. Reality wasn't as kind. Everything was blurry and shapeless because his date took his glasses along with most of his clothes. Without being able to see, he couldn't get his bearings.

What he could see, he didn't want to. His muddy, blood-spattered hands. His cold sweat-slick skin covered with twigs, pebbles, grass, and mud. He shivered. His jaw clanked shut. Time to cross the last item off the list. Tovin looked back. Why not? The beast chasing him had to be caught up by now. Plus, looking back had to be the free space for whatever vengeful deity was playing chase-scene bingo.

Nothing moved. For a moment, Tovin thought Garvey gave up. Maybe werewolves were fundamentally lazy, maybe something scared it off, maybe Garvey wasn't a werewolf at all, just some random weirdo the boys from the bar found on the internet to fuck with him. That last thought sounded plausible. Yes. The last bit. That *had* to be the case. Werewolves. Tovin snorted at himself and then took a step toward the direction he came.

Some pixilated brown blob came forward from the green of the bushes. With a yelp, Tovin fell backward, twisting his ankle in the process. Air rushed from his body as he struck the ground. Whatever it was *tsked* at him and tossed something. Dirt shot up into his face. "Asshole," Tovin shouted back at it, wanting to believe that the whatever above him was some type of prank.

The thing held his hands up to his chest as though wounded. Then pointed to the ground. "Glasses," it said back.

Tovin struggled to pick them up—his tingling fingers felt bloated and numb and struggled with the nuanced movement required to place the thin frames behind his ears. It took several humiliating attempts before ground and shrubs came into sharp focus, making the threat to nonthreat contrast evident. Shrub. Rock. Tree. Small tree. Werewolf. It made a sweeping gesture with its paw, *Go ahead and run. Cool by me.*

Expectations insisted the monster be taller than six two, be bulky, and have no genitalia or genitalia that would be acceptably covered by a pair of tatty pants that had torn themselves graciously into a pair of boxers. Today was a day of disappointments. Garvey as a werewolf, looked pretty much like an especially menacing gray wolf with his dick showing.

The teeth were larger, the claws like curled fingers, the feet and hands an obvious human-dog hybrid with elongated phalanges, but the face was pure wolf—tufts of hair building around the neck and face, coarse vibrissa around a somewhat elongated snout, pink tongue lolling out of its mouth, fuzzy cheese-wedge ears that were perked up and rotating slightly, and dingy yellow eyes that reflected sharply like sunlight hitting mica. Each time the wolf turned its head and the light reflected, Tovin's nervous system overloaded.

None of the monster's movements were especially threatening. The hybrid dropped to all fours, shrinking almost to the size of a normal dog as it strode toward him in a smooth, easy manner—head and ears erect, tail wagging slightly. From what little Tovin knew of dogs, none of these were bad signs, but each step taken toward him ratcheted up a queasy feeling in his bowels. "Stay," he said to it. "Stay."

Tovin could have sworn he heard a chuckle in response. *Wolves don't chuckle*, he told himself.

The wolf was close enough that the fingerprint-like notches and grooves of its nose became visible. Tovin tried to scuttle away, pulling himself across the ground. Other than cutting up his hands, he didn't achieve much, but the wolf sat and stopped advancing when more howling in the distance caught the wolf's attention.

It turned its head slightly in the general direction of the noise. Its chest heaved upward then down. Air whooshing made the soft, wet lips flap. *Wolves don't sigh,* Tovin told himself, *and this is a wolf.* It turned back on Tovin quickly and grabbed his bad ankle, squeezing it tightly before tilting its head back to howl in return. Immense pain popped in the back of Tovin's head as he tried to scramble backward to escape, but the wolf only tightened its grip and let its tongue slip out, mouth falling open in a delighted grin that said without saying, *I knew you were going to do that.* A whimper came despite Tovin's best efforts to suppress it and then another as the monster pulled Tovin toward it.

"Why did you bring the glasses?" Tovin didn't care about the answer and dimly realized it was himself who had asked the question. He wanted the wolf to stop pulling. Which it did. Briefly. And then simply clucked its tongue and made another small gesture with its head and paws that could have meant any number of things. *Choose your own adventure.*

When the monster pulled at the ankle again, Tovin blurted out another question, "What are you?" This time it released Tovin's ankle and stood back up on two legs and in a sort of shrugging gesture collapsed back into his human form.

Transformation from ominously naked wolf to awkwardly naked man took only a few seconds. Wolf eyes turned to large, round brown human eyes that seemed in constant waggish movement. His blockish, straight-jawed face was once again framed by his much-loved brown hair.

"I'm sorry, sweet treat," the man version of the monster said. "This isn't normally the part of the process where I take questions." He grinned again, the two elongated front incisors pinched at the lower lip, the only remaining evidence that there once stood a wolf. "But to answer your question, I thought you might need them. I was being helpful. I can't help but think if you had them earlier, you wouldn't have run deeper into the woods, though I did appreciate it. Well done. And you know what I am."

"This town is like 80 percent woods." Tovin blurted out his thought from earlier.

Garvey chuckled. "Good point. Hold up a tick." Garvey walked back into the bushes and returned with the backpack.

Tovin looked at it in confusion.

He grinned again before dumping the contents on the ground, a sort of good-humored recognition of Tovin's confusion. Sweatpants. A sweatshirt. Tennis shoes. Garvey explained, "I bring them with me anywhere. As it turns out murdering someone and eating them is not something most people call the police for. They assume it's not happening. Walk around with no pants on, though, and suddenly you're in the back of a cruiser and then in therapy because they think you have a pathological need to expose yourself.

"Now I know what you're thinking," Garvey continued while he pulled on his pants, stopping the narrative to include Tovin, a polite host. "Why not eat them all? Well, that's what I would have done at some point, and those were the good days, but now the Boo Hags have all these rules and policies about who you can kill and eat, where you can kill and eat them, how much time you spend killing and eating them. If you violate any of the damn rules, you have to fill out forms and go before a council. It's all so civilized." He rolled his eyes, tilted his head up, and sighed. "I prefer therapy."

"Oh." It felt stupid, and Tovin was sure it sounded clueless as well, but how did one engage in social rituals and niceties with a *something*?

The wolf simply clucked his tongue and ignored the response. "Okay, now that we've had our chat, are you ready to go, sweet treat?" When Tovin made no response other than to curl himself into a tight ball—assuming *go* was some type of standard euphemism for *are you ready to die?*—the brown eyes narrowed slightly, the first time the werewolf looked anything other than bored, and again, "Let's go." A direct, emphatic hand gesture. *This way.*

"Go where?" Tovin shook his head. It didn't make sense.

"To the van. I'm not going to carry you. That ankle doesn't look that bad, and I'm not the type of werewolf who lugs people around."

There was a van? When Tovin said nothing and did not move, the werewolf grew impatient. "Did your jog through the woods shake something loose in your brain? To the van, sweet treat. This way." When Tovin failed to move or respond, the werewolf's gestures became more agitated and the expression less good-humored.

"All right, then." Long legs covered the distance between them in seconds, and Tovin was brought to his feet too quickly. The sudden jounce hooked his head to the side and sent the glasses flopping to the ground. Garvey sighed and let go of his arm as he bent to retrieve them.

Of course the twisted ankle gave out, and Tovin fell to the dirt with an undignified "thump" and then a "whump" as the air pushed out of his body. The glasses were thrown alongside him. "Okay, here you go. Put them on and look at me." Tovin complied. Brown eyes—reflecting some gold—took another inventory and grew hard. "Now get up and walk, sweet treat."

"Can't." Tovin pointed to his ankle and then thought, *Also my ribs, and my knees, and my entire left side of my body since you dropped me on it, you total dick.* "Why? Eat me here. I'm not going to run, and I'm not going to walk. I'm here. You're here. We're here. Seems like we have all the necessary elements for this event to occur. So kill me here or carry me to your damn van." Tovin paused. "Asshole."

Garvey maintained eye contact through Tovin's entire spiel, but once it was out, he dropped his head. The pain and the fear caught up, gained the upper hand over the desire to die in a somewhat dignified manner. There was a pause, and Tovin kept his head bowed to the ground, willing himself to remain with himself a bit longer, to not think too much about the mechanics of being eaten. It was tough. He was a mechanics and process sort of guy.

Nothing happened for what seemed an eternity in scared-shitless time. When Tovin finally willed himself to look up, Garvey appeared to be making the rounds in his own head. He stared off into space while rolling his tongue along the roof of his mouth. Two more howls once again caught his attention. Garvey howled back in four quick, disjointed bursts of, Woo, Woo, Woo, Wooooooo! For a moment, Tovin could imagine he just said, *Hold up a tick!* in wolf language.

The other wolves howled back, theirs long and protracted.

Garvey rolled his eyes and complained, "So impatient, those two." When he saw Tovin looking up at him, his face split open in the same confident, swagger grin from earlier—now with sharper teeth. Softer hands gathered Tovin in an embrace, and he felt himself being lifted— first his upper body and then his legs.

"Sweet treat, if I were going to kill and eat you, you'd be dead, and I'd be digesting you by now. There are other plans for you. Now, I'm going to take you to the van, and you're going to go along unless you can think of a better, independent plan that doesn't involve running away because—and now I'm being frank—that is never going to work out for you."

Tovin was out of responses, so he relaxed while his once-date carried him, allowing his mind to linger on the smell—almost like wet sagebrush—and feel of a body next to his. "Time for some real magic." Before Tovin could ask him what he meant, a large hand covered his eyes and most of his head. Tovin heard some strange words and felt his body relax and his brain shut down. There was a moment when he woke up propped against something soft and a strap was brought down around him, and he dimly realized, *I'm in a car.*

No, he was in a minivan. Not a modern-day, trying-to-be-cool-young-couple's minivan. It was a your-mom-in-mom-jeans minivan admitting, *I give up...I'm a minivan.* As much as he could respect the practicality of such a vehicle, Tovin couldn't help but feel a little confused. Was he being abducted or was he on his way to soccer practice?

Kidnapped as it turned out.

Garvey fanned large knuckles across Tovin's cheek and said, "Sorry, sweet treat." Then a door slid into place. There was a metallic thud above Tovin's head, a curled fist hitting the roof of the car, universal for *Good to go.*

CHAPTER EIGHT: BLAME IT ON GARVEY

Yuri and Nadine were well on their way to the distribution center with the heavily sedated humans sleeping behind them. Yuri looked in the mirror to check in on the crop, a small reassurance that everything else had gone according to plan. There was Tovin. Yuri's eyes narrowed when she got a glimpse of his battered face. The reflection tore at her for a variety of reasons. Right now she had to focus on the primary concern—she and Nadine were in some seriously deep shit. Her companion was too much of an in-the-moment wolf to realize it.

Small circles of smoke made their way past Nadine's mouth from time to time. She attempted to indulge in her habit in a way that didn't draw too much attention. Despite her best efforts, it was clear what she was doing. As always, she overlooked minor details, such as opening a window to let the smoke out. Giving her friend a pointed look, Yuri rolled hers down; fresh air whooshed through the van. So far, Nadine had at least repressed her chatter until, finally, she broke with a strained voice. "I'll handle Lavario."

Yuri snorted. Like hell she would.

"He's a softie. I'll tell him..." she made little circles in the air with her hand, trying to draw inspiration, "Tovin wasn't fully drugged, woke up, Garvey chased him, and he fell a few times. No biggie. All Garvey's fault. Maybe we'll just be looking at a formal reprimand."

Yuri snorted again.

"I hate it when you do this. Talk to me, Yur."

"Why did Garvey do this?"

Nadine shrugged her shoulders and took another drag. She was a soldier. As far as she was concerned, the big picture only involved her as she was ordered in and out of it. The rest of the time it was a backdrop for a smoke break. She gave the first answer that came to her mind. "He was horny?"

"It wasn't suspicious to you that it's Lavario's servant?"

"No."

Yuri gave her a long, level look. Lavario and Garvey had more history than Rome. Practically everything the False Moon bastard did was to annoy his maker in some way, and if he wasn't trying to annoy Lavario, he was trying to get under someone else's skin.

Nadine grimaced. "I mean, a little, but this isn't the first time. He likes to have fun."

"He likes to have fun." Yuri mimicked her then flexed her hands to push her claws outward. It gave her satisfaction when Nadine leaned farther onto the passenger-side door. "What are we going to do if Tovin gets rejected?"

Something finally clicked in her head. "Shit."

"Uh huh."

She twisted in her seat to give Tovin another glance over. "Erghhh!"

"Yup."

"Lavario is going to beat us half to death."

"That old softie?"

Nadine turned pale enough that the freckles on the bridge of her nose started to melt together. Her hands developed a mind of their own and flapped up and down, joints snapping with the force of it. "Shit. Shit. Shit. What are we going to do?"

Yuri didn't know. Rules governed all aspects of the pickup and distribution of humans. Those regulations were in place to make sure the process went in a smooth, orderly way. Problems were dealt with through a standardized routine that even the dumbest wolf could follow. Occasionally, humans had to be discarded, but that was inevitable in an undertaking so large and important. Yuri never thought much of it. Then, she'd never been in a situation where the extraction of a guardian's servant went so horribly, horribly wrong.

Tovin was a mess. Any number of theoretical solutions were available. She or Nadine could heal the boy, he could be healed at the distribution center, or Lavario could take him and heal him. Each option was against procedure for various reasons, none of which applied to their situation. A bureaucracy that Yuri could write a love letter to on most days had turned against her. Garvey would be thrilled. He frequently said, "If it made sense, it wouldn't be called bureaucracy." He was wise to take another van.

Yuri sighed and extended her claws again.

Nadine sat up with a jolt of sudden inspiration. "We could kill him now. Blame it on Garvey. That way we never had custody of him when he was alive."

"No." Yuri shook her head.

"Why not? It works. Not like anyone is going to question Garvey fucking up, doing something dumb. With the kid dead, Garvey gets beat to shit instead of us, Lavario gets a new pet. Everyone's happy, happy, happy."

Yuri shot her a sour look.

"There is something you're not telling me here. What gives, Yur?"

"I said no." She pounded her fist against the wheel for emphasis.

Nadine made some type of protracted grunting noise that went up in volume and pitch the longer it went. Doing her best to ignore her friends protesting, Yuri kept her gaze focused, straight ahead on the road. As always, Nadine's first solution was the easy way out. Finally, her friend gave up that line. "What then? What are we going to do? He's going to be killed anyway."

"Maybe not." She looked at Tovin again. Yes, he was a mess. But. "He's Lavario's."

* * *

Dazed, Tovin blinked a few times and tried to get his bearings. The two women from the bar were in the front seats arguing with each other. Bits and pieces of the heated discussion zipped back to him in isolated fragments. Pink Flower Dress hit the wheel—once, twice, three times. It was only a series of dull thuds to his ears, blurred movements to his eyes. Overall meaningless.

Pain caught up to him. Tovin began to feel every cut, scratch, and gouge littered up and down his body. It took a great deal of effort not to groan, whimper, or otherwise verbalize his discomfort.

Now what could he remember? According to Garvey, Tovin was en route to a distribution center where he'd be catalogued before being sent to his werewolf overlord. He wasn't sure if any of that was true, the tale certainly seemed implausible. Then he remembered the forest, the way Garvey's skin fell away until a giant wolf stood there—massive, terrifying, very real. Best case scenario, the two women were crazy people, not real werewolves. A born skeptic, Tovin had to cling to that notion to keep himself from going totally insane. *No such thing as werewolves,* he told himself. *The wine Garvey gave me was drugged or something. These people are just crazy.*

Trapped in a van with the criminally insane probably wasn't much better than being in a van with monsters. He was still a captive and heading to who knew where. Tovin forced himself to remain calm and appear unconscious.

There were other people with him. All drugged from the looks of it. None of them rested in a position that could be described as comfortable or natural. One of the males, a thirty-something guy in a cheap suit, faced the wrong direction as though he had been placed there by a careless child who didn't want to play make-believe that her dolly was a real person with joints or a spine. Two other women overlapped, with the head of one shoved firmly in the seat cushion. Tovin wondered if they had similar ill-fated nights out.

Better safe than sorry was the creed he'd said to himself countless times before, along with prepare for the worst, hope for the best. A life without risk—work, bar trivia, Matlock reruns, then bed—and ritualized living from the socks he wore each day to the meals he ate in the evening. Tovin thought he was tired of it. His date with Garvey was going to be the start of something new. *Oh dear,* Garvey had said. Now Tovin knew why.

None of it mattered anymore. The situation was what it was. Tovin focused on listening, hoping to pick up some detail that would get his ass out of this mess.

"We need to kill him, Yur. They're not going to budge on the rules. Not even for Lavario."

That came through loud and clear.

Tovin did the only thing he could think of at that point. He unbuckled himself, opened the door, and fell out.

* * *

"What the fuck was that?" Nadine twisted in her seat.

"What?!" Yuri shouted back at her before continuing her tirade. "If you'd just think this through instead of just doing whatever Garvey—"

"Oh shit. The boy bailed, Yur."

Yuri slammed on the breaks and looked back at the empty seat where Tovin was supposed to be. "But he was drugged. Motherfucker must have used magic!"

"The kid?" Nadine looked at her in disbelief. "You think he teleported?"

Restraint. Restraint. Restraint. Yuri felt white-hot heat saturate her entire being. She loved Nadine, but sometimes her friend could be so dense. "NO. *Garvey* used magic." Her companion continued to stare, perplexed. "On the boy. Instead of drugging him."

Now she got it. "That dickcheese rat bastard!"

That pretty much summed up Yuri's feelings. Magical slumber was only effective for a short period. The evolutionary purpose of it was to prevent prey from screaming, attracting unwanted attention to the hunter. Typical of Garvey, he'd used it to fuck with people.

Tovin couldn't have gotten very far. Yuri got out of the car, sniffed the air, taking in the smells—the pine, the burnt rubber, and finally the traces of cheap cologne that she knew to be the scent of the boy. "This way," she jerked her head to the right. "Come on." Nadine followed half-heartedly.

Mess before, catastrophe now. Tovin was somehow awake and alive, lying on the ground moaning and clutching at his side then at his leg where a bone stuck out at the shin. Yuri cradled him. The boy's green eyes were squeezed shut. That was probably for the best. She didn't want to see them right now.

Joyful, Nadine clapped her hands together with a snap. "Leave him. Drive over him. This is a gift from the Goddess. The kid *fell* out of the car...and died. Tragic. Bummer. Sorry, Lavario." She shrugged. "The universe is giving us this one, Yur. It's got a bow on it."

Decisions had to be made. Nadine's position was clear. Killing the boy certainly had more advantages than disadvantages. Her friend's simple solution was the best in this circumstance. This extraction was, at the very least, going to result in a demotion. Yuri would be lucky to end up on a novice bloodhound team after this fiasco. Tovin's death resolved that. More than that, it kept Yuri's secrets safe.

Curled up in her arms, Tovin probably didn't know what he was doing. Shock, pain, fear whirled around inside of him. Yuri felt every least bit of it through her bond with him. Perhaps, long shot that it was, he could be okay. She needed him to be okay. "Tovin, Tovin. Listen to me."

He moaned but opened his eyes. Yuri's heart constricted at the fear she saw there. It wasn't supposed to be this way for him. He was supposed to be on his way to a wonderful life, to live with one of the most powerful of their kind as a companion.

She forced her tone to be stern. For his sake, he needed to be afraid right now. "Do you want to die right now, or do you want to be still and quiet and *maybe* live?"

Nadine flung her hands up in the air. She transformed slightly. The rest of her dress ripped off with the force of the gesture; jigsaw bits of it fluttered around her torso. She tried to piece them back together. Recognizing it was useless, she tossed her hands in the air again, and kicked out at nothing.

Yuri ignored her. "Tovin, answer me."

Although she didn't assign a numerical value to the options, the boy held up two fingers. It was understood well enough.

"Good. Then, you'll need to sit still and be quiet. You try to run again, you're dead. You talk, you're dead. You do anything other than sit in the car. Dead." Comply or be dead. She didn't ask if he was okay with these terms or if he understood.

"This is the dumbest thing I think you've ever done." Nadine looked down at her, at Tovin. "Someday, you're going to explain why. For now, let me help him with the pain."

She couldn't tell her friend she'd bonded with Tovin, thought of him as a son. It wouldn't be fair to drag her into the quagmire of her situation, which only got worse. She was, however, grateful for her friend's understanding. "Thank you, Naddie."

Nadine's expression softened a bit. "We can kill him. Putting that out there." When Yuri only gave her a grim smile in response, Nadine relented. "Okay, got any spare of the Rohypnol?"

"No."

Quickly, and with surprising gentleness, Nadine eased Tovin's pain and once again put him in a magic-induced sleep.

CHAPTER NINE: SENSELESS BUREAUCRACY

The building was all sharp angles and no-nonsense geometry. Squares beside squares beside rectangles. Functional. Yuri loved the design of it. Whenever she saw the edges of it peek out of the foliage, she knew she was home. Under normal circumstances, this was her favorite part of the process. Accolades were normally her due after a night of hard work. No one was going to tell her she'd done well today. She might be a False Moon wolf by the end of it. She and Garvey might even be packmates. The thought brought rage then dread.

Yuri had never cared for Anton—normal circumstances or not. Today, he was possibly the ugliest, shortest, dumbest, and dullest werewolf to ever live. *Generous description of the swollen toad,* Yuri thought unkindly as Anton bustled up to them with his clipboard posed, ready to record.

"Smooth?" Anton asked as though he were too busy for full sentences.

Yuri took a deep breath and started in, "Well—"

"Problem?" He raised an eyebrow.

Yuri stepped aside and pointed at Tovin, who was once again magicked to sleep and tossing fitfully in the backseat of the van. Drugs lasted longer, sleeping spells only kept the prey quiet for a quick feeding, but Yuri was unsure he'd ever wake again, drugged or magicked. Bloody and bruised, his face was hardly recognizable as the boy whose photo Yuri sent to Lavario.

Garvey arrived minutes later. He hit the lock button until the horn honked—not once but twice. "Holy shit, sweet treat should have gone parasailing," he chimed in when he saw Tovin. Later, if Yuri was around to see it through, she'd slap the smug off his face.

As if guessing her thoughts, he gave her a lopsided smile and a cheery wink.

"Eresna will make you pay for this," she assured him.

His grin became a crescent moon, waning until it vanished. He shifted from one foot to another, as though eager to leave.

"This is bad." Anton stated the obvious in an air that managed to be grand beyond his rank, yet nervous.

Tactless, Nadine went in. "We know. Things—" She waved her hand in the air, searching for the right words. "—got messy."

That's when Lavario and Mazgan came around the corner. Yuri had hoped for a little more time to clean the boy up and to get their story straight. By the time everyone was done with the formal greetings, she was nowhere near a satisfactory explanation to offer the powerful guardians. She was especially nervous about Lavario since Tovin was meant to be his servant. Guardians had the luxury of handpicking whom they'd feed from, and Lavario was known for being demanding. Eresna was the only exception. The Alpha Guardian of the Isangelous accepted whatever servant her pack gifted.

Yuri fidgeted as he approached. If Lavario noticed her distress, he gave no indication. He was his typical grand self, dressed in a fine wool suit that had a higher thread count than any of them had years to their lives. As always, he was immaculately groomed—his slightly curly, dark hair smoothed back with a light product, his fingernails cut into round moons, eyebrows arched with haughty superiority over light-green eyes. Considered to be one of the most beautiful of their kind when transformed, he was equally desirable in his human form.

And scary. Anton gulped. "There were some problems with the extraction of your servant, Guardian Lavario."

"What sort of problems?" Lavario's green eyes narrowed as he scanned their faces. Yuri noticed Mazgan puff himself up. Something resembling a smile crept to his face, but he suppressed it quickly.

"Garvey chased him through the woods, Guardian Lavario." Nadine distanced herself and Yuri from blame and tossed Garvey under the bus in the process.

Garvey didn't seem to mind one bit. The mocking lilt was back in his voice when he responded, "*Followed*. To be fair I followed him through the woods."

Lavario ignored the lack of formal address, almost ignored Garvey completely. "Let me see Tovin."

Reluctantly, Yuri, Nadine, and Anton stepped aside to allow full view of the wreckage. Eyes narrowed as they scanned Tovin's bloody clothes, bruises, scratches, broken bones, and matted hair. Although Lavario seemed calm enough, even serene, as he looked over the young man's injuries, no one was fooled. Collectively, wolves felt the energy of transformation in waves that coiled through them, the feeling was either exhilarating or terrifying depending on the context.

"That was how he was delivered, Guardian Lavario." Anton rushed to drop all blame.

"I see. Yuri, you oversaw this extraction?" Light-green eyes fixed on her.

"Yes, Guardian Lavario," she answered.

"And did you know what Garvey intended to do?"

"No, Guar—"

"That's enough, thank you." He turned back to Anton. "Get a healer down here. Take care of this."

"You know that's against the rules, Guardian. They must be healthy enough to travel before distribution. This is to *everyone's* benefit. You wouldn't want him to die after the first feeding." Clearly, Anton went over this in his head before spitting it out. He rushed through the explanation with quick, breathless urgency.

"Healing him now solves those problems. Heal him, distribute him to me."

"I can't." Anton said again, holding his clipboard in front of him as though he could call upon the powers of bureaucracy to save him from the wrath of the irate guardian. Yuri believed in the power of the system to do many things, but she was sure Lavario, a very old, very powerful werewolf, could cut through Anton until guts hung from claws like so much red tape. Anton must have come to a similar conclusion. "Alpha Guardian, Mazgan, I'm very sorry for Guardian Lavario's upset, but you understand we cannot give Tovin to you?"

"Of course," Mazgan said smoothly. "But we will be compensated for the loss."

To Yuri's ears, he sounded far too pleased. She could have sworn she'd seen him exchange glances with Garvey a few times. It had to be her imagination. The Alpha Guardian from the Varcolac was far too arrogant to associate with the likes of a False Moon.

Relieved he at least had one of the guardians on his side, Anton let go of the breath he was holding with a loud whoosh that fluttered the papers on his clipboard. "Absolutely, Guardian Lavario is free to choose his replacement. Whatever one he wants."

Mazgan smiled. "Excellent. You hear that, Guardian Lavario?"

Perfectly groomed fingernails gave way to hooked claws, a translucent white at the tip, then opaque black to the root. "I heard."

Lavario did not use Mazgan's title. All of them, even Garvey, stepped back as the disrespect hung in the air between them. It was no secret that there was no love between the two, yet Lavario had always at least outwardly gone through the motions of deferring to Mazgan. Rank was everything. If the two major packs—the Varcolac and Isangelous—agreed on one concept that would be it. Varcolac wolves like Mazgan were especially prickly about status, believing they'd earned theirs through combat.

"Pick one, then." Teeth out and seething, Mazgan did not press it or strike out at his subordinate. Everyone was surprised, only Garvey was disappointed.

Lavario didn't say anything else until he reached the last van, the one that contained the servants of the Isangelous guardians and other higher-ranking wolves in the pack. Yuri did not like where this was heading. Not one bit. Even less when he ordered them to unload it with clipped precision.

Carefully, Nadine and Yuri obeyed his orders. Humans were hauled out and placed on the sidewalk for Lavario's inspection. Fine, expensive clothing worn by the potential bloodservants gathered white dust from the ground below while the guardian paced up and down the line.

Finally, he selected. "This one."

Yup. Bad to worse. Yuri closed her eyes and begged for it all to be a bad dream. Lavario pointed to the bloodservant of Alpha Guardian Eresna.

Guardian servants in the Isangelous were not simply food no matter what the pretenders in the Varcolac said. The man the Isangelous extracted for Eresna was a symbol of their commitment to their queen. He was affluent, intelligent, attractive, confident, secure, and talented. A gift to her. Abducting him was a risk. People would look for such a man, perhaps for years. Such a companion was worthy of a leader.

"Be reasonable, Guardian Lavario. This one belongs to Guardian Eresna." Anton was practically on his knees when he said this, doing what he could to pacify the irate wolf. Lavario simply offered a slight smile sans teeth, sans mirth, sans *smile* and pointed at the man again—Eresna's bloodservant, Vincent. *This one.* Seeing a lost cause there, Anton turned to his former ally. "Alpha Guardian Mazgan, surely you must understand this is not possible. Have him select another."

Mazgan looked beside himself with joy. "Your mistake. Your problem. Guardian Lavario wants this one."

Mazgan's words surprised everyone, including Lavario whose face fell into defeated, agitated lines. Bold move, stupid move. Either way, it was now another mess for her and Nadine to clean up later.

Governed by rules, by process, Anton gave into the whims of the higher-ranking wolf. Lavario got Eresna's bloodservant. Tovin remained behind.

CHAPTER TEN: ACCIDENTS

Lavario came in behind Yuri as she placed Tovin on one of the bunks in the holding area. She greeted him as gracefully as she could. Terrified of what he might do, Yuri still had her pride to uphold. No matter what, she'd face Lavario's wrath with dignity—her back straight, her head held high, her shoulders square. A soldier's stance.

He was not impressed. "A word, Yuri."

"Guardian—"

"Cut the titles. Show respect by answering questions honestly."

"Always, Guardi—" She stopped herself, swallowing hard. "Of course."

"Why did you suggest Tovin to me?" Yuri could see the accusation that she had been a part of something on his face. What happened with Tovin was bad for Lavario. After exile, he was no longer an Isangelous Guardian. Life as a Varcolac meant he needed to be in control of what was his, powerful enough to maintain it. Losing anything—even if it was a pet—because of Garvey's shenanigans made him seem weak, foolish. Asking Yuri if she was also involved was a courtesy he was willing to extend given her history as a no-nonsense, apolitical workhorse.

"I thought you might like him." Not a total lie. True enough she believed Lavario would be attracted to Tovin. More importantly, she saw Lavario as the one to take Tovin away from a bigoted, terrible world.

Lavario's voice was a low growl. "Come now, Yuri." Lavario tilted his head to the side and lifted his lips with derision, showing his fangs. Violence wasn't Lavario's style—Yuri had only seen him lose his temper a handful of times during her little part of his long life—but he was making it clear things could go that way. This had to be far bigger than she imagined.

"I had nothing to do with what happened today. I swear it to you."

He gave her a long look before withdrawing with a deep sigh. "Garvey?"

Obviously. "Yes."

"And Nadine?"

Yuri didn't want to throw her friend to the fire, but Lavario would know one way or another. "She did not know what he planned. She assumed he was up to the usual, having sex, fooling around. She would never knowingly cross you."

He showed his teeth again very quickly and without too much malice. He turned his attention to Tovin, resting somewhat peacefully on the bunk. Yuri tucked him in while the rest of the possible rejects were scattered on the bunks, stored without much consideration until their fates were decided. "You care for Tovin."

Yuri said nothing.

"Interesting."

For once he seemed sincere when he said it. To him, Yuri was little more than a signpost on an endless stretch of highway: something he acknowledged with casual interest but never lingered on beyond its immediate utility. Now he was studying her intently, trying to gather up what she knew, what she was hiding. He wanted to make it his own.

Dry-mouthed, Yuri changed the topic. "How bad is this for you?"

"Depends."

"On?"

Lavario gave her a dark look. Willing to drop the title but less amenable to forgetting rank, he took exception to a wolf of Yuri's status questioning him. Apologetic for not showing her former guardian the proper respect, Yuri demurred, "Forgive my prying in your private affairs, Guardian."

He waved his hand. "I am on edge, Yuri. The outcome depends on how much my daughter wishes to keep her status in the Varcolac. Mazgan told her she must choose between us."

Bad. Really bad. Yuri thought of the stern-faced Kijo. Those dark black eyes of hers were born hard, lacking sentiment. Loving her father wouldn't be enough this time with her pack on the line. Unlike Lavario, Kijo knew how to walk away from the past.

Angry for her former guardian, Yuri asked, "Why don't you challenge Mazgan? What happened today won't matter then." No wolf from the Isangelous understood why their former guardian allowed himself to be ruled over. He'd gone to the Varcolac as an exile, but he was powerful enough to claim the role of alpha. Mazgan was a poor copy of Lavario, from his hair that was slicked back with a heavy, oily product to the shoes that were expensive because someone put a sticker on them rather than because they were well crafted.

"It is a legitimacy issue. I cannot rule the Varcolac unless they suddenly decide I am one of them." He wasn't one to be taken off topic for too long. He pointed again at Tovin. "What is the likely outcome of this, Yuri?"

"Tovin will be killed." She did her best not to wince when she said it. It was a statement of fact about a process she'd gone through so many times before, not an emotional moment.

"How do you feel about that?"

That part was something she knew he'd already guessed on his own. Dangerous as it was to say too much, it was equally dangerous to do nothing. Lavario would make her pay for inaction. "Do you want to help me save him?"

He considered. "Small win from this mess."

"I have an idea." She looked him in the eye. "I'll need your help."

"I am at your disposal."

Well, if that was the case...

As a human, Yuri had been far more adventurous—living and taking with impunity the way beautiful, rich people could. Life as a werewolf made her far more reserved. Now that she was staring down the barrel of two guns, she lost very little by taking a risk. The worst he could say was no. "There is something you can do for me now."

"Tovin will need—"

"This part has nothing to do with Tovin."

He tilted his head to the side again in an invitation to explain herself. Instead of using words, she stood on the tip of her toes to nibble at his lower lip. That should get the point across clear enough.

* * *

"Have you lost your damn mind?" Nadine asked Yuri fifteen versions of the same question every minute or so as they traveled down the hall on their way to Eresna's chambers, Tovin in tow. The little group reminded Yuri of her dinner plate—of all separate elements not daring to overlap. Worked for her, especially since Garvey and Nadine seemed uncomfortable.

"Lavario made you do this?" Nadine asked.

"Smells like he had her up against a wall," Garvey chimed in.

Nadine licked her tooth. "He give you a real hard time, Yur?"

"This could save Tovin." She assured both, ignoring their stupid little innuendoes. The two of them could go on forever like human children if she let them.

"What exactly do we gain if it does?" Nadine wanted to know.

"Lavario's good opinion of us, which is somewhat strained. He asked about your involvement in this." Yuri gave her friend a hard look. Pale, Nadine nodded her head and gulped. Getting back into the good graces of the powerful wolf was reason enough for her. Being on the wrong side of Lavario was not where she wanted to be. Soldiers were only as happy as those who gave them orders. She was on board with the plan now.

Garvey wasn't. "Time for me to go."

"What type of wolf creates all this mess and then leaves, Garvey?" Yuri spit back at him.

"A smart one. She's going to slap me until my teeth fall out. Worst you two will get will be a stern lecture. You're her favorite fetchers. Good dogs the both of ya."

"You're a False Moon accident that does nothing but create other accidents. Why can't you do your job?" Yuri felt her lips lift into a sneer.

"This is the longest this hall has ever been." Nadine rolled her eyes at both of them. "We need to figure out what we're going to do here. What's done is done. Can we all agree on that?"

Yuri never understood why Nadine liked Garvey so much, why she defended him. Reckless, feckless idiot. His only function was his ability to extract. Unlike most of their kind, he kept up with the fads, the trends, the slang, and the culture of humans. Yuri did the same to a lesser degree. Garvey immersed himself, glorifying in the fun of it, while she mimicked.

Nadine gave them a mock thumbs up when Yuri stopped fighting and Garvey agreed to stay. They continued down the hall in silence until Nadine said, "Right then. Here we are."

Before them was the entrance to Eresna's servant's chambers. Ancient, the mahogany double doors were a carved atlas of the pack's life—its ancestors, its battles, its symbols. Entwined through it all was a diamond-scaled, sapphire-eyed dragon Eresna was said to have rode on in the last great pack war. Rumor had it that the dragon's soul was trapped in the wood, waiting for the queen's touch to release it for another battle.

All to guard the entrance to a servant's quarters.

Yuri acknowledged it without any resentment. Eresna was the Alpha Guardian of the Isangelous. Their pack was the only true one in Yuri's mind. The Varcolac were little more than bullies who'd taken power by threatening to destroy the bloodservant system, by promising mass-scale bloodshed. Their "might makes right" way of governance was a sham from the start. Eresna had been powerful enough to make them stay, but she wasn't cruel enough.

The power on display here was the pack's.

The man Tovin replaced was meant to be theirs, too. He was supposed to be a symbol for the risks the pack would take on the behalf of their leader. A gift. Instead of the posh, handsome man Eresna was due, she'd end up with young man of no means.

No one would look for Tovin. Beautiful though he was, he was like any other of the hundreds of thousands of people who vanished each year. There might be flyers, perhaps a few posters. Close family excluded, resources would not likely be spent beyond those few token gestures. Forgotten quickly, Tovin was the type of companion a wolf like Yuri might own.

After a few minutes of wrangling the details, the three of them settled on a plan. Tovin might not be what Eresna wanted, but he'd be what she got.

CHAPTER ELEVEN: STUPID AND CHEAP

Gentle shaking jarred Tovin back to consciousness. He blinked a few times until he could make out the jutting triangle of a face. The Asian woman from the bar stood on the other end of a pale arm that looked like blurred lines through bad binoculars. The floral print of her dress seemed to stretch outside the hard lines of her body. Little pink blurs everywhere.

"Tovin," she shook him again.

"This is stupid." He heard another woman say. "Really stupid. Like Garvey-thought-of-it levels of stupid."

Pink flowers ignored her. "Tovin, wake up."

He didn't immediately respond. His body felt like he was stepping outside of a dream into a nightmare he had previously abandoned. He tried to roll back the other way to reboot himself into a better situation. It worked for the computer at the library, after all. Turn it off. Turn it on. Problem solved.

"Sweet treat," Garvey called out.

That son of a bitch. Tovin's eyes flew open along with his mouth. He was about ready to give the man a piece of his mind when he caught a glimpse of all three of them. His eyes focused. Six pointed incisors in total. Right. Werewolves. Or crazy people—he had to keep telling himself that. Not that it mattered either way.

Then there was the pain. Tovin groaned. Memories came back in one solid heap. The date, the forest, the minivan. Panicked, he tried to look down at his leg. He remembered the white of protruding bone and his torn, bloodied pants. Pink Flowers pushed him against the cushions of a sofa. "There, there." she comforted him awkwardly, rubbing her hand along his temple as if checking for fever.

But he didn't need to see the fracture to know it was there. It was the epicenter for the agony sending shock waves through his body.

Standing beside Pink Flowers was the other woman from the bar, the redhead who was good at trivia. Her dress was gone and replaced with an odd assortment of styles—yellow glasses frames with no lenses, a printed tee, and leggings. Tovin especially loved the leather jacket that had a giant wolf face on the back of it. He saw it whenever she turned her back on him, which was often. Werewolf or not, he had to applaud the fashion statement she made.

"You think this is going to work?" the redhead asked while she gave Tovin a doubtful look. "This kid is handsome but not exactly as..." she flipped her hand through the air. Whatever word she was searching for never came. "Look, all I'm saying is that you could have cut your tongue licking that other man's nipples."

"Sweet treat is adorable. Look at him with his big green eyes and blondish-brown hair. Oats and honey. Human Build-A-Bear. Eresna can dress him up in all sorts of cute outfits."

Garvey crinkled his nose at Tovin.

Redhead responded, "Oats and honey it might have been before you let it tenderize itself against every rock in the forest, but now it's black beans and curdled milk. Two things I wouldn't eat separately, let alone together."

"I'd eat it." Garvey gave her a toothy smile.

Both shewolves exchanged glances. Red shook her head again slightly and looked at Garvey the way a mother looks to an errant child whose disappointments were becoming too numerous to bear, a look that only made Garvey's smile expand.

"Right," Pink Flowers eventually said. "Let's get him cleaned up."

They all argued for a bit about what they were going to do with him. Red worried about bonding with him. *Yuck* was tossed out there as a descriptive word. She pointed at his leg, his other injuries. Garvey wanted to dress him up to impress someone. Pink Flowers stomped her foot, tiny heels clicked. Tovin couldn't follow any of it. The most he got from the entire exchange was the redhead's and Pink Flower's names: Nadine and Yuri. He wanted to assure them all they were most certainly not going to bond, not in any sense of the word as he understood it.

"All right, time for Garvey to fix this. Come here, you." Garvey bent down and stretched his arms out toward Tovin.

Pain shot up from his leg through his entire body, coiling tightly in his groin, as he swatted at the werewolf. Vomit surged from his mouth, hitting the floor with a splatter. He drooled the rest on his clothes. Too weak to turn over, he swallowed down the leftover acid, the bile. "Yuck," Nadine said again. And again. And again. He got the idea.

"Lesson learned." Gleeful as always, Garvey picked him up and carried him to a bathroom Tovin would have appreciated under other circumstances. Very modern. Glossy gray tiles covered the floor and the walls, highlighting the stark whiteness of all the fixtures. Everything gleamed and shone under a chandelier that floated like a jellyfish above them.

The large shower room Garvey eventually plopped him in was equally amazing. Several spouts jutted from the marble walls, each at a different height. The largest showerhead hung from the top; it was a massive rectangular fixture directly above a small bench. When Tovin looked at it, he wanted to shut his eyes and let the water gently coax away the filth and grime from his body.

It was the type of thing he wanted for himself in his normal life.

"Pretty cool, huh?" Garvey said. "It's all yours if you don't get your neck snapped."

Tovin couldn't help it. He whimpered.

"Oops. Made it worse." Garvey shook his head at himself. "Cheer up, though. We have a plan. Ever bring a stray home to your parents and promise them you'd pick up its poopies and take such good care of it?"

Tovin hadn't. But he got the general idea, so he nodded.

"Good. You're the stray. The werewolf who's coming here soon is our parent. We, the kids, are going to look at her with big eyes and say, 'Please.' You need to continue looking pathetic. Yes. Like that. And maybe whimper again some. That even got me going a bit."

"This is so stupid," Nadine said again. "And cheap."

"Well, we're committed now," Garvey responded with good cheer.

Garvey was gentle enough undressing him. Even when Tovin made a few perfunctory gestures of defiance, mostly born from the notion that he should protect his nudity, the werewolf shushed him and then yanked off the remains of Tovin's clothes.

When the actual shower began, Tovin's protests became less superficial, Garvey's admonishments less congenial. The water was far too hot for human skin and left red splotch marks wherever it touched, searing rather than coaxing the grime and dirt from Tovin's body. Garvey scoured his flesh as though Tovin was an especially troublesome skillet caked with egg. Contusions and scrapes were met with greater force as though the werewolf felt his level of vigor would correspond to greater results and the marred parts of Tovin's body would yield accordingly.

It hurt. Tovin kept twisting to get away, and Garvey kept dragging him back, his hands slipping on what parts of Tovin's skin were slick with soap. Occasionally the werewolf tugged on his bad leg, and the pain made him moan and cry out, all to his shame. "I'm trying to help you. Hold still." But Tovin couldn't and continued to claw his way around the shower stall to find a spot where at least he would be protected from the sting of the water.

"It's too hot," Tovin protested.

Nadine chuckled. "I'm going to hug it and squeeze it and call it—"

Yuri, pale with fury, stamped her foot again. The noise scattered like a shotgun blast around the room. "Enough. Move. You're hurting him."

For the first time, Garvey looked angry. "For fuck's sake, Yuri. I'm trying to—"

Pink flowers showed her teeth and jerked her thumb behind her. "Move."

Garvey bared his teeth back at her.

There was a lot of growling and posturing. Eventually, Garvey averted his gaze with a huff. He tossed the washcloth to the ground and got out of the way. Fiddling on his smartphone suddenly seemed like something he wanted to do all along. He said something to Nadine about someone in his LARP group having a birthday. She told him it sounded like the perfect time to role-play a character who was cheap and forgetful. They both laughed.

Pink Flowers, now known to him as Yuri, fixed the water first, continually looking at him to ask, "Comfortable?" as she adjusted the temperature. When he finally nodded, she knelt beside him, gathered him into her arms and washed him more gently than he would have ever thought her capable, all while mumbling platitudes—shushes, tuts, and there nows.

Nadine looked concerned. "Jesus. You're already fully bonded to him. What's going on, Yuri? How did that happen?"

Yuri didn't have a response to that question. She rested her chin on Tovin's head and said, "We're going to be fine."

CHAPTER TWELVE: OVERTHINKING IT

Through clacking teeth, Tovin asked, "What's going to happen? What's going to happen if Eresna doesn't accept me?" He kept repeating. They kept ignoring him.

At least they'd sort of healed his leg. It was still red and throbbing, but no longer broken.

Naked except for his underwear, Tovin was surrounded by personal details that didn't belong to him. He was not a cellist, did not wear finely tailored suits, was not a briefs sort of guy, and had never worn a bow tie or read much classical literature. In his head, Tovin heard the fine, expensive objects in the room titter in Miller's voice that something so fine would never belong to a fag like him. Thinking it stung. The more he tried to unthink it for his own sake, the more the word repeated. He'd been called that so many times before.

Pawing through it all and oblivious to any and all resentments was Garvey looking for pajamas. Each item he found had its own brief narrative—the gist of which was simply, *These are not pajamas*—and then was discarded summarily onto a growing pile of nonpajamas on the floor.

All of them avoided eye contact with Tovin. Occasional spin-the-bottle glances where eyes never quite chose to look at him darted his way.

"We need something adorable," Garvey told the two shewolves. "What's more adorable than pajamas?"

Yuri, staring off into space, didn't turn to him to respond. "I hope she beats you until you're full on your own blood and can't feel your fangs, Garvey."

"Drama, drama," he snapped back.

The hostilities between the two hadn't waned. They went on like that for a bit. Garvey wisecracking, Yuri retorting, Nadine mediating. Tovin drifted in and out of it until the doors opened. In wisped with airy grace what had to be one of the most beautiful women Tovin had ever seen. A slender, smooth-muscled statue who had dark, flawless skin, all soft lines and shine, and a trove of curly hair that geysered from her scalp and shook with each little movement. Lacking immortality, she would have had a timeless face—the old woman with smooth skin, impossibly white teeth. The three of them snapped to attention, and said as one. "Alpha Guardian Eresna."

"Who is this?" The woman's voice was soft, her expression curious when she looked at Tovin. "Where is my companion?"

"Garvey messed things up, Alpha Guardian Eresna." Nadine pointed at the cowering wolfman, who lingered behind Tovin's shoulder.

"Explain," the newcomer demanded with the haughty air of authority.

Though the request was directed at Garvey, Yuri answered. "Garvey thought it would be fun to have sex with Lavario's bloodservant. When that failed, he decided it would be equally fun to transform and then hunt down the boy. During the chase, the human injured himself to the point where Mazgan was unwilling to accept him, stating that the boy's injuries would result in death during feeding. Lavario got to choose another to take this one's place. He chose your companion. There was nothing to be done since the fault was ours."

"I see. Why is he here?" Eresna gestured to Tovin.

"He's a gift." Nadine rushed in to explain, cutting Yuri off with a sideways glance in the other shewolf's direction. "From Lavario."

She looked at Tovin down the line of her nose. "How very considerate of him. Why did you three bring him to me, and why is he awake?"

Nadine rushed in again. "We thought you might actually like him. Great body. Unusual eyes, stunning really. I know you can't see it now because of all—" She circled her hand in the air again. "Well, he's kind of dinged up. Healed, he's quite good looking. He was *Lavario's* after all."

If she was meant to be impressed by the last bit, she wasn't. Distant, suspicious, she held herself back from the group. Although he wouldn't bet his life on it, Tovin thought he saw some humor here and there—quick flashes of light in her deep-brown eyes. It kept him from hating her completely. "Gay—or at least bisexual—for Lavario's pleasure, I assume?"

"Well. Yes. Gay."

"Not much fun for me." Eresna raised her lip in a slight, chiding smile.

"No, but. Uh. Uh. Erm." Nadine paused, searching, searching, searching. "I bet you'll enjoy his company. He's real good at trivia."

This was the point at which Tovin decided he'd like a more articulate advocate than Nadine. Yuri, the one who was so gentle with him, was the only other one keen to speak. Each time she tried, Nadine cut her off in hurried spurts of garbled arguments amounting to nothing more than the elongated *please* Garvey mockingly suggested earlier.

Eresna was having nothing of any of it. She made some guttural noise, cutting the babbling redhead off. "Garvey?" Eresna turned his direction. "Did you do all this because he was to be Lavario's?"

Garvey's smile bubbled to the surface like it wanted to come out but knew better. "We have our history."

Questions stopped. The woman began to strip. Nudity didn't bother Tovin, but the controlled way she stepped out of her elegant gown made him want to look away. It was lethal, driven by an intent the more primitive parts of Tovin's brain immediately understood. Outside of her gown at last, she folded it, still calm, and handed it over to Yuri for safekeeping.

Regally, showing the same care she'd shown for the gown, she transformed. Reactively, Garvey followed and hunkered down into a defensive posture. Side by side, Garvey's form appeared mangy and domesticated, close to ridiculous. Eresna's form was more what Tovin expected in a werewolf: massive, lacking identifiable sexual organs, and terrifying yet beautiful in its own way.

No suspense. She beat the shit out of him.

Garvey, for his part, endured. He made no attempt to fight back, no movement to protect himself. Each bite pierced skin, each blow landed. The longer she wailed on him, the more doglike he became, physically shrinking until he was the size of any standard wolf. Only when the shewolf's maw descended on his throat did he make any sort of proactive, voluntary maneuver—rolling onto his back to whimper. Eresna hovered above his throat, growling softly.

Tovin wasn't going to lie. It felt so good at first—like the first few bites of ice cream on a hundred-degree day. Before too long, Tovin couldn't help but feel bad for Garvey. Not that it mattered. He was nonexistent, tucked away in the corner of the room to observe and wait until they were ready to tell him his fate. Neck snapped or forever food.

Worst participant in a chase scene, terrified captive, then possible slave to a werewolf queen. Tovin cared little for his story arc so far. "Stop," Tovin did his best to stand when he said it, but he couldn't manage much with this leg. It throbbed. The pain bit at his resolve.

All heads turned his direction. Eresna looked at him briefly before returning to her task.

"Stop," Tovin repeated.

This time Eresna acknowledged him. Bits of flesh dripped from her paws, blood pulled away from her canines like liquid on the side of a plastic cup. Slits of amber narrowed on his face. Was she angry? He couldn't tell. Maybe. Probably. Heavy breathing, the scuttle of her claws against the wooden floor, and the frantic beat of his own heart kept him company as he closed his eyes and prepared himself to die for the second time today.

A gentle touch where he was expecting a strike startled him. Yuri touched his shoulder. Her face had an expression that reflected his thoughts, *Really? For that asshole?* As much as it could emote, Garvey's battered-dog face echoed the sentiment. Eresna hadn't moved at all. "She would never kill Garvey," Yuri said to him before turning to Eresna. "You see how kind he is, Guardian?"

"Or dumb," Nadine said.

Yuri gave her a sharp look.

Apologetic, Nadine amended her previous statement. "He's very kind. Just the sweetest."

Wolf changed back to woman and she glanced at Tovin with sad eyes before fixing her gaze back on her petite companion. "Yuri, the boy is not suited for me."

Yuri looked to her feet. Nadine shook her head. Garvey hopped out of his wolf form. Bent to the side, his nose pouring blood. The rest of his face was red, beginning to blacken. There were welts on this body, long claw marks turning purple at the edges. Despite the injuries, Garvey tried to advocate for Tovin. "But he's so adorable."

Everyone ignored him.

"He is not suited." Eresna stressed it again, draping a long, silken robe over her nakedness. "My people will be disappointed. You know my bloodservant is a gift from them, Yuri."

Yuri gave Nadine a brief glance, as though asking for permission. The other shewolf grimaced and then nodded. "We've already bonded with him, Guardian. It happened on accident after he fell out of the car. Please spare us by accepting him."

Eresna turned to Nadine with a raised eyebrow, disbelief etched into her features.

"Yes, I'm bonded to him. I love him. I'd be devastated if anything were to happen to him," Nadine assured her. None of it was intended to be sarcastic—at least Tovin didn't get that sense—but the shewolf was a terrible actress. Lines were blurted and clunky, eyes wide and straightforward as she recited them. It didn't make him hopeful that whatever it is they were doing was working.

"I see you care for him, Yuri." Eresna's face softened some as she continued. "Perhaps we can work something out. What type of servant did you get?"

The question was directed at Yuri. Garvey laughed before answering. "She got some sort of animal trainer with a paunch and a gambling addiction."

Eresna made a face Tovin couldn't quite interpret. She turned to Nadine, who quickly answered with, "Hobo." Eresna's eyes continued to probe. Confused, Nadine went on qualifying. "Drunk, sort of crazy, smells like urine, bad teeth." She shrugged. "Hobo."

Eresna's frown said no to Yuri and Nadine's bloodservants. She touched the side of her subordinate's face with the tips of her fingers. "I'm so sorry, Yuri."

Tovin repressed another whimper. For whatever reason, he was so sure this was going to work out. Now that it wasn't, he tried without result to crawl his way out the door. Where was he going? He didn't know. Away. Away from this mess. Or two feet. Yeah, he got as far as two feet before the pain cramped him.

Yuri watched him with tears in her eyes. Nadine focused on the floor.

Garvey called out before Eresna left. "Wait!"

The hem of her long robe skidded on the smooth marble of the floor. She turned back around, considering the wolf. "What is it, Garvey?"

"Take him for political reasons."

Eresna indicated he should continue.

"Control over Tovin gives you some measure of control over Lavario."

"Perhaps. Why would I want this?"

Garvey tilted his head to the side as though he couldn't believe she asked him such a question. "Because he's powerful. Because he'd owe you a favor if you kept Tovin. Because you want to fuck with him. Pick a reason. Use your imagination. I've never known you to be a thoughtless killer. You know, like—"

"You?" Eresna finished for him.

"You got it."

Mad as hell was the response Tovin expected after Garvey's rant. The accusation at the end made him wince. Eresna, however, appeared amused. The smooth lines of her face rippled into a smile. "Something is off here, Garvey. I'm starting to think you're smitten with this boy. Odd for a Moondog. Tell me what you got out of this mess."

"Going to release vampires. Kill some people." While everyone laughed, Garvey mashed his lips together. Tovin saw something dark in his former date's eyes, quick flashes of real anger. The moment drifted away. Humor settled over Garvey's features like a fog over a valley. Fog was dangerous. Unwary travelers who thought they knew the terrain always got in the worst sort of accidents. Garvey laughed, too—a long, clucking chuckle that made Tovin uneasy.

Yuri saw it, too. "You're going to kill people with vampires? How?"

Nadine sighed at her friend and said, "Lighten up, Yuri. Vampires are dead. Garv is just being himself."

Garvey agreed, "Yes, I know. I'm so silly. Really, though. Eresna, I bonded with Tovin in the woods. He's a tricky little devil."

Tovin's heart squeezed. Somehow, it felt true, too.

For the first time since she'd walked in, Eresna actually assessed Tovin. Contemplation made her brown eyes dark tunnels. Tovin could only hope he'd see the light at the end. "Please," he begged her.

Eresna relented. "Very well, we will keep him for political reasons. Our official story is we spared him for Yuri's sake. Understood?" All the werewolves nodded. Her lip curled some when she said, "Garvey, since this is your handiwork, find the healer, get him some clothes, check in with distribution."

"Thank you, Guardian," they all said at once like a room of schoolchildren.

Another day for them. They were ready to move on from it.

Tovin wasn't. Yesterday, or was it a week ago, he was standing in the grocery store aisle sniffing bottles of deodorant, taking all the time in the world to make what—at the time—seemed like an important decision. How was he going to smell for Garvey, the date that was going to change his life? His sister had leaned over his shoulder. *Overthinking it*, she'd said five minutes into his process. *Really overthinking it,* she'd chastised him after ten. In the end, he'd walked out with the same brand he'd always used.

Change had always been small, controlled, and on his own terms, meaning mostly nonexistent. Things were not going to work that way here. Invisible, he sat off to the side while the three werewolves planned his future—his clothes, his smell, his food. Judging by their level of interest, none of them were going to take the care he'd take.

CHAPTER THIRTEEN: THE BOO HAG EXILE

Guest halls were meant to be a place of celebration where the pack gathered to bless its accomplishments. Lush gardens, gushing fountains, and foods from all over the world were available to any wolf who wanted to take part in the festivities following a successful hunt. The bloodservant system was the pride of the Isangelous pack—hated by the False Moons, who derided it as cruel and lazy, but coveted by the Varcolac wolves. Today, the hall was a place of awkward, forced socializing. Lower-ranking wolves, or the submissives as they were called, were there, but none of them were in very high spirits given the atmosphere.

Eresna sat at the head of the table. The Alpha Guardian took several token sips from her wine glass, nibbles from the honey ham. Other Isangelous wolves did the same. The two guests from the Varcolac—Lavario and Mazgan—hadn't touched any of the food.

Mazgan hovered, grinning from ear to ear with an erratic manic energy that no one could mistake for actual happiness. Beneath it all—as always—was a violence that could manifest at any time, for an insult real or imagined. Since he refused to sit in the presence of the submissives, the chair placed for him at the table remained empty.

Lavario sat. Good manners were important to him even under the worst circumstances. Eresna acknowledged his courtesy with equal grace. There was a time when the two of them would have talked early into the morning hours about old times, great adventures and pack politics. But Lavario was Varcolac now. Neutral was the most forgiving word Yuri could think of to describe the relationship between her queen and the exile.

Tovin slumbered. He was propped on the chaise off to the side, the only bloodservant in attendance. A healer tended to the boy's wounds. Contusions, deep cuts, and broken bones all mended under his skilled fingers. "Want me to fix the eyes or do you like the glasses?" The healer asked once all the critical injuries were attended to.

"Fix them, please." Eresna favored him with a nod and a smile. "It would be a shame to obscure his best feature with those hideous things."

Mazgan turned to Eresna and said, "Even cleaned up, this one is not quite as handsome as the servant you selected. Your people went beyond their duty to extract something so special for you. Such a shame for Lavario to snatch it away and replace it with this."

It was a shame. Eresna was no doubt furious. Lavario too. Hard feelings were set aside for the sake of pride. Neither guardian would admit they'd had something taken away from them by Mazgan, who gloated inelegantly, constantly drawing attention back to the botched extraction. The more he went on about it, the politer Lavario and Eresna became until they were eventually talking about the entire situation with a strained good humor.

When Eresna responded, her tone was light, musical. "Tovin is a dear boy, I'm sure, Alpha Guardian. Lavario gifting him to me was quite thoughtful."

"Indeed. We all know how much Lavario likes his pretty boys with no real substance." Mazgan looked to Lavario and then to Garvey as he said it.

Garvey waited for the focus to shift from him. He then batted his eyelashes at Nadine and mouthed, *I'm so pretty!*

Nadine smirked. *No real substance*, she mouthed back and licked her tooth.

Garvey nodded, mouthing, *Sounds about right.* He held up his index finger before he continued. *But pretty!*

Lavario ignored Mazgan and Garvey. "Thank you for accepting my gift, Eresna. My apologies for the circumstances. I only hope you understand my distress regarding the boy's situation."

Although her queen went through all the motions of accepting Tovin into her service, an uneasy feeling landed like a persistent fly in Yuri's subconscious. She swatted it and tried to focus on a short list of her duties. Be available, be silent, be knowledgeable, and be a representative of the Isangelous above all else, especially with Varcolac wolves present. Mazgan in particular. She wouldn't disgrace her kind by asking her queen out-of-turn questions.

Mazgan disgraced his kind well enough for all of them. "What is Tovin again? Some sort of salesman? The other guy was a cellist? And a boxer in college? Athletic. Good looking."

"Yes, I believe so, Alpha Guardian." With thin-lipped patience, Eresna changed the subject once again. "Where is Kijo? She normally loves the pastries."

At the mention of his daughter, Lavario's jaw clenched with a spasm. He gave them a quick explanation everyone understood to be a lie. She was in the car. Tired, Lavario explained, from the stress of the day's travels. The entire time, his face was pinched, angry.

Mazgan rushed in as if he'd been waiting for that moment the entire night, "I wonder why she remains there. Perhaps you can tell us, Lavario." He didn't give his second-in-command any time to respond. He continued, "She did not want to watch you humiliate yourself over some human. That is my guess."

"Plausible." Lavario sounded bored with the topic. Yuri knew him too well to be fooled. Transformed into a wolf, he kept his human eyes—a light green that stood out in stark contrast to his black fur. It was unique to him. Other wolves had yellowish, golden eyes regardless of their human features. When angered, Lavario lost some of his control. The animal took hold and flecks of gold yellow began to creep like sap seeping out through timber. Yuri saw it now.

That's when things went from awkward to bad.

"You forget yourself again," Mazgan's nostrils flared. "Address me properly. I earned my rank. I am no pampered Boo Hag who runs about creating False Moon bastard wolves."

"We prefer Moondogs over False Moon, Alpha Guardian," Garvey said with a smile.

"And we prefer Isangelous, Alpha Guardian," Eresna said without one.

Mazgan snorted at them both. "I will use whatever term I wish."

Wolf eyes, full like the moon but glowing hot like the sun, took over Eresna's face. She was about to respond when Lavario cut in. "You earned that title, Alpha Guardian. You bit, you fought, you warred, and you killed for it. And I did none of those things."

"Yours was given," Mazgan snarled back.

Lavario nodded. He had regained his calm. His green eyes were sharply focused. "Undeserving as I am, perhaps you challenge me, Alpha Guardian. Challenge me. Defeat me. Cast me down to live with the low-ranking wolves.

Speechless at last, Mazgan considered Lavario with claws drawn and teeth bared. Anger gathered up as a tight ball of energy in the room, concentrating around the irate Alpha Guardian, who was a few moments away from losing control entirely and transforming. Loose cannon, rule breaker, human-lover, and possessing all the mannerisms of Isangelous royalty, Lavario was everything Mazgan hated.

Wolf it up, Yuri said to herself. *Fight Lavario and see what an Isangelous guardian can do.* A Boo Hag in charge of Varcolac wolves would be the sweetest revenge for the arrogance Mazgan and his kind showed. Yuri knew Eresna, for all her power, wasn't in the position to do it herself. It wasn't her place. She wasn't Varcolac.

"Challenge me," Lavario said again in a way that gave Yuri a thrill.

Control was regained in patches. First, Mazgan pulled back his teeth a little bit, claws followed. Eyes lost their golden hue and became the same brown that reminded Yuri of dung—both in color and density. His white skin, which had turned into a sort of ugly red, turned back to its normal bloated macaroni state. He was human when he approached Tovin. "Such a pretty one," Mazgan brushed the hair back from the boy's face.

Lavario stood.

Even Garvey, who had watched everything with an amused, casual air, popped to attention. It startled Nadine, who was nodding off.

Eresna arched her brow. "He is mine, Alpha Guardian."

"Not yet," he responded.

True. Eresna had not bonded with Tovin yet. By their own rules, it wasn't official until she did. Mazgan knew it. The Varcolac loved to exploit such policies. He shook Tovin awake with enough force that they heard his teeth rattle. Eventually, the boy woke up. Upon seeing Mazgan, his face leering down with incisors slightly extended, Tovin drew back with a yelp.

Mazgan shushed him. "I want to show you what these Boo Hags mean by 'companionship.' This will only hurt for a bit."

Yuri was bonded to Tovin. Pain shot through her the moment Mazgan's fangs punctured his jugular. Fear followed, then the desperate, panicked realization that this was how death came.

Luckily, Eresna was too busy being outraged by Mazgan's gall to notice Yuri's extreme discomfort. "That's enough. You made your point."

He pulled back. Blood ran down his chin. "Lavario, have I made my point?"

Lavario lifted his head. For a moment, Yuri thought he was going to continue his defiance. Tovin was already almost dead anyway. Then, finally, "Yes, you made your point, Alpha Guardian."

"Tell me what my point is."

"I am a Boo Hag, Alpha Guardian."

"To the bone," Mazgan responded.

Lavario was cursed. Unlike all of her other brothers and sisters, Yuri understood that to be the truest thing about their exiled guardian. Being forced to feel for humans was called a gift, a way for wolves to understand their servants and live fully through them. Bullshit. It was all about resource management. Humans were food, but wolves couldn't afford to cull too many. Her kind went through the motions knowing this, bonding themselves so that they'd be more likely to conserve rather than kill or discard.

As a pack guardian, Lavario was the first to take the gift back when it was conceptualized. It worked a bit too well at first. He became an empath, able to feel emotions and sense general thoughts. Another way he was unique.

Until Tovin, Yuri only understood the burden of it on a surface level. In the moment she thought the boy was going to die, she was a pinball machine. Bells went off. Lights blinked, blinked, blinked and stopped as the ball plummeted right down the middle. To feel that for every human as Lavario did would be a terrible thing. To live that way as a Varcolac would have been torture.

PART TWO

THE WORST WEREWOLF

CHAPTER FOURTEEN: FATHER AND DAUGHTER

Lavario sat inside the comfort of his limousine while Kijo discussed the night's events with Mazgan. He could hear bits and pieces of their conversation, mostly loud posturing from Mazgan. No doubt their Alpha Guardian stressed the prostration that occurred after he nearly drained Tovin. Thinking on the night's events made Lavario extend his claws in agitation.

The bloodservant he only knew as Not-Tovin sat on the floor, a gift from Mazgan. *A chance for you to bond with your new companion,* he said as though he were the smartest wolf to ever howl at the moon. Lavario did have to admit this was good. One of Mazgan's plans might pay off for him.

Much depended on Kijo.

"She is my daughter," he said to himself. "She will not challenge me."

His fingers tapped as he said it. He wasn't so sure. Kijo adored him, he had no doubt, but she also loved her pack and they her. Thus far they had endured her relationship with Lavario, hoping one day she would cut ties as progeny often did, but they grew tired of waiting. Century reminders became decade reminders became yearly reminders. She needed to choose her camp.

Lavario came to the Varcolac as the lusty, foolish guardian of the Isangelous who usurped the power of his alpha and made his human companion a wolf. He came as a rule breaker. Garvey. His first stupid thing. His accident.

Varcolac wolves cared little for the transgression itself. Members of the pack could turn humans with pack support, only with the understanding that the test would weed out the weak, the unworthy. But a wolf had to have a certain respect for rank, and Lavario had defied his leader without directly challenging him for power. Only the weakest of wolves wangled results. The noble among them achieved their ends legitimately. Lavario was simply a powerful cheat to most of his brothers and sisters.

Lavario sighed. Nothing he could do now but wait.

Memory kept him company. Sometimes it was a polite guest, letting him dwell on the happy parts of his long life. Mostly it pricked, needled, and twisted the knife far better than Mazgan ever could have.

There was the conversation he had with Kijo before they went to collect their new servants.

Boo Haggish, Kijo called his eagerness to meet Tovin. It was said with more force than normal.

Daughter, he had responded, *it is the same as it has always been.*

Now he knew exactly how different it was. Now he knew *Boo Haggish* was the worst thing she could have called it.

Beside him, his sleeping bloodservant farted. Lavario wrinkled his nose at the sharp smell, but allowed himself a dark chuckle. Life cared little for his situation. It went on, and on, and on, and on.

* * *

Kijo got in the car with Lavario. A good sign. Once again she was by his side, her black eyes fierce and distant. She looked down at the sleeping servant before addressing him. "Blood is blood and tastes like metal, salt, and oxygen no matter whose arteries it comes from, Father."

"It is not the blood I want to taste."

She snorted and shook her head. "Your stupid thing was unraveled by your previous stupid thing."

She was, of course, referring to Garvey's role in this mess. It was one thing to be thwarted by the Boo Hags, who were well known as rigid, long-term thinkers with single-minded devotion to duty. More than a few wolves had seen better plans fall apart due to their interference. It was quite another to be thwarted by Garvey, who was seen—even by his own pack—as Lavario's accident, a farce.

Worse, Garvey did not plot. Garvey just did things. He was the quintessential id-driven monster of lore, running about chasing people in a mad frenzy. Very unwolf. Very False Moon.

"Yes, our brothers and sisters will be displeased, no doubt," Lavario replied. "I imagine they will believe I am weak because I lost something to my bastard's nonsense."

"They will challenge you, Father."

He raised an eyebrow at that. "And they will lose."

"Mazgan—"

"Would lose."

"Challenge him," she pressed him.

"I will never be the leader of the Varcolac, my daughter."

"But if you win by force—"

"Then I will spend the rest of my life ruling through force." Lavario looked to his Kijo, who was so sure her packmates would accept him if he won power in their version of a legitimate fight. "I would rather have sex with some pretty men and women and enjoy my gardens."

Her black eyes compressed so hard Lavario thought they might turn to diamonds. "Your Boo Hag frills are costly. We have both paid for them."

Yes, that was true.

Rebellion was a rite of passage and expected. Unwillingness to do so could be misconstrued as weakness, often resulting in more challenges for power from submissives, which meant more chances to be marked or killed. Kijo had suffered a lot in her 200th year when she failed to bare her teeth to Lavario, her Boo Hag father.

She defeated them all, even killing one who had dared to call her by her human name. Jun. Kijo ripped the wolf's head off and drank his blood as she would a human's. Subsequent challenges stopped. She was strong, his Kijo. Smart, fierce, ambitious, perceptive—a true guardian, one of birth. She was not the type you ever had to sternly tell, *This is not a joke*. She almost never laughed. Her face was a canvas of haughty scorn, quick calculation. Pure Varcolac.

And a fierce opponent.

"Will you fight me?" He had asked the question before and almost always the answer was a playful nip at his chin and her saying, *There, you have been challenged, Father*. This time he dreaded the answer.

She ignored the question. "We can act as though this was planned. You did not lose Tovin. You took Eresna's bloodservant."

Lavario looked at Not-Tovin, now the emblem of his humiliation. Soigne, talented, educated—a beautiful human, as fine as any Lavario had ever fed from, a companion who was no doubt fit for a guardian as powerful as Eresna or Lavario himself. What a petty thing to lose his power over. Stupid, stupid thing. "Mazgan will not allow that."

"They need to know you're no Boo Hag, Father. I need to know it."

"I am no longer Isangelous. They have made that clear."

She gave him a deep, dissatisfied growl. "Then do not sit there and let it end this way between us. Do something."

Lavario was her personality flaw. Powerful wolves fell to such things by either failing to acknowledge or address the issue. It was one of the first lessons he ever taught her when she was his little Jun—before Kijo, before politics, before the Varcolac.

Lavario fought back the urge to remind her of the girl she once was, his little moon, some bedraggled waif left to die because her human father wanted a boy. She had not done very well for herself in the forest that night. Her crying was incessant, and she asked the advice of the stuffed bear she had been dumped with, as if it could tell her where to find food, warmth, comfort, and love. Not as practical back then.

Newly exiled, he intended to kill her, to clamp his jaws over her throat and drink her blood in the type of callous fashion his new Varcolac peers would find acceptable. When he approached her, she looked up at him with such fearless black eyes and her gaunt arms reached out to him. *Gǒu*, she called him, despite the fact he stood over eight feet tall and had his face fixed in a snarl.

Instead of killing her, he licked her face—taking all her snot, her tears, her pain into himself. When she came back to the camp with him, her fist curled around his tail, his brothers and sisters made several challenges. He beat them all. She continued to sleep curled against his chest, the stuffed bear cupped under her chin, for seven more years until she was old enough to insist on her own fine bedding and other vanities.

Kijo was born soon after.

The stray in tattered rags morphed into a petite young woman who wanted nothing but the finest silk dresses. One night, his little lady in silk brought her human father into the pack's camp. There was a welt on the side of his head where she struck him with a broom.

Feed from him, she told Lavario.

That night, he did something he rarely did and refused her, fearing that she would ask it of him only to regret it later. *Child, this is your father*.

Jun took out a knife, cut the man's throat open, and drank his blood herself. When she was done vomiting it back up, she turned to him and said *You will now call me Kijo. I am your daughter*.

He obeyed her that time. She became his second legitimate offspring to survive the test and be confirmed wolf.

A waif in rags, a lady in silk, a werewolf guardian who conformed her dress to the standards of her pack. Now everything she wore was a rebuke to beauty. She kept her glossy black hair tightly bound and wore shapeless clothes that made her some frumpy khaki-clad warrior. Lavario loved all incarnations equally but for different reasons. She had been his moon for so long that he did not want her to become just another object in space drifting away from him.

More, he did not want her to challenge him. Kijo did little halfway. To truly separate herself from him—from him and his rule breaking, from him and his Boo Haggishness, from him and his humiliation—she would have to kill him. Simply marking him wouldn't be enough to assure her brothers and sisters she was no longer his ally.

For him to win meant killing her. She would not lie down, even when beaten, Lavario knew. He disliked both outcomes. He did not want to die, certainly. And no father wants to feel life drain from his child. Yet a challenge seemed forthcoming. Lavario could feel it building within her, gathering its momentum as her own excuses for continuing to allow him to be her burden ran their course.

Excuses ended. Then so would they.

CHAPTER FIFTEEN: LAST OF THE GOOD TIMES

Kijo granted Lavario a generous amount of time to consider where he went wrong. Silence between them was usually as familiar as it was binding. Now it was wearisome. Lavario ran himself in exhaustive circles trying to piece together what each minuscule variation in her expression meant. He'd have better luck using the entrails of a chicken to divine the weather than he would interpreting his daughter's mood.

The only thing keeping him company was his empath's burden.

Even sleeping threads of the bloodservant's thoughts found their way to Lavario. Images of family, friends—happy times of barbeques on the lawn and fireworks. It felt as though he were there, that it was him telling puckish kids to stop chasing their younger siblings with spitting, hissing sparkler flames.

Minor details of the bloodservant's life bedeviled Lavario, too. An endless collection of unpaid bills, dental worries, and traffic jams. Sorting through the clutter to find his way back to the current situation proved much more difficult while also under the onslaught of Kijo's quiet, overhanging rage.

Lavario fought the urge to kill the bloodservant, ending at least some of his torment.

But losing control would not help his situation. Lavario taught Kijo that only weak wolves frenzied; strong wolves were deliberate, spoke softly but meant every word said. Allowing himself a fit of temper would only make him appear powerless in her eyes. *Plus*, Lavario thought, *I'd be out several meals.*

"I would have killed Jun." Kijo broke the silence with the odd confession.

Lavario didn't quite know where she was going, but he was at least relieved to be talking about something other than his bloodservant disaster. "Yes, most certainly."

"Why did you save her?"

"I love her."

She made a face. "Jun was not worthy of love."

"Worthiness was never a consideration. Kijo and Jun are the same to me. You make a distinction. I surrender to your right to do so."

For a moment, it seemed she would strike him. Her top lip subducted beneath her lower, a pressure formed there as the jutting soft flesh of her beloved mouth trembled. "I live as I do today because you are a sap. A fool." Orey-eyed, she turned to face him, looking over the lines of his features scanning for a sign of denial.

She needed him to argue, to reassure her that she was not a stupid thing, a product of statistical probabilities that had worked in her favor. Truthfully, Lavario created many children after Garvey. The Varcolac turned most human bloodservants as a matter of courtesy at the end, allowing them at least some chance at immorality. Most died during the test, usually in the first few minutes, unworthy as they were. Unlike the rest of the Varcolac, Lavario looked back on his failed children with fondness, even love and regret.

"Yes," he said at last, "you are here because I am weak. A Varcolac would have killed Jun as you say. What have you told yourself all these years? That Jun was different from Garvey? From Tovin? Nonsense, Kijo. You are no pup, and I never lied."

What story *had* she told herself? Lavario did not know. It's not something he ever bothered to ask since it always worked in his favor. Denial has its own type of inertia. Immortals were no different in that. New wolves believed that everything would change for them once they were turned. They would be better versions of themselves somehow. In practice, it was the old self with added hair, fangs, claws. Very rarely was it transformative beyond that. His daughter was no exception. She lived both lives in a state of repression.

Trying to lighten the mood, Lavario jested, "Perhaps I can get myself exiled again. Live as a Moondog."

She shook her head, considering as if he'd been serious. "Mazgan will not allow it. This was planned. He said I would understand the depth of your weakness after tonight, that I would understand how foolish you look and how foolish I am through association. He wants you dead. He wants all guardians who were born to their post dead."

"All?" He looked at his daughter pointedly.

She snorted. "Not me. He loves me."

Mazgan's affections for Kijo were unrequited and hilarious. Even Kijo, who laughed as often as the moon was blue, chuckled.

She sobered up quickly. "He is right. I cannot keep power for much longer, Father."

Lavario reminded her that this mistake was not remarkably different from any of his others. He had found, screwed, and even loved humans for centuries now. It was one thing that never got old.

As if sensing his thoughts, she explained, "It is not only this situation. Each time you blunder, your mistakes are added to the others. The pack cannot think of one without thinking on them all until it's a totality of errors. What Alpha Guardian Mazgan said holds true. I look weak through you. I'm a child born of your folly who lives in your folly." She stopped, trying to take control of her face, which was swelling with emotion. "I love you despite it."

"What will you do?"

She didn't answer.

Scenery blurred by, slowing down when he focused for a few moments. Her hands drifted, rising and falling like little white petals caught in a breeze. She couldn't pace as she thought through her options, but she couldn't hold still, either. He was sure she was fighting with herself. She certainly talked to herself the way she always did when confronted with a problem.

She gave him the briefest of smiles. "Maybe we can both be Moondogs."

Lavario laughed at the notion.

"Yes," she said, "that was the conclusion I came to."

Once again, he saw his jaws around her throat, hers around his. It made him shudder.

She must have seen the same thing. Normally stoic, his Kijo was on the verge of tears, something he hadn't seen since her human days. She tried to hide it under anger, resentment, but Lavario knew what he saw.

He placed his hand over hers. "Kijo..."

She let herself be comforted by his touch before jerking away. "Do something," she told him again, a slight, almost undetectable break in her voice.

"By *something* you mean kill Mazgan, yes?"

Kijo confirmed. Comfortable, once again logically detached, she reasoned, "Between the two of us, you are the one in the position to do so *right now*. My challenge would be considered fence jumping until I beat you."

"Lest we forget the rules," Lavario rolled his eyes at the absurdity of the process. The Varcolac existed because of Mazgan's brashness, his willingness to attack political opponents for power. His ascension was nothing but a long series of jumped fences. Pointing out the hypocrisy could wait. "I didn't survive ten thousand years to terrorize submissives while wearing uncomfortable pants. The pack does not accept me, daughter. They love you. Lead them."

"And if I could bring them to your side?"

"You would require one hell of a rolled-up newspaper."

Humor was inappropriate. Always. But especially now. If possible, her eyes became harder, less forgiving.

He flipped his hand up in the air, yielding to her strange optimism. "Very well, prove me wrong."

"Hand me your bloodservant's wallet," she commanded him.

Lavario did as she instructed.

Her brow furrowed as she looked through the pictures. Kijo mused, "Good, he has kids. I worried it would not be the case."

There were several pictures of the man's family inside the wallet. His wife was equally beautiful, as were his three children. Two daughters, one looked like she was in her twenties and the other in her late teens, and a boy who was a pup. Full grown, he'd be a handsome fellow.

He already had his father's sharp features and hazel eyes. In family pictures, he was little bits of flesh peeping out of massive coats, caps, and sports jerseys. For professional portraits, they had him dressed as a little man in bow ties and sweater vests, his delicate little hands clinging to a violin as he grinned the grin of a child who has not yet mastered artifice well enough to know that the expression made him look half-crazed.

"Delightful. My bloodservant loves his family at least."

"They are mostly of the boy. He must love the boy."

Lavario noticed a dearth of pictures when it came to the two girls and their mother. The bloodservant's son was front and center, it was true. It made sense that his Kijo would see it. Few wolves could hold a grudge the way she did. Most forgot petty slights from the past and kept focused on the now and the future, but his daughter remembered every cut, every snub, and every injury. Her father was the first. Even after all the blood spilled from him, she visited his corpse in the woods where he remained unburied, rotting.

It didn't take too much imagination to see her visiting his body in the same way. Swallowing, Lavario focused on now. "What good does his family do us?" he asked her.

Instead of answering him, Kijo hit the glass pane separating them from the driver, Dip. The gangly beast answered her, "Yes, Guardians?"

"Park here," Kijo ordered him.

She was on the phone the moment she got out. Hours later, almost long enough for Lavario to worry about the bloodservant waking, she was back in the car. Her black eyes were glossy from her excitement. Whatever she'd arranged held promise.

Lavario allowed himself some hope. "You have a plan, daughter?"

"We're going to contrive a story that will be good for us or good for me. Your choice."

Plotting and politicking were a team effort, not business either of them soloed. Accustomed as he was to their usual back and forth, it took him a while to realize he'd waited for her to disclose the entire scheme. His eyes fixated on hers with embarrassing neediness, desperate for her to act as though things were normal between them. Tarlike, her black pupils took him in and swallowed him whole.

"Pack first, pack always," she told him.

CHAPTER SIXTEEN: DISTANCING HERSELF

Lavario lost track of how much time they'd spent driving. All he knew was his long legs felt cramped and the animal inside him wanted out of its cage. His daughter appeared atypically serene. Instead of sitting upright the Varcolac way, she leaned her head against the cool window and watched the scenery. Indulging, Lavario thought, in the simple freedom of being herself away from all the expectations of her family.

Lavario found himself remembering who his daughter was before Kijo came along and extirpated Jun. Serious, always. But also an introspective, freethinking young woman who was comfortable with ambiguity. Not anymore. *Pack first, pack always*, she said, so certain it was the right answer.

Outside, the evergreen trees turned to quaking aspens. As they approached residential areas, there were more flowering crabapple trees and giant lilac bushes. Lavario's stomach lurched. Whatever waited for him at the end of their journey wasn't going to make his day any better. Already frustrated, he prepared himself to be furious. And sad.

They turned down a secluded street. The houses got farther and farther apart.

The long driveway leading to the traditional Cape Cod home was paved by affixing loose rocks to tar. During the summer months, heat would bring out a pungent odor, almost unbearable to a wolf's sensitive nose. Mercifully, it was cold outside tonight. And wet. The constant drizzling rain and foggy haze rising from the road matched Lavario's mood.

The cheery homestead did not.

Under normal circumstances, he would have appreciated its quiet, modest charm. There was very little embellishment on the home itself aside from wooden shutters with cutout hearts and a wrought iron rooster, rusted now, stuck between roof dormers. It turned in the wind, making an awful ruckus.

Haughty in his anger, Lavario sniped at Kijo, "Are you thinking of a real estate investment? What will your brothers and sisters think of something as lavish as a painted door?"

His dig at the sparse living style of the Varcolac was wasted. Seconds later she left the still-moving limo. The door remained wide open as the vehicle came to a stuttering stop. Typical of her, she tramped ahead, ceding nothing to her surroundings.

Spring was a dirty time of year. Lavario got out of the limo with slow precision, making sure he didn't step in puddles. The ground around the pavement was muddy, even the standing water was gorged with blobs of unidentifiable yard waste. When the hem of his wool coat licked the ground, he growled at the line of dirt and the impending dry-cleaning bill.

In an instant, he stopped fussing with the garment.

Fear has a smell you can taste. Lingering long afterward, sometimes for days. Lavario tasted it now. It mired his tongue, making it feel swollen and foreign. The wolf inside wanted to open its mouth, sniff the air. Tiny hairs stood on end. There was danger. To him? After today, he couldn't rule it out.

He stood beside Kijo. He wasn't even paying attention to the way the rain made his curly hair frizz. Something here was very wrong. Instinct shouted it loud and clear. All the bite was gone from his voice when he asked, "What did you do?"

"Created opportunity."

The door to the home opened. Two of his daughter's lackeys appeared, Geri and Freki, scraggly dogs always looking for an influential hand to lick. Geri, the bolder and more talkative of the two, bowed to Lavario and made a sweeping gesture like an old-time carnival huckster inviting him to take a ride.

Lavario went inside.

Thirty or so wolves, a little over half of the Varcolac pack, were present. Although they kept their heads low and eyes averted, deferring to his authority, they managed to make it clear they found his clothing repugnant. Elegant tailored suits were Boo Hag garnish. True wolves didn't need to cloak themselves in finery to show power. They used force. Each one sniffed at Lavario's expensive threads, showing teeth.

Lavario did not show them his. Most of the time he thought the gesture was redundant, not to mention stupid. These pups felt his bite.

They knew the address to his fangs, the zip code of his claws if they wished to journey there. "Yes," he told them, "you are an imposing flock of sheep in wolves' clothing."

The jab brought their heads up. One charged forward.

"Guardian Lavario," Kijo interrupted. She collared the affronted wolf by his scruff, flinging him backward behind her. "Follow me."

Lavario kept his tone equally formal, only inwardly reminding himself he spoke to his daughter. "Delighted to, Guardian Kijo."

She escorted him into a formal sitting room filled with furniture that still had its factory smell. Lavario could imagine the owners guarding it for decades, redirecting grimy hands to a timeworn sofa stashed in a comfortable room.

The care they'd taken went to waste. Their formal room was covered in blood. Splatters of it reached as high as the ceiling. Bodies piled up like leaves took center stage. A child's leg poked out underneath the body of his mother, his sister. Tiny spaceships, aliens, and the stars of the boy's pajama bottoms were awash in a new abyss of gory muck that was perhaps as unfathomable as space. Lavario did not know. Did not want to know.

He swallowed his rage, whispering out, "Kijo."

Impassive, she scrutinized the carnage she'd ordered but said nothing.

He kept his voice low, hissing toward the end. "What is this?"

She addressed everyone—him and all the Varcolac forming a half circle behind them. "You have been brought here to decide. Are you Varcolac or are you a Boo Hag?"

He gave them a short barking laugh he cut off at the end, disgusted with the sound of it in the room. Judging by the clothing of the Varcolac wolves—completely intact—none of them transformed for the butchery. He was about ready to remind them merely their presence there was forbidden. The scolding words suffocated in his mouth.

A girl was brought forward kicking and screaming. Her college sweatshirt, torn and bloodied, knotted around her armpits. The way her feet paddled in the air elevated her heart rate. She pushed and pushed and pushed but went nowhere. Her pain, her fear, and most of all her rage chipped at him the way the tide chiseled away at bits and pieces of the shoreline.

The eldest daughter. Lavario recognized her from the photos in his bloodservant's wallet.

She was slung on the floor at his feet.

"This is Amber, Guardian Lavario," Geri introduced her. "She's pleased to meet you."

Panting, Amber looked at him with wild brown eyes full of fight, not an ounce of flight. Beside her was a fire poker. She clutched it, stood up, and whacked him over the head. Once, twice, three times. Many after. Although it didn't hurt, Lavario recoiled from the furor.

Geri chuckled, continuing his mock introductions, "Lavario, Guardian of the Varcolac everyone."

None of the other Varcolac laughed. Golden wolf eyes shone at the anticipated upcoming bloodshed. Eagerness made their predator mannerisms more pronounced. Heads low, they formed a tight perimeter around the girl, shifting their bodies in response to her slightest movement. They bobbed and weaved, blocking her exit should she decide to flee.

Amber shook. Her lips trembled. "What do you people want? What do you want?" she shouted.

"Shush," Lavario said to her. "Be still. Be strong. Do not frenzy."

Kijo had received the same speech 456 times. The number of times he held her to his chest. The number of times he felt her small hands tangle with his ears as her tantrums ran their course. The number of times he ran his thumb across the contours of her red, tear-blotched face. *Four hundred and fifty-six times, Jun. I counted each one until you stopped your wailings, stopped your frenzies, and became my daughter. I taught you how to be Varcolac.* He needed to tell this girl once. Her terror ripped through him.

"Kill her," Kijo instructed. "Kill her and be of this pack."

Lavario transformed.

Amber dropped the poker. There was no clank, no clatter. Hardly a sound at all when it hit the carpet. She knew. In her eyes, he saw the entire event unwind, the finality of it. Soon, her dumfounded expression would turn to terror, terror to acceptance, acceptance to nothing. Now it was inescapable. Now she would die.

CHAPTER SEVENTEEN: PACK FIRST, PACK ALWAYS

Normally his wolf form made him proud. Over eight feet tall, he towered. His black coat gleamed with a silver luminance to it in the moonlight. Marks from previous battles, the most prominent of which were claw marks on the left side of his muzzle, were his accessories. Each one was in a perfect spot, as well tailored to him as any of his suits. Even his harshest critics in any pack could not deny him the power of his beauty. Any wolf who looked lusted.

Amber's eyes saw none of it. She saw a monster.

And for good reason.

As if from a great distance, Geri laughed. For once, Lavario wished for more Varcolac sensibility and discretion. Merriment was forbidden to them the same as comfort. Surely one of the younger hot-headed wolves would silence the fool.

Kijo showed Geri her teeth. Instant, blissful quiet. Lavario took back everything he said about the foolishness of the gesture. His daughter came back to him. "Kill her," she urged him. "Choose Varcolac. Your pack is here to witness. Ready to embrace you."

How fantastic. Lavario shut his eyes. Whatever it was his daughter had planned, he'd never expected it to be this. Perhaps he should be grateful for the opportunity she provided. He was certainly beholden to the fierce, protective love in her dark eyes. They urged him to kill, to conquer. They urged him to lead with her the Varcolac way.

But he could not be what she asked.

He returned to his human form. Naked now, he overshadowed the terrified girl. Standing despite everything that had happened to her, she looked at him with a mixture of awe and absolute hatred. Offering her comfort was off the table. He knew how she'd interrupt such a gesture.

Instead, he turned to his daughter, bracing himself for her disappointment. She looked hopeful, something he thought she'd lost centuries ago. "I cannot."

"You *won't*."

"Is there a difference?"

"A great deal."

Lavario said nothing. They'd lost, as ridiculous as it was.

Open wide, her black eyes burned. In her anger, her lower lip trembled. For a moment, it looked like she was a child about to tantrum rather than the powerful guardian she'd become. Maybe it was only his way of attaching sight to memory. No matter how much she grew, there'd always be a part of him that saw her as a pup. "Do not frenzy, my daughter," he chided her gently.

She nodded, a short, final bob of her head. Her expression was set, her gaze fixed forward. "Bring me the father."

Lavario's bloodservant—Eresna's old one—was dragged inside.

Amber perked up when she saw him. "Daddy!" Her voice was so full of childish expectations—Daddy was here, Daddy would make things right, Daddy would stop the monsters. She tried to run to him, but Geri pushed her back.

Daddy was unconscious. One of the Varcolac wolves roused him.

"Mfaman," the bloodservant mumbled. "Mfaman," he said again, and his eyelids fluttered. "Wolfman!" he shouted at last, sitting upright with a jolt. Lavario sighed. Garvey must have extracted this one as well.

"Yes," Kijo confirmed for him. "Wolfmen indeed. Or women. If you believe it possible."

She walked around him in a loose circle. Here to create a spectacle one way or another, she let her brothers and sisters see how far she was willing to go, how cruel she could be, how unlike her father she was. *No Boo Hag here*, she was telling them, *but one of you. Fully. Pack first, pack always.*

Transformation came in waves. First teeth. Then claws. Horror built. It knotted in Lavario's stomach as it twisted the bloodservant's. Fully wolf at last, she let the bloodservant crawl around the room, herding him with her body toward his living daughter and the rest of his dead family.

The man gibbered. "Please God, forgive me. What did I do, what did I do, what did I do?" And then he begged the untransformed monsters around him. "Help us. Please. I have money."

"Money." Geri snorted at him, at the stupidity of it.

Angry at last, he wailed, "What game is this? What do you want?"

"No game. The needs of my kind are simple as they should be," Kijo came out of her form to answer. Though she directed it at the bloodservant, Lavario knew the speech was for him. "Your kind is more difficult. You want your money, your frippery, your easy living. Me, I only want blood. *Your* blood."

Wolf again in an instant,

Thinking it was soon to be over, Lavario closed his eyes and waited for the beat of the man's heart to cease and for both of their torments to be over. But Kijo protracted even the man's death. Draining him slowly to make him pay for the sins of her father.

Stalwart, Amber stood. Shakier, her legs kept her upright even when Kijo, her maw wet with her father's blood, approached. Lavario prepared himself for her death to be equally gruesome.

Kijo did nothing but speak. She grabbed the girl by her chin and forced her to look at Lavario. "This is his doing. He brought us here. He ordered it. Your life is over. You belong to us."

Lavario thought about the little boy's pajamas, a fake universe limning the stars with smiles and twinkling dreams. He tried to place himself in the canvas of the fabric as one of the cheerful balls of light, but the image would not last. He was a neutron star in any version of events, a stellar remnant drifting along in the remembrances of when it first started producing iron. *This is the end*, he told himself then. Apparently not.

When it was over with, Kijo had another rebirth. There was no renaming herself, only slight hints that the loss of her father tore at her as it always would. She had always been so stoic but now there were cracks, deep welts within her composure. Pain and anger seeped through, cooled, resurfaced. A new world was forming on top.

I want to die on my own terms. The thought sprang into Lavario's mind. It took him awhile to figure out it wasn't his. It was Amber's. Kijo dragged her along with them.

* * *

They were back in the car together. Lavario didn't know what justification she'd used for it but she was here.

In that space, Jun and Kijo existed together. The girl who loved her daddy slipped through in tears. The wolf she became allowed them to fall without quarrel. Within that time, Lavario thought she might understand the dilemma of needing two incompatible things, both with equal vigor.

An image of her in the forest holding her teddy bear crept in on him, the way she continually snuck into his bed. Other memories followed. She was right, one could not think on one thing without thinking on the others. So he sat as his mind recycled old memories. The way she could not say his name and called him Lario, the years of cradling her on his chest while she ran her hands over his ears, the way she'd lift his lips to admire his teeth, and the way she'd grab one clawed finger in her small hands.

She took his hand and told him, "Be still. Be strong. Do not frenzy."

"I love you," he told her.

"Father—"

He cut her off, not wanting to hear the rest. "It is your time. Be with me until you cannot."

Chapter Eighteen: Rival

Daughter to rival.

Kijo put distance between herself and Lavario the moment the car door clicked behind them. Most of the pack gathered in a tight, horseshoe-shaped formation of codependency. The "guardians," Lavario mentally put their title in air quotes, were up front. Oscar, the pack's current fourth-in-command, spoke first, "We were nearly ready to go fetch you both."

You fetch because you are dogs, Lavario thought to himself.

Mazgan looked at Kijo, the girl, and the dead father. Obviously he thought the two of them had conspired on their way home. His plans—Lavario doubted they were careful—might come undone in the process. With a red-faced fury, he launched, "What is this? What have you two done?"

"I have done nothing, Alpha Guardian," Kijo insisted. "Guardian Lavario went into a rage after he was denied his toy, became desperate when I did not support him. He killed my servant and his own, leaving the bodies in the woods to be found by anyone. He took this girl."

Mazgan cheered up immensely after Kijo spoke. His back straightened. He smiled. She'd finally made the right choice. "Stand beside me."

Lavario swiveled his head to follow his daughter's walk to the Alpha Guardian's side. There was a soldier's precision to her gate—a steady one two, one two, one two. Duty over love. Pack first, pack always. Although Lavario kept his expression blank, his gaze steady and straight forward, her footsteps felt like tiny little cuts on the tips of his fingers.

Mazgan continued once she was by his side, "Now tell me why this happened."

She went through all the formalities, titles and affirmations, before she began, "Lavario wishes to be exiled, me along with him. To live as Moondogs. False Moons," she spat. Too serious to laugh, too contained to boo, too stoic to gasp: the Varcolac stood around like cargo-pant-clad statues while his daughter continued her tale. "He disobeyed the edicts. He put us all at risk by exposing our true form to humans, by killing in the open. He brought these violations to our very door. I obeyed his orders, but he is my superior. I was duty bound."

The pack, even those who had witnessed what happened, nodded in sympathetic agreement. Kijo had no choice since Lavario outranked her. Momentarily annoyed by the pack's forgetfulness, Lavario fought back to the urge to remind them all of the very long history between he and Kijo. But this was Kijo's moment.

She continued, "But now I stand before you to repudiate his actions. This Boo Hag is not my father."

Mazgan's eyes brightened to a glossy gold in his excitement. "What do you say to Kijo's accusations, Lavario?"

Lavario didn't say anything in his defense. Kijo could have told the pack that he rode a polar bear into a bank and then took out a home loan with twenty percent interest, and their reactions would have been the same. Whatever lies, truths, or half-truths got Lavario to the other side of the Door worked for them.

"Very well. Lavario has nothing to say for himself. What say you, Kijo?"

His daughter swallowed. With some satisfaction, Lavario noted she was fighting off her emotions. "I issue a formal challenge to Guardian Lavario, second of the Varcolac."

"Lavario?" Mazgan tossed it his way with a sneer, without much ceremony.

"I accept," he replied.

There was a smell to the air, like a memory he found and then forgot. Maybe it was just the leaves on the ground. Some crinkled and cracked when he stepped on them, some mushed. All rotted.

Lavario turned to leave, thinking it was done.

His daughter stopped him. "Alpha Guardian, I have a suggestion regarding Lavario's punishment for this mess." She pointed to the living girl and the dead father, the remains of the family they slaughtered. Punishment was Mazgan's right as the leader, and so Kijo's arrogance made the alpha's lips twist. He was about to refuse her, he had already turned to address the pack, but she leaned forward to whisper in his ear, her hand tugging almost ladylike at his sleeve. Despite his predicament, Lavario gloated inwardly. His daughter was going to run circles around this buffoon.

"Very well," Mazgan said to her, "I would allow you this, considering the insults he has visited upon you."

She gave Lavario a sly little quirk of her lip. "Give him his stupid thing. Give it to him. Let him live with it."

CHAPTER NINETEEN: HIS STUPID THINGS

Trauma brought on a persistent fever, leaving Amber too weak to feed from. Lavario ended up in the exact situation the Isangelous sought to avoid at the distribution center when they refused him Tovin. There was a humor to it he declined to appreciate.

He could take care of Amber's condition. Only healing her meant fully bonding. For him, fully bonding meant seeing himself through her eyes, knowing most of her thoughts. Knowing her thoughts meant constant misery. And then she might die by Mazgan's hand. Horribly. The entire situation vexed him.

Lavario's hunger hooked its fang deep in his belly. An ungracious killer, it reminded him dallying was no longer his privilege. He could feed from her—healed or not—or wither away until he expired.

He approached the bed where Amber slept.

Garbling insults, she lashed out at something in her fevered sleep. *Probably me*, Lavario mused, *or one of the other Varcolac wolves*. He wrapped his hand in a cool cloth before touching her sweaty cheeks, patting them the way he'd seen concerned mothers do on television shows. Even in her sleep she flinched away from his touch. Even through the cloth of the rag, her subconscious found its way to him.

In her dream rain fell on a roof, rushing off the nearly rotted shingles and pouring to the concrete below where it landed with heavy-handed irregular splatters. Children with their mouths open wide caught some of the water before it hit the ground. They were too young, too happy-go-lucky to care about things like bacteria. But Amber saw herself as full-grown. "Yuck!" she yelled down. Her condemnation only made the giggles louder. One of kids raised his hands to fling the dirty water Amber's direction.

Lavario smiled, happy because Amber was. Elated, he ran down the stairs with her; taking them one by one, two by two, three by three. Their gait was reckless, confident, youthful. The door opened, flinging wide. They bolted through it. And stopped.

Blood ran from bodies and from the roof above. A monster that pretended to be a man played in it. Green eyes twinkled when he threw his head back and opened his mouth to drink. He looked at her and giggled in voice of a thousand slain children. Gracefully, each movement calculated, he pulled his body to the side so she could see her family strewn out on the ground below his feet.

Alarmed, Lavario stumbled backward from the horrific images of himself. He shook off his foolish surprise. How else was she to see the werewolf who'd supposedly ordered the slaughter of her family? When she woke, she'd be with him until one of them died, constantly reliving the ordeal. Moved by pity he resolved to end her suffering. He tilted her head to the side. Fangs out, sharp and white in the lamplight, he bent over her throat.

Kijo's voice cut through the haze. "Earning your Boo Hag title."

"Yes, I…" Harsh words dried on his lips. "What is this?" He pointed at the large garbage bag she towed.

"The rest of your punishment."

He waited for an explanation but got none. Hunger dulled his senses. To figure out the contents of the sack he had to sniff at the air around him like a common ally dog pawing through the garbage. Once he knew, he leapt to his feet. Snarling, he bore down on Kijo. Accomplishing nothing.

She straightened a strand of his hair, smoothing the top so that the pointed ends all went the same direction. "You are more poodle than wolf."

He felt the weight of his fangs on his bottom lip. "This poodle has killed more wolves than you have years, Jun."

Kijo stopped grooming him and raised her lip a fraction above one tooth, more ironic than concerned. Her tone was as close to humor as she got when she chastised him in their old, familiar way, "You frenzy, Guardian Lavario."

He wanted to go back to the time when her saying this would have followed a pat on his cheek. He wanted it more than he wanted to live. The sentimentality nipped at his heels.

"Feeling sorry for yourself?"

"Yes," Lavario answered his daughter.

"You must be terribly inconvenienced."

"I have had better weeks."

"I imagine so." Kijo glanced at Amber. As if on cue, the girl moaned in her sleep. "You would kill her—in her sleep no less—after what she endured to live?"

"There is no need for her to suffer."

"True," Kijo considered, "but she chose to fight. And you chose to save Jun."

Lavario wanted to keep the dialogue going. Talking to Kijo was as close to normal as he could get. Protracted arguments were not on his daughter's itinerary. She left him to make his own decisions.

Familiar magic worked its way through him. Lavario surrendered his control, allowed it to guide his hands as he mended Amber's ailments. When her breathing was no longer ragged, Lavario opened his eyes and rubbed her head. His hand felt massive against her delicate brow. Curled up against one of the long pillows, hugging it close to her body the way children clutched teddy bears, Amber appeared peaceful.

When she woke, her world would be nothing but constant uncertainty, continual change. Amber wanted to fight. He hoped she'd feel the same way once she woke.

The bag Kijo brought in contained the body of Amber's father.

* * *

Staging the scene as a wake rather than degradation worked for a day or two. Amber grieved. She held her father's hand and thought about all the bad things she'd ever done to disappoint him. Last time they talked, he'd called her a whore for sleeping with a college boy. *Spreading her legs*, he'd said, *instead of getting an education.* Brokenhearted, she'd come home to mend their relationship. She was so wrapped up in what she could have said to bring peace that she forgot Lavario existed.

Maybe she didn't recognize him. To say he wasn't quite what Amber remembered would have been an understatement. Hair, so carefully groomed when she saw him last, puffed at the top and clung to his neck in a nest of sweat and grime at the bottom. Green eyes, menacing in her dreams, were bloodshot, puffy and dull.

She probably wouldn't recognize herself either. As the body in front of Amber stopped being her father, the more it grinned and stank, she became manic. She talked gibberish, often wailing and slapping herself as though she were trying to come out of a dream. Fine bedding that was to be Tovin's became sticky with sloughed off skin and rank from discharged body chemicals. His stupid thing. *Let him live with it*, Kijo had said. He assumed she meant the girl. How wrong he'd been.

"Please," she was in her begging cycle, "bury him."

"Soon," he promised her even though he had no idea how much longer it would be.

Grief became the squatter in Lavario's chambers, laying claim to his space. Whenever he tried to reclaim himself, Amber would wail, or her father's body would break apart, morphing into something newly hideous. Even when the head slumped away, Geri or Freki found a way to unite skull and neck once again. Remarkable for such stupid wolves.

Humans in distress were a terrible burden, and putrefaction was a tiresomely long process. Sleep was the only peace he got. Otherwise, it was screaming, sobbing, and the stench of the dead.

Grudgingly, Lavario applauded Kijo's stratagem, even felt a bit of pride at the ingenuity of using the thing the Varcolac hated about him to destroy him. Nostalgia tugged. No matter how much he willed his feelings to be disapproval, hatred, or scorn, he could manage nothing outside of wounded love.

Jun. Jun. Jun. He'd taught her how to be Varcolac instead of like him. He truly was a giant Boo Hag.

A pot hitting the side of his head brought him back to the present. Amber shouted, "Bury him! Bury him you monster."

"I cannot," he responded.

She sneered at him. "Do you have a shovel?"

He was dumfounded. "A shovel? No."

"Never mind. I'll dig with my hands if I have to."

Lavario didn't fully understand what she meant until she dragged the body out the door.

CHAPTER TWENTY: BURIAL

Amber's father, once proud and handsome, seemed to bump into everything. She tried to be careful at first, gently guiding him along by gripping his pant legs. Fear made her desperate. Grief made her clumsy. She came undone when she imaged him saying, *This is your fault. Whore.* Soon after, she sobbed while she yanked and pulled the body down the hall.

"Amber," Lavario tried to pull her away.

She shoved him.

"Do you know where you are taking him?"

"Go to hell," she shot back. She stood up and walked past. Thinking she'd given up, Lavario prepared himself to drag the body back to his room. A minute or two later, she reemerged holding his linen curtains, the ones with the embroidered trim. Circumstances being what they were, Lavario still cringed when she tossed the delicate fabric on the floor and rolled her father onto it.

She tied the edges to form a handle. It worked for about two seconds until the knot came undone and the body fluids soaked through.

Varcolac wolves watched events unfold with various degrees of involvement. To them Amber's suffering was a nuisance, an obstacle preventing them from going in a straight line to their destinations. Had she been the bloodservant of any other wolf, they would have used physical force to remove her. Being Lavario's gave her more license. For now their fear of him outweighed their hatred. Amber didn't know this. She still glared back at them in open defiance, going so far as to growl at one.

Eventually, she had to admit defeat. She wasn't strong enough to move the body on her own. Failure hit her full force. She couldn't do right by him in life or in death. Crying, she sat down next to her father and told herself she couldn't let the monsters see her fall apart. Tears came anyway, followed by sobs she tried to muffle by biting her hand.

"Amber," he gently touched her shoulder.

She didn't answer, only blinked away tears and grabbed her knees tighter to her chest.

Lavario picked up the body and draped it over his shoulder. Smell and texture worked in tandem to nauseate him. He fought through his dizziness and made peace with losing another good suit. "Come with me, Amber."

When she failed to move, he walked away, leaving her to decide for herself if she'd see her task through. Being strong on her own was the only way she'd survive her ordeal.

He was relieved when he heard her light, fractured footsteps behind him.

All the hallways in the Varcolac complex were the same. Each room was sparse, devoid of personality. No pictures, no rugs, no curtains, very little furniture, and gray walls. The entire massive complex was like a construction zone or a part of an office building that should have been marked off with a semi-transparent plastic curtain. Lavario sensed Amber felt lost in the vast space and sure he was going to take her through the twists and turns only to ditch her and her father.

"We are close now," he told her as they started to climb.

And then they arrived. She blinked her eyes when the afternoon sunlight hit her face. "What is this?"

"My garden," Lavario answered.

The peonies were in full bloom, filling the area with their sweet, almost roselike smell. The flower reminded him of old southern graveyards filled with massive stone angels towering above the dead. It was an appropriate image for what they came here to do.

He got a shovel from the shed. Before he started the grave, Amber grabbed the tool from his hands. *This is my job*, she thought but said nothing. Lavario surrendered the task to her.

In the early part of the process, when she was full of certainty and renewed vigor, dirt got flung everywhere. Wide and wasteful, her movements were testament to the youthful belief in unlimited energy. As Lavario expected, the inability to pace herself cost her at the end. Hands bleeding, her breathing ragged, Amber finished the task fueled by stubbornness alone.

She climbed up from the grave and brushed off at least two shovel scoops of dirt from her face, hands, and clothes. Moonlight outlined the waterlines on her face where tears and sweat merged. It made her brown eyes look black.

She looked at the cloth covering her father's body and swallowed hard. *I can't lift him,* she told herself. An image flashed into Lavario's mind, one of Amber's father flopping into the grave the way sacks of grain hit the bottom of their barn. Those sacks would often split open.

Lavario lowered his hand onto her shoulder. "I am here to help you lower him. It is time to say good-bye."

She'd been ready to put her father to rest but not ready to for things to end this way between them. She didn't want to be alone in the world. She approached his body in small increments. Dragging herself toward the end of their time together felt like carrying her father's weight all over again.

Tentatively, she took the last few steps forward. Guilt tore through her, zigzagging though Lavario's mind as well. She didn't want to touch it anymore. Whatever her father was in life—a musician whose graceful fingers made art from air, a boxer whose fists cut through air like lightning to make thunder, an intellectual whose book shelves were, as he often said, like air to someone living under water—he wasn't that now. He had no more breath left in him. Before her was a grotesque bacteria-filled mass stripping everything down to its frame. Inevitable but ugly.

Lavario transferred the body to the grave. Although he offered to fill it in, Amber insisted the task was hers by right of blood. Pain laced with fatigue made the undertaking last until the sunlight crept in from the west. By then, she was on the verge of collapse. Stooped over, she used the shovel to create the illusion of standing tall.

Lavario asked Amber, "Is there anything you would like to say to honor him?"

Her thoughts broke through to Lavario. Absurd images of garden gnomes acting as a tombstone came to her. Those stupid creatures were scattered in their yard back home. Her father loved them, especially the ultra-cutesy gnomes with pudgy bellies and rosy cheeks. The notion of one standing vigil over the grave made her spit out a grief-filled laugh.

Such thoughts felt inappropriate. She could see her stern-faced father standing beside her, saying something about responsibility. Guilty again, she searched for clever, meaningful words. None came to mind. She stood over him clutching a makeshift bouquet. "He was..." she started. Then stopped.

CHAPTER TWENTY-ONE: WRAITH LOCH

Patches of sleep came and went. Nightmares plagued Amber's rest each time her eyelids closed. Through her, Lavario experienced the terror and a hopelessness that came with being a captive facing an uncertain future. Relaxation was a scarce resource.

And when she wasn't having bad dreams, she was awake and plotting.

Too afraid to verbally express her anger, Amber fantasized about the day she'd kill him. More than once he saw her standing over his dead body, kicking it in triumph. Sometimes in her visions, she sawed off his head and took it to her father's grave. Wishful thinking.

The more time she spent with him, the more her confidence waned, the more bad dreams she had. She thought about killing him a lot less and instead worried, "What's going to happen to me when you die?"

"My death is not certain," he'd remind her

She considered her lavish surroundings with a critical eye worthy of a Varcolac wolf. To Amber, his apartment was some type of museum library hybrid. Tasteful but old-fashioned. Lots of dark wood, carvings, drapes that cascaded down from the ceiling but covered no windows. And shelves and shelves of books. When he searched Amber's mind for a description of himself, all he heard was *snobby geezer with hoarder issues.*

The description rankled. He did *not* have hoarder issues.

She opened his closet, going so far as to grope undergarments. Lavario raised a haughty eyebrow at the intrusion but said nothing.

"What's this divide for?" she knocked on the wood board separating his wardrobe.

"Right side for nonwolf days, left side for wolf days." She gave him a confused shake of her head. Exasperated that it mattered to her, Lavario sighed and explained, "When I believe a day will anger me to the point of transformation, I wear something from the left side. When I'm reasonably confident the day will be stress free, I select from the right. No need to ruin my nicer clothes if it can be avoided."

"That is... you are..." She puffed out her cheeks. "What's going to happen to me when you die?" It might have been amusing if not for her tear-saturated brown eyes.

When he didn't answer, she went back to mauling his possessions with her clumsy hands. His keepsake box with wolves, elk, and flowers carved into the sides crashed down on the floor. Amber flipped open the silver lid and rummaged through the contents. She pulled out a stuffed animal. "Is this a teddy bear? What's a werewolf doing with a teddy bear?"

Kijo's. Lavario's heart gave a painful squeeze, reminding him of what he'd lost. Though he'd done his best to preserve Mr. Bear, its white stuffing peeped out from behind ripping seams. One eye was missing. That happened centuries ago. He grabbed it from Amber more roughly than he intended.

She glared and rubbed her hand. "You are the absolute worst werewolf."

He put the box and the bear on a higher shelf. Satisfied it was safe for now, he turned his attention to Amber and asked her, "And what is your idea of a good werewolf?"

Lavario got the sense she knew what she'd said was ridiculous. She didn't have many other werewolves to compare him to. Knowing this didn't prevent her from doubling down with, "I dunno. Go out in the forest and eat campers."

Lavario sniffed. "Even the word campers smells bad, and I hate the forest."

"The *worst*," Amber repeated with venom.

"Come with me," he gestured for her to follow. He took her by her elbow. Mindful of her tender skin and the strength of his own hands, he guided her until she followed on her own. They came to a wall.

"A-plus wall," she told him. "I really love how you accented the brick with wood. That's going to get you a lot of resale value."

"Very amusing. Stay here."

He placed his hand in the center of the invisible door there. Magic opened it. He didn't give Amber time to quip. Once again, he grabbed her elbow and pulled her along.

Darkness didn't hinder his vision. Amber fumbled along, sliding her hands along solid stone and shuffling her feet across the uneven floor. Instead of helping her, Lavario left her to find her own way. If she ever came back here, she'd need to navigate the terrain without him.

Eventually they came to an underground lake. Its waters were always quiet and clear. You could see through but never to the bottom. Lavario didn't know if it had one. He often came here when he needed to escape. The idea of a lake that continued onward to eternity appealed to him at those times.

"What is this place?" she asked.

"It is Wraith Loch. There is a romantic tale that the dead speak here."

Her voice was a hopeful whisper, "Is that true?"

"Doubtful but possible." Lavario told her. "I have never heard their voices. But it's a quiet place to read and would be a peaceful place to die."

She didn't take his meaning at first. Her mind was caught on the idea of the dead speaking. Hopeful, she sunk down on her knees at the edge of the shore. Water instantly accommodated the shape of her knees, bending around the imprint of her body. Amber called out the names of her family members in her head. She said them over and over again when she heard nothing.

Lavario tried to reach out to her with his own thoughts, knowing full well it didn't work that way. Cruel as it was, he'd have to spell it out for her. "I will leave the door to the passage open to you," he said. "Should I die, you can come here and slip away or you can stay and try to fight. Your choice."

Sudden jolts of fear notified Lavario she'd received his message. Outwardly, she continued to stare at the lake, begging it to give her a sentence or two of comfort in a familiar voice. She'd settle for a word. A sign. Her thoughts hiccupped as though interrupted by weeping.

CHAPTER TWENTY-TWO: OH YEAH, REVENGE

Mazgan came into his apartment without invitation. Lavario and Amber smelled of the lake, like earth and magic. Lavario didn't think anything of it until Mazgan said, "You took a *human* to the Loch?"

The fact the Alpha Guardian cared about the lake was news to Lavario. In all his years visiting the area, he'd only ever seen Mazgan on its shore during binding ceremonies, unions similar to human weddings. To say the alpha's anger felt situationally advantageous was an understatement. Unimpressed, Lavario waved him off. "Yes. Yes. I took her there."

"Sacrilege!"

Lavario chuckled at the pretension. "Who are you here to impress? Certainly not me." When Mazgan showed his teeth but remained silent, Lavario tiredly asked, "*Why* are you here?"

Mazgan corrected him, "*Alpha Guardian.* You keep forgetting, Lavario."

Sensing he was in for a protracted ordeal, Lavario slipped on his comfortable house shoes and coat and sat down in one of his plushest armchairs. After he felt Boo Haggish enough, he repeated, "Why are you here?"

Chest puffed out, head elevated as though looming over an entire crowd of enraptured servants, Mazgan grandstanded. "I am here to tell you I won. Kijo is mine. Your days are over. I look forward to watching you die."

"There. I have been told." Lavario swept his hand in the direction of the door. "Off you go, then."

Mazgan struggled for mastery of his emotions. Feeling smug, Lavario watched him get tangled in the leash of his own temper. More than anything, the alpha wanted to use violence. Lavario could see it in his posture, the way he fought off transformation. Would he be fool enough to make it physical between them? Lavario certainly hoped so. Such an altercation wouldn't change Lavario's situation, but it would prove satisfying.

Using one claw, and one only, Lavario tapped on the wooden arm of his chair and pushed again. "Anything else?"

Mazgan swallowed hard. Rage was as unfriendly going down as it was coming up from the looks of it. "Mercy is not below me, Lavario. I offer you death at my hand. It would save our darling Kijo the heartbreak of killing her maker."

"How very un-Varcolac of you. And for her."

"It would be public. You would submit—"

"Oh yes. You want it to be your big moment. Proud Boo Hag Lavario brought low by the rightful Alpha Guardian of the Varcolac."

"It is for Kijo's sake."

"Kijo is fine."

Mazgan lashed out at the nearest wall. Unsatisfied, he scanned the room for something better, something to make Lavario regret his disobedience and his haughtiness. His gaze settled on Amber the same way it settled on Tovin back at the Isangelous dinner hall.

Apprehensive, Amber had watched the exchange very sure Mazgan was the stronger of them. Anger and hair-trigger violence were familiar tools in her world, and they worked well enough in her estimation. Sensing his advantage over her the way a base animal might, Mazgan approached, claws and teeth on display.

"What you did earlier today was sacrilege, human. You have no place at Wraith Loch."

Terrified, she cringed away. But she refused to be totally cowed. Stubbornness or insanity took hold as she said, "It was a lake. Not like I peed in it."

Amber felt pleased with her own bravado until Mazgan yanked on her arm, forcing her to face him so he could slap her across her mouth. Lavario felt as much as she did—the pain of the indignity and the throb of the nerve he'd struck.

A blow to her stomach coerced Amber to her knees. She grabbed herself in a tight embrace and vomited. The smell of it and the taste of acid made her vomit again. Blood wasn't pouring out of her, to both their relief. Most of it got caught up in viscous snot and trailed out in a dull red ribbon from her mouth. She tried to spit as much of it as she could outward, toward Mazgan. *Fuck him,* she thought.

Lavario agreed. *Fuck him.*

Warnings were mandatory in these types of situations. Fighting back his rage, he kept to the rules. Lavario clucked his tongue. "She's mine. I intend to keep her," he cautioned Mazgan. Rules regarding property in the Varcolac were clear. Taking it meant you had to fight for it. This applied to Alpha Guardians. Hopefully Mazgan was too wrapped up in his display of power to take heed.

He continued to posture, herding Amber around the room, flaunting his superior strength.

Calmly, Lavario stripped out of his clothes. He'd lost enough good suits in the last few days and wasn't eager to rip any others. Transforming felt good. Even better when he saw Mazgan stumble backward, finally realizing his error. Ears back, teeth showing, Lavario took the alpha on a nice tour of the apartment, forcing him wall to wall.

But before he had a chance to raise his paw, Mazgan surrendered. "Enough of this," he ordered with as much authority as he could manage while he cowered, "I am not taking your precious pet."

Amber laughed at him, clenching herself tight from the pain of it.

The alpha's liquid gold eyes fixated on her.

Hilarious as it was, Lavario felt himself cringe for Amber's sake. Should he fall during his battle with Kijo, she'd need a quick path to the lake. Her death would otherwise be the worst Mazgan could make it.

* * *

Lavario leaned over Amber, tending to her injuries. "Hold still."

"I don't want your help," she sniped at him, swatting at his hands.

"Could you be more of a ridiculous child?"

"Yes," she assured him.

He didn't doubt it.

She tried to sit up. *Pssshhh,* was the sound the air made as it hissed through her clenched teeth. Pain might force her cooperation after all. Slightly mocking, Lavario inquired, "Would you like me to heal you now?"

"Yessss." She surrendered and lay back down.

"Splendid." Using gentle hands, Lavario navigated the bends and curves of her body the best he could while also considering Amber's modesty. Usually, by now, he and his bloodservant were up all night pleasuring each other. Amber certainly thought about it, especially when his long fingers touched the tender line of her neck, but she hated herself afterward.

Self-loathing was front and center now. Her racing thoughts, always laden with fear along with guilt, distracted him. Inconvenient. Reaching out with magic taxed his energy. Stress, not to mention sexual frustration, made him terse. "I should leave you some scars to remind you."

Amber's nostrils flared. "Of what? That you *own* me? That I'm *yours*?"

"No, to not be so foolish."

"But also that you *own* me."

"If you feel so powerless, you can put me on a leash and walk me around. Would you like this? It would certainly be much closer to the time I envisioned for myself. You can call me bad. Insult me." He put his mouth next to her ear and whispered, "Spank me."

She flushed. "You're..." she sputtered. "You're an old horndog."

He chuckled. She stewed. Scandalized outrage bought him a lasting silence he enjoyed thoroughly until a word popped into her head. *Revenge*. She was going to get so much revenge. Against him. Against Mazgan. Every last werewolf in the world would feel her wrath. And fucking vampires, too. If they existed.

She also went back to being afraid.

"One day you might be a werewolf," he told her. "The Varcolac change their bloodservants at the end, allowing them a chance at immorality. And vampires are already dead."

She sprung upward, pulling a blanket protectively around her as though he were a Peeping Tom rather than an empath. "You can read my thoughts?"

"Yes," he confessed. "Sadly so. For both of us, I think."

Indignant, Amber sputtered a few times. "Fine. Fine. I'm not ashamed, not afraid. No, no, no. *After* I turn into a werewolf, I'm going to kill you. I'm going to kill your insane daughter. I'm going to kill that alpha whatever. You know, the guy who is pretty much one giant bad comb-over. You'll all die the way you killed my family. I'll kill you by..."

She'd been pointing at random objects around his house while giving her Hamletesque soliloquy on who she was going to kill and how. By the time she was done, Lavario knew all the details of her unrealistic plots. Stuck wagging, Amber's finger shook a few more times in his face before she finally brought it back down to her side.

"There are quite a few errors in your thinking."

"Such as?" She did her best to keep her face confident, her chin up.

"The most obvious is pretty simple. I am the one who would turn you."

"Your point?"

"You promised to murder me. I do not feel incentivized."

She shifted her weight. Uncertain. "Another will turn me. I'll find one."

"Where? Craigslist?"

Her nostrils flared. Her eyes shone with unshed tears. He was about ready to comfort her when she hit him with an ash tray he forgot he had. He hadn't smoked for at least seven centuries. "Hoarder," she shouted as though she could read his mind.

And thus began a new phase of their relationship.

CHAPTER TWENTY-THREE: SOME TYPE OF TRICK

The day before the fight.

Kijo had her rituals. Lavario had his. He could almost picture her nose scrunched, hands clenching and unclenching, eyes intense while she restlessly fidgeted around the room, trying in vain to find her happy place. Young, impatient for the fight—Kijo never much cared for the wait and was especially unsettled the night before. Lavario simply went to his happy place. Bad TV.

"Really?" Amber asked. She sat on his bed—an audacity he was sure she wanted him to rebuke—and pointed to the teenage supernatural drama on the television. "You know your insane fanged spawn is getting pumped up for the fight right now while you sit here and watch this crap?"

He gave her a quick "Yes" and went back to his show.

The more she spoke, the more Lavario became nostalgic for the days when she was all hostile glares and angry silence. Time had worn down those avenues of defiance. She had moved on to destroying his possessions, constant backtalk, and—for a more modernized nuisance—she deleted unwatched shows from his DVR. He regretted his efforts to make her feel more comfortable. He should have let her stay afraid of him, at least until the fight was over.

Attempts to stop her behavior or bring her comfort were met with hostility. *Don't frenzy*, he told her. Amber simply responded by telling him to shut up and called him a psycho douchewaffle. He did not understand what a waffle made of douche contents would look like or how to take it as an insult. Google only helped him so much.

Amber tossed herself back on his bed, displacing some of the decorative pillows in the process. A gesture that apparently didn't go far enough for her. She picked one up, considered it, tossed it to the ground. "Then what's with the chill attitude? Shouldn't you be hitting a punching bag or *something*?"

"I do not see that helping."

"*This* is?" She tossed a pillow at the television.

"About as much as hitting a punching bag."

He didn't look in her direction, but he could sense her anger and could see the corresponding expression in his mind. Beyond that, he could feel the fear underlining it all, the constant burden of knowing if he fell, then she fell with him. Over and over she wondered where she'd be after tomorrow.

"You're the worst werewolf," Amber told him yet again. "Why don't you go abduct some more dumb people?" His entire bed was a mess now. She was starting to eye his bookcase.

"I abducted you."

"Kijo abducted me."

Details. Details. "I suppose that's mostly true."

"You suppose." She was standing beside him now, dressing him down with her hands curled up into fists placed on her hips. "Don't you want to win this thing?"

A feeling of ridiculousness settled over Lavario as she glared down over him. Maybe he should at least hit her. No. Lavario could not bring himself to simply strike the girl. Ruling through intimidation and fear was the course of a lesser wolf. He would not devolve into a bully. Still, Garvey was the only one who had ever talked to Lavario the way she did. At least they fucked afterward. There were no such perks to Amber's chivying—just the noise and mess.

"Do something!" she commanded him again.

Lavario snorted. He paused the show, though he wasn't sure why he bothered. He already knew how it ended since Amber had kindly told him. "There is nothing more to be done. The fight will be what it will."

Once again, Amber shifted herself. Left foot, right foot. Left to right again. Moments of silence to be enjoyed. Her throat constricted as she swallowed. Before he could see the distress in her facial features, she turned from him and retreated to his bed. This time when she tossed herself down to his bed, he could feel her anxiety building, which took some of the bite out of the defiant gesture. It felt good. Then it felt ridiculous that it felt so good. "Where do you want to go from here, Amber?"

"What do you mean?" Pouting. Not very wolf.

"How do you wish to proceed? Continue down this path or make peace with things as they are? We will be together until one of us dies. There is no need to make the time unpleasant."

"I will never forgive you for what you did."

It was as resolute as anything he'd ever heard mumbled into his sheets. Lavario was never quite sure how to take his young companion. Confident, brave, intelligent, Amber had many of the marks of a fine wolf. Though often unwisely, she confronted him with as much force, with as much determination as any of his brothers and sisters. Other times she was a pouting, insecure, impulsive child wrapped up protectively in the college sweater she was wearing the night they took her. She'd refused to change out of the ragged thing.

Lavario turned to her and smiled a somewhat tight smile. "Yes, but I can always simply tie you to a chair or to a bed and leave you there until I feed. You can live bound down, only moving when I allow it. Is that the type of life you want for yourself?"

It was as though he did strike her. Her head jerked back, her teeth snapped together, and she winced. Panic and determination teetered along her senses, which was expected. Only her surprise confused Lavario. She should have thought about that as an outcome. She was not stupid. Lavario allowed his expression to soften before he spoke to her again. "It doesn't have to be like that, Amber. I don't require forgiveness. Just that you stop with your nettling and that you cooperate."

"In exchange for what?"

Never had Lavario considered himself to be even slightly impulsive or prone to fits of violence. Kijo and Garvey both gave in to their immediate whims—though in different ways—despite his attempts to teach them otherwise. It was not a trait he understood until now. The girl was a fool to think she was in any position to bargain with him. Urges to shout at her and call her an idiot were fought down although Lavario could feel the claws and fangs of the half transformation from his ire. *I am not Kijo. I am not Garvey. This is not my stupid thing. I will get what I want and let fools be fools.* So Lavario told himself and tried to smile. "I would train you for your test."

Her mood perked up, and she sat up on his bed with a jolt. "You're going to train me..." Her expression fell immediately. "...so I can kill you... This is some sort of stupid trick."

Yes, absolutely it was. But if he could Mr. Miyagi his way out of this mess, he'd wax on until her mouth shut off. It's not like he had anything else to do. Worst case was she somehow managed to become a werewolf and would be yet another of his kind who wanted him dead.

"No trick. I'm simply buying myself some peace. And I would train you for your test, which very few prospects pass. You, in your current state, would not pass." He tried not to sound too skeptical of her ability overall. The young woman was obviously proud, expressing any form of disbelief might tip her back over the edge to show-deleting-bed-destroying territory, forcing Lavario to eventually make good on his threats.

Her face was scrunched up into its skeptic lines. "What about the whole fight with Kij? Thought you said you might get your ass stomped tomorrow. And, no offense but..." she started to trail off, looking for the right words to say. It was a start.

"But I'm the worst werewolf *ever*? A bitch? A psycho? A waffle made of douche?"

"A douchewaffle. Otherwise," she pointed a finger-gun at him. The gesture said *nailed it*.

He continued to smile down at her, though he could feel the tightness of it and only assumed it was bordering on a grimace. "She might win. If she wins, she might kill me. At that point you will want to revisit your options." Not that there would be any. She'd be killed. Yet the young woman sat there and considered. Adorable. Sensing she was on the fence, Lavario pressed. "Training, even if it is from the worst werewolf ever, would make you more prepared. Not all humans get such a chance."

"Okay. I'll agree to a cease fire." She sort of tossed her hands into the air. *Why not?*

"Fantastic." It was difficult to edge the sarcasm out of his voice. He reached for the remote and started the show up again. The young men and women were about to "hook up" as Amber said. As they kissed, Amber walked around the room, searching for something. Each time she moved an item on one of his shelves or displaced a curio from its location, Lavario felt the muscles in his face twitch. "What are you looking for, Amber?" He tried to keep his tone casual, friendly, signifying their new relationship.

"Some paper and a pen or a pencil." She looked inside some antique pottery and then moved it with her elbow when she did not find what she was looking for.

"Are artifacts from the Shang Dynasty where you would store such things?" Lavario couldn't help himself. It was unbearable.

She shrugged. "It's a clay pot. Pots are vessels. Vessels hold stuff. It follows."

The young man and woman in the show were just starting to brush lips. Finally. After seven years. Seven years he'd waited for them to finally just admit they wanted to fuck and then subsequently fuck. Oh well. Lavario turned off the TV so he could find Amber her pen and paper.

She took it from him at least somewhat graciously. "What's my first lesson?" She waved her hand at him just as he opened his mouth to speak. "Skip to the most important one in case you're too dead tomorrow to keep teaching me." She sat in front of his chair cross-legged, the notepad resting on her lap and pen raised. The college sweater she wore had seen better days. Only the "U" remained. The other letters signifying her college of choice were represented only in vague outlines. Pity, despite her many petty annoyances, found its way back to Lavario. She was trying to go back to some form of normal.

Lessons. Training. Agreements. A reality she was going to have to face very soon. "Are you going to plot against me?"

"Probably."

"Do it quietly. Have you ever called Kijo 'Kij' to her face?"

"No."

"Don't."

"What exactly is the lesson here?" She tapped the notebook with the end of the pen, looking up at him with some censure as if to point out: *You're not keeping your end of the bargain.*

"Be quiet. Stay alive. Dead people don't get revenge."

She wrote it down. Big, bold letters. *Dead ≠ revenge.*

Close enough.

CHAPTER TWENTY-FOUR: THAT'S HIS THING

Lessons only took them so far. Amber was smart enough to know it was a sham, a way for Lavario to manage hostilities. The leftover child chained herself to the illusion. She followed through, digging at him for satisfying answers. She chose being his student over merely being his cooperative food. He couldn't fault her for it.

Lavario began his lesson.

"Two forms. Human for magic. Wolf for physical strength. My people live in a world of dichotomies, rules and regulations that sort one thing from another with disregard to what's possible. The Isangelous advocate human reason. They see the wolf as a manifestation of brutality. Isangelous are the Boo Hags," he clarified when he saw her confused expression. She'd never heard their true pack name until now. "The Varcolac assert wolf superiority through force. A very long time ago, I thought as they did. I thought the wolf inside of me was incompatible with the human. One of them had to win. One of them had to be dominant. I could be a wolf or a human, not both."

"You are *not* human," Amber told him with force.

"I am human, and I am wolf."

"You are *not* human," she repeated.

Lavario continued. No point in arguing. "When I thought that was true, it allowed me to do terrible things. Certainty is troublesome that way."

"Like kill entire families?"

"Yes, exactly like that, only without any reflection afterward. How can you regret what you say is your true nature?" Lavario arched his eyebrow. "How can you murder something you have no association with? Do you murder grass when you walk over the top of it?"

She puffed air through her cheeks. "Kijo said something similar."

"Makes sense. That is the way she sees humans. That is the Varcolac way."

Anger skittered across her features. For once, she mastered it and moved on. *Progress*, Lavario thought. "What does this have to do with your fight tomorrow? Are you going to defeat them with hypocrisy?"

"They defeat themselves with that." Lavario thought of his Varcolac brothers and sisters and the horrendous clothes that they wore in public and the uncomfortable furniture in their sitting rooms. Silks and lounge chairs were stashed away along with secret desires to have other frilly and nonsensical things. "But in a way, yes, that's what I will do."

"But you think you're going to win?" Amber straightened, again youthful and full of hope.

"The fight is mine to lose."

She bounced a little bit in her chair. The enthusiasm cheered Lavario a bit. Part of him wanted to rein her in, to draw her back down to reality, but he began his speech to bring her some form of comfort. She'd spent the entire night spooling through all the possible things that might happen to her if he was defeated in the morning. She alternated between making peace with the horror of it and promising herself that she could make it back to the lake to die in peace.

"But how?" she asked. "Kijo sounded pretty confident."

"She should feel that way. She's very skilled." Truthfully, her skill might override his plans. Amber, already jumping out of her skin, didn't need to know that.

"So *how* are you going to beat her?" she pressed. She hated to repeat herself. Asking the same question more than once was a personal affront.

"Two forms—"

"You went through that already!" She tossed her hands in the air.

"Two forms. One for magic and the other for brute force. This is one of the rules that Kijo lives by. She believes that you must choose between wolf and human—teeth and claws *or* spells and incantations. This is how all wolves believe. Wars have been fought over it. I will choose both."

"So... you can use magic as a wolf? That's your thing?"

Lavario hid a smile at her phrasing. "Yes, that is my thing."

"How does it work?"

"Imagination."

She snorted at him with scorn while rolling her eyes. "You're fucking kidding me. Next you're going to tell me the secret to being a werewolf is to believe in yourself."

Lavario chuckled. "I wouldn't dare. Magic is an exercise in possibilities. Someone who believes the world operates according to immutable rules can only think of a few, mostly things that serve an immediate function. Sleeping spells and healing, for example. Powerful magic requires more flex, more flux. It requires the user to hold several ideas all at once. That is why other wolves fail. They cannot sustain the concentration it requires to hold their wolf form while they use magic."

"And you—"

This time he cut her off. "Here. Watch."

He transformed, quickly touching her shoulder with gentle care to let her know he was himself. Humans always associated their wolf forms with uncontrollable bloodlust. Not that he could blame them. They certainly cultivated that reputation for themselves. He held out his paw, concentrated. Fire emerged. He let it build, then let it dance around him as tiny flashes that came and went like the blinking lights of fireflies.

Fear drained her face of its defiance. "You can do anything."

Lavario snuffed it out. "No, we can alter the physical world, elements that exist. Wolf magic is not powerful enough for much else."

She puffed air out of her cheeks again. "What's the lesson in all of this? I can't do magic!"

And they were back to the start. Lavario searched himself for something to say to the young woman other than, *I told you this because you're a frightened child who has night terrors. I hear you crying at night, thrashing, and I thought it might help if you felt your future was more certain.* He couldn't say that. Comfort was only something she appreciated if left unsaid between them. "You want the magic—?"

"Yeah, that's the idea."

Lavario began again. "Any time you act, you choose. There is no neutrality in deeds. Even if you sit idle and allow something to happen, you made a choice. Only in the mind can opposing views have equal play. You can love your father while hating your father. You can blame yourself while you absolve yourself. You can miss your brother while believing he's better off not living this nightmare. You can want to die while wanting to live. You, like Kijo, are trying to eliminate parts of yourself so that you only love, blame, or hate all in the name of consistency. That is the antithesis of magic. You must choose who you are now, but you don't have to choose who you will always be. Keep the opposites around for a time when you wish to change your mind. Others might call you a hypocrite, but be that instead of an ideologue entrenched in your certainty.”

“What about both at once?” She was being sarcastic with him. “A hypocrite and an ideologue?”

Lavario gave her another chuckle. “Those are the worst of all.”

CHAPTER TWENTY-FIVE: HIS TO LOSE

Lavario dressed in his most ostentatious garment—a floor-length robe made of silk from golden orb spiders—and nothing else. Bright and vibrant, embellished with floral designs, the robe was a stark contrast to the attire his brothers and sisters wore. If not for their fangs and claws, they could have fit comfortably in any advertisement for cheap khaki pants and chambray shirts. "You don't exactly fit in here." Amber tied the knot of his sash right below his chest, rather than at his waist as it was intended. "Think you should go change? Put on some *pants—*" she looked to Kijo "—and maybe a something nice made out of boiled leather? Some *pants,*" she stressed again.

"I am dressed as I should be." Today might be the day he died. He wasn't going to show up looking even slightly contrite, as though he just recently got the message they found his mannerisms troublesome. Fussy until the end. Boo Haggish until death. "Putting on cheap clothing isn't going to make them reconsider this whole thing. They hate me in my silk robe. They'd hate me in uncomfortable pants."

Amber rolled her eyes and continued to fuss with the knot to the point where it almost looked like a giant phallic boondoggle, which somewhat injured the effect he was going for. "Whatever you say, werewolf Liberace. I'd hate for you to get your ass kicked in anything less lavish. Or in *pants.* Seriously," she put herself up on her tiptoes to do her version of whispering in his ear, "I can see your dick."

Lavario pushed her hands away and undid the knots she tied. "You can go wait in the room if you like. My penis cannot be seen from there, it's far more comfortable, and you would also escape the notice of my brothers and sisters."

Lavario tried once again, hoping the toothy glares and snarls shot her direction would press home his point, which was that she was not welcome here. The robe was a conscious decision on his part—a final *fuck you* if things turned sour—but Amber's presence was unwelcome fuel to the fire. Her trying to fix his sash or adjust his clothing was simply one of his stupid things messing with his other stupid thing. At the end of the fight, the robe might be burned, buried, soiled. But it was an item, lifeless. Lavario hated to think they'd compound her punishment in response to her presence here today. She already faced a very hard future without him if Kijo won.

She shook her head again. Stubborn. "I need to see this." She pulled the fabric over his torso again. "The fight. Not your dick."

Lavario relented. Putting her to sleep, using restraints, or simply locking her in the room all had individual appeal, yet Lavario could not bring himself to do any of it, even if it was for her own good. It was an informal part of her training to be a wolf. She had to find her own way. He could only hope the consequences she faced would be minimal. "Very well. But I strongly suggest you remain right here." He pointed to the spot where she currently stood. "Remember what I said last night about revenge?"

"Dead girls don't get any."

"Correct."

She gave him a quick salute and then made a gesture toward the open part of the robe where he was exposed. With a final shake of his head, Lavario left her to whatever fate befell her.

No one cheered as Lavario and Kijo came onto the floor. Such a thing was considered unseemly, beneath the importance of the ceremony. Fights between guardians and lesser wolves could take place in an instant. It was not uncommon for higher-ranking wolves to spontaneously assert dominance over unwieldy new wolves who did not fully comprehend their place in the pack. Conversely, battles between guardians were rare and signified shifts in pack mentality or direction. It was a fight for the leadership of the community itself, not over petty, personal grievances or individual power.

Each pack was represented. The Isangelous. Lavario could see Eresna and a few of his other Boo Hag kin, all of them dressed in their best ceremonial garb; cloaks, dresses, tunics all made of fine fabric, expertly tailored, flashy and frills but nothing overwrought or distasteful. The False Moon, or Moondogs as they preferred to be called. Some of them took the event seriously and were dressed appropriately and others wore baseball caps and even cowboy hats. And of course his brothers and sisters of the Varcolac, doing their best to imitate a very boring cult. In the middle of it all stood him and his daughter. Their eyes locked. When she looked at his yellow robe and gave him a supercilious twitch of her upper lip, Lavario smiled and cocked an eyebrow in return.

Mazgan walked to the podium where he began a long speech that only the tiresomely loyal listened to. More theatrics. Unlike the rest of the pack, he was dressed in finery. Gold chains, jewels on his fingers, and silk wraps. Lavario could picture the buffoon practicing it in his chambers as he looked at himself in the mirror, preening to imaginary thunderous applause. Lavario knew Mazgan saw this as his moment, not Kijo's.

At least it provided cover for him to talk with his daughter one last time before they fought. There was so much he wanted to say to her. Very little in his heart was relevant given the context or would be appreciated given their new relationship. Worse, it might come across as though he were begging. *Stick with the practical*, Lavario decided.

"Kijo," he said, "if I fall today, let the girl go to the Loch if she so chooses."

"That's what you're worried about right now?" She looked incredulous.

"What else is there to worry about right now?"

She thought for a moment and then gave him a quick affirmative gesture that could be interpreted as disdain to any onlookers. Lavario repressed a smile.

Finally, Mazgan stopped his grandstanding and got down to business, ten minutes later. "A challenge has been issued. Kijo, do you accept the consequences of this challenge?"

"I accept, Alpha Guardian," Kijo said, her spine straight and stance proud. Lavario could feel the collective pride of Varcolac wolves. His daughter spoke with their voice. Lavario felt a twinge of pleasure as well. His daughter was a fine wolf.

"Lavario, do you accept the consequences of this challenge?"

"I accept," Lavario said with a dismissive wave of his hand. He never quite understood the need for any of this. There was no real choice. It was accept and fight or don't accept and fight anyway.

Mazgan twisted his lips at the gesture and the lack of formal address. Perhaps he thought it didn't matter anymore since he continued without demanding the title be said. "I, *Alpha Guardian* of the Varcolac, sanction this challenge. The dispute is settled through death, forfeit, or submission."

With that, he raised his hands to the air. Howling—the only form of socially acceptable camaraderie at the event—broke out in response. Lavario remained silent and watched as his daughter celebrated with her peers. Losing oneself to the pack, joining your voice with theirs, was about as basic and primal as one could get. Lavario considered himself neither of those things.

While they carried on, he focused until the world around him stopped. Noise, emotions, wants, desires, fears were locked away for later. Echoes dissipated. It was time to get the show started. Lavario disrobed to transform. Shifting to wolf was fluid and seamless, an action as natural as any other body motion.

Kijo stepped backward, as surprised as he thought she'd be. Wolves fought in the physical realm, and she expected him to use magic. Spells, mere trickery according to her, were the fallback for Boo Hags who associated more with their human selves. Her shock only lasted for a second and was probably only visible to Lavario, who knew the nuances of her expressions as well as he knew his own. Within moments she was also wolf—ears back, tail erect, eyes fixed—and rushing toward him with all her considerable strength.

Lavario lifted one paw. A flick of his wrist sent her flying backward. The entire room, silent before, was filled with the cracking of chairs as wolves from every pack shuffled uncomfortably in their seats. For once, they were all on the same page in a collective shock. Somewhere in the crowd, Garvey said, "Whoa. Shit."

Kijo looked up at him from the floor in disbelief, her expression conveyed betrayal, ever-present anger. She thought Lavario had taught her everything he knew. In a way he had. *Be careful what you share and who you share it with* was advice he gave her many times over. That especially applied to children everyone had slated to kill you, children who then surpassed you in rank and also had the temperament and ability to do just that. "My apologies, Kijo. You are my daughter, and I love you." He flicked his wrist again. She crashed into one of the walls and fell to the floor with an undignified thump.

It was a strong blow—stronger as a wolf than it would have been in his human form—and Lavario had the element of surprise. Thrilling as it was to watch her fly across the room, Lavario suppressed the urge to gloat, either internally or externally, while Kijo shook herself and got back to her feet with unsteady, almost drunken unease. Arrogant. The word was an apt way to describe him. But then his daughter was, too.

She thought it would be so easy once she forced him into a melee battle; her superior strength would overcome any Boo Hag trickery he could conjure. Pride was no doubt wounded right now, but he knew it was not over. Fight was all Kijo knew. Finally back on her feet, she charged him again, her paws hitting the ground with heavy thuds, intent on making it a physical confrontation.

The fire he created for Amber was for show, nothing more than little lights flashing around him before blinking out in a puff of smoke. The fireball taking shape in his paw now was massive. He struggled to maintain enough concentration to hold it together when it flared. Hair burned, releasing a sulfurous odor into the air. *Not yet*, he told himself, clamping his jaw in a long-toothed grimace to keep himself from roaring in pain. With difficulty, he focused his mind away from the burning sensation and brought his magic under control. The fireball solidified into a tight, condensed coil of energy waiting to be released.

He hurled it when she was about ten feet away from him, thinking she'd be forced to revert to human form to counter the magic. His failing concentration made his aim poor, though. He hit her leg rather than her chest as he intended. Enraged, she howled but continued toward him. Lavario crashed to the ground as Kijo slammed into him. Claws dug into his sides, fire scorched his belly, and her teeth penetrated deep into his right shoulder. Blood welled then suffused as she shook her head side-to-side to deepen her hold and open the wound. She only just barely missed his throat. He'd be dying or even dead by now if she hadn't.

She wanted him to bleed out.

Strength failing, Lavario placed his hand on her chest and sent her flying backward once again with less force. Perhaps thinking she had the time given his injuries, she reverted to her human form to counter his magic. Instinct took over Lavario. Until this was done, she was not his daughter. She was vulnerable prey.

Lavario jumped on top of her and jabbed all five claws into her side. He felt her body jerk and spasm when he got to bone. It was not a fatal wound, but she was done.

He'd won.

This was a moment Lavario pictured a billion times over. The details imagined then reimagined came to focus. The shock of his peers, their crestfallen faces as they realized the extent of his power, even Garvey in the audience saying something ridiculous, out of touch, and inappropriate—the least popular of all his stupid things spiking the ball for him. Only Kijo's presence deviated from the idealized version of events so far. In fantasy, Lavario never fought his daughter, never so much as touched a hair on her head. It was Mazgan. And Mazgan was dead by now.

He looked down at his daughter, impaled by his own hand. She did not succumb to anger as he anticipated. She maintained her calm and went for an early kill as he taught her. "Submit." He whispered it in her ear. Black eyes narrowed in response, nostrils flared. She tried to rise, but Lavario twisted his hand inside her. "Submit. It's over." Defeat was an odious look on his Kijo, the intended savior of the Varcolac. Part of Lavario wanted her to win probably about as much as she wanted to beat him, if only to avoid this moment. Fantasy no longer, this was what Lavario had always dreaded the most. He knew she would not yield. Yet he was not above begging. "Please, my daughter. Submit."

"Never."

She meant it. Trumped up as this fight was, she could hardly escape the backlash, the disappointment, of defeat. She was panting heavily. Lavario felt his own strength ebb as his shoulder wound nagged at him. Both of them needed to heal. "Then I submit to you." Withdrawing as he stood, Lavario looked down at Kijo, who looked at him as though he was insane. Maybe he was.

"I do not accept your submission." She spat at him with vitriol that stung.

"Then I forfeit." She gasped at him, clearly stunned. To submit was shameful enough, to forfeit was to exit in disgrace. Worse than exile, worse than death. Forever marked as a coward, he'd live his life scorned, without rank. But he would not lose his daughter. "I forfeit." He said it loudly, so all wolves could hear.

Official responses had apparently dried up. Mazgan stood at the edge of the fighting stage with a dumbfounded look. But the fight was over. Kijo had no choice but to accept a forfeit. Lavario transformed back to his human form to heal his shoulder, leaving only a few of his daughter's teeth marks as a decorative badge from the fight. Slowly, showing some uncertainty, Kijo did the same to her wound.

Miraculously unsoiled, the robe tarried in the spot where Lavario left it. Wrapping himself back in it felt good, felt right. He was the wolf with the frills after all. Rule breaker. Loner. Lavario looked to all his kith and howled on his own, a private celebration for everyone's favorite sentimental, Boo Hag fool.

CHAPTER TWENTY-SIX: UNDERSTANDABLY DISAPPOINTED

"What the fuck was that?" Amber shouted at him. "You are the worst. *The worst.* You had that shit in the bag, and then you were just..." She trailed off into a series of flustered hand gestures.

"Your disappointment is noted." Lavario sat perched on one of his favorite ornamental chairs. He'd enjoy it while he could and to the extent Amber would allow. Good-bye comfort. Good-bye luxury. Good-bye elegance. He was sure Mazgan and his daughter would be here soon to repossess everything that made life worth living.

Amber would certainly remain. As she continued to seethe and Godzilla his stuff, he became more and more sure of it. The girl was on a binge. Promises had been broken in her estimation, and he was going to pay the price. Under it all—the pageantry of her anger—she was simply terrified. *What's going to happen to me?* An emotion she broadcasted over and over again. Lavario wanted to comfort her, but realistically she would share in whatever fate Kijo and Mazgan brought to his door. He had no idea what it might be. He just knew it wouldn't be very good. There was little comfort to offer.

"And put on some goddamn pants." She went to his dresser, flinging out all his sorted laundry—all of it once cleanly folded and slotted in its proper spot—until she found some trousers. "Here." She flung them at him. Lavario grabbed at them before they hit him in the face. Tiredly, he did as she told him. Maybe he *was* the worst werewolf ever. Taking orders from a human teenager. Forfeiting fights he should have won.

Lavario was on the verge of giving her what might count as a pep talk when his door flung open. "Hey, kids." Garvey. Lavario growled. The presence of his errant progeny was only slightly better than Mazgan and Kijo coming to kill him or take his possessions. "So how's it going?"

"Who the hell are you?" Amber blurted out immediately. The child had no filter, no conceptualization that other wolves might actually hurt her. Luckily for her, Garvey was a different type of fool.

"My apologies. How rude of me not to introduce myself to Lavario's new keeper. I'm Garvey, Lavario's first and worst mistake." He bent down, grabbed the young girl's hand and kissed it. "Delighted to meet you. Please feel free to join in and continue to lambast Lavi-doodle here." Lavario snarled at the pejorative. "Do you like that? It's a combo of your name and poodle, sort of a sissy breed of nonstarters. I don't know if he's the worst werewolf *ever,* though. Close. Probably pretty close. What do you think, Lav?"

"Are you here to gloat?" Lavario asked him with gravel in his voice.

"I'm in the process of gloating. So yes." Garvey leaned up against the frame of the door, smiling his typical big-toothed grin.

Lavario was in no mood for it. "Task accomplished. See yourself back out."

Garvey ignored him and continued to address Amber. "He's always this way. In case you were wondering. Enjoy your life of sulking and skulking followed by some quiet reflection and soul searching."

Amber's mouth hung open in shocked silence. Perhaps because she finally met someone who was a bigger pain in his ass than she was, or maybe because Garvey—outlandish and talkative—was unlike any werewolf she'd met so far. She was finally unable to come up with a retort.

Urges to kill or at least maim Garvey worked their way through Lavario. His wayward son's foolishness had cost him dearly. Kijo would be his daughter and the fantasy of killing Mazgan, either himself or through Kijo, might have come to pass. Instead, he had an annoying teenage girl as his bloodservant and his daughter was his enemy. Disgraced. Facing an uncertain future. All because of Garvey. He wanted to kill the other wolf. Or fuck him. Lavario was never entirely sure which it was. "This is your doing."

Garvey acted as if he had no idea what Lavario was talking about for a while. Until, "Oh, the whole Tovin thing?"

Lavario's claws seeped into the wood of his chair. "Yes, the whole Tovin thing."

"Jesus, Lav. That chair forfeits. It's too fabulous to fight. Leave it be, why don't you?" Garvey tsked him. "And Tovin. Oh Tovin. Such a sweet little treat he was. You," he paused to point at Lavario, "you definitely would have enjoyed him."

"You were going to have sex with the other guy?" Amber butted into the conversation. For once Lavario was grateful. He was nearly to the point of jumping out of his chair. Frenzy. Frenzy. Frenzy. The one thing he always told all his children *not* to do. Only Garvey could ever bring him to this point so quickly and with so little energy spent on his part. "I thought you and Kijo..."

She trailed off as Garvey cut her off with a laugh. Then he stopped himself to turn back to Lavario. "Wait, *did* you guys ever get down and dirty?"

"No." She was always his daughter.

"Yeah, that would be weird. She never stopped calling you Daddy." Lavario only snarled in response. "Right. 'Father.' Formal, dignified wolves you two." Garvey smiled and turned back to Amber. "So is this fine young lady to be your new baby or new paramour?" Amber gave him another confused glance. With a quick wink, he explained, "Paramour is a fancy way of saying fuck buddy."

"I know what the word means." She was defensive, then angry again. "I want to kill him. He murdered my family."

Amber never missed her chance to remind anyone and everyone of her ultimate goal. Lavario started to see it as her statement of comfort, a verbal security blanket she could retreat back into when the situation got out of her control: *No matter what's going on now, it's okay. I'm going to kill him at the end of it all.* Despite the undesirability of the outcome, he could appreciate the mantra at its core. It was important to have long-term goals. But if she was looking for sympathy from Garvey, she was not likely to find it. He had killed more than his fair share of humans.

"Perfect." Garvey beamed at Amber. "We all wish you the best of luck with that. For now, though, take your revenge monologue on the road." He shooed her, pointing repeatedly to the bloodservant's chambers. "Go on now. Be a good little nondead girl." She left. Reluctantly. There was a moment Lavario resented the exchange, her willingness to obey his idiot progeny over him. It passed. At least she was in the other room. At least she was quiet. Garvey closed the door behind her, locking it.

"You should probably end that particular plotline. Nothing some teeth in the old jugular wouldn't solve." Lavario declined to comment, though he sort of agreed in spirit. "Munching an entire family, though. Pretty dastardly stuff there. I'm not sure your Boo Hag buddies would approve." He stopped to wink.

Difficult as it was, Lavario ignored him. When it became clear Lavario wasn't going to engage, Garvey wandered around the room, picking up various items. Eventually he found the picture of Tovin that Yuri sent Lavario among the items on the desk.

"Oh Tovin. Sweet little Tovin. I was really sorry he got caught up in this, by the way." Garvey directed the comment at Lavario but kept his eyes locked on the picture. For once, Garvey sounded as though he might regret his actions. Lavario almost believed him. As if Garvey sensed he was on the fence, he continued, "No. Really. He is a kindhearted little fellow. You should have seen the determined way he tossed himself over me when Eresna was about to beat me half to death. He was such a gallant little speed bump. And a good kisser once you get him going. Right up until the point I became a giant, unfriendly wolf monster, I'm pretty sure I was the best date that boy had ever had."

It was hard for Lavario to picture anyone—let alone the contusion-covered young man Lavario saw at the distribution point—throwing himself in front of an enraged Eresna, especially to protect Garvey. Who, other than himself, would ever be that stupid? "He is doing all right?" Lavario knew he was being baited into the conversation, but he allowed it. Engaging Garvey under this circumstance at least got him the information he wanted.

"Yes, Eresna took him in at Yuri's request. It was close, though. Sort of reckless of you to trade him for a guardian's servant, don't you think? I would have gone for a scroggling if I wanted to keep the boy alive. Most of the lower-ranking would have been thrilled to receive your cast off. Another guardian...not so much. Picky lot." Garvey waved his hand to encompass Lavario's room as if to say, *do you see what a bunch of decadent assholes you are?*

Lavario fretted after the exchange of servants. He thought he might have doomed Tovin in his own selfish bid to maintain ownership. He made many mistakes that night. To keep Tovin safe, he should have taken a scroggling, the servant of a lower-ranked wolf, as his choice. The Boo Hags went through a lot of trouble for Eresna's bloodservant. Kidnapping unwanted unknowns was simple. Few—aside from scattered close friends or relatives—ever looked for them. Kidnapping affluent or even middle-class humans was far riskier. National news levels of risky. Only a guardian could demand something so lavish and impractical, and Lavario gambled on their unwillingness to part with such a status symbol. There were moments when he halfway expected Eresna to show up at his door to reclaim the man.

Lavario snorted uncomfortably. "I hoped they wouldn't make the trade at all."

"Ah. Guess that makes sense...if you're a selfish prick who just wants to Stockholm some poor guy until he's comfortable enough to take off his pants." Garvey smiled, a sort of lopsided gotcha-grin. There was also a resoluteness Lavario rarely heard. The thought Garvey did care for the boy tipped him over the edge. "Anyway..."

Lavario did not let him finish. With speed that surprised even himself, he whirled out of his chair and charged Garvey into the wall, pinning him there with an elbow across the chest. Pots clanked together, some fell off the shelves on impact. The other wolf cringed back involuntarily, avoiding eye contact. The proximity. The smell. Lavario tried to hold on to his anger. "You would have killed him."

"Yes," Garvey bit it out, "I would have killed him. I wouldn't diminish him."

"Is that what I did to you?" Few could anger Lavario the way Garvey did. Everything Lavario held dear was lost when he made the other wolf—family, status, reputation, community. Still, Garvey resented him. Still, he hated him. "Did I diminish you?"

"Yes." For once, there was no embellishment, just a simple affirmation.

"Look at me."

The other wolf kept his eyes fixed on the ceiling. "Doesn't this count as a frenzy, Lav?" It was an attempt to come off as chiding, nonchalant. Lavario knew better. Garvey was far from unconcerned. But he had a point. Control was no longer present.

Lavario slammed him up against the wall again. Curios everywhere. "Look at me."

Hesitantly, Garvey lowered his head so that his eyes met Lavario's. "Good. Now tell me how I diminished you. I made you immortal."

Instead of answering, Garvey twisted and turned until Lavario simply let him go. Once free, Garvey transformed. Most wolves found Garvey's—and the form of the other False Moon wolves—comical, something they might have dressed up for at Halloween as a lark if they had any sense of humor. Stunted, dog like. Lowly. "You made a joke." His huge paws clenched into fists. "I and my 'false moon' brothers and sisters are mocked, abused, killed. And this," he gestured once again to Lavario's room, his belongings, "has been your punishment. Rather a great deal more lavish than you deserve."

"I gave you the option to stay with me." He paused, trying to draw nearer to Garvey. "I wanted you to stay with me."

"They called me your pet. Your mistake." Garvey shook his head. "And you never even considered coming with me, living outside of the true packs."

It was spat at him with such force that Lavario winced away. Denying it was useless. Lavario never considered living with the False Moons as an option until it came down to that or killing Kijo. He was one of the originals, one of the oldest, a true wolf, but he had loved Garvey. No one could not deny him that. "I never saw you as a pet or as a mistake. Garvey, my—"

"I am not yours."

Lavario continued. "My love...I did what I did to keep you alive. I could not lose you."

"You're such a benign collector, Lav." It was said with less force, a sad resignation.

"I have been selfish, I admit." Each bloodservant since Garvey had been a new Garvey, an attempt to reclaim what he had before. It was a foolish, stupid desire and one that never failed to disappoint. Lavario was far too old to call it anything else. "I never saw you as an object for me to collect, as a mistake, or as a pet. I never wanted to diminish you." He was standing right beside Garvey, and—for once—the other wolf did not pull away. He reached out to touch him but stopped himself short. In fantasies, Garvey turned to him at this point. They made love the way they used to. Garvey forgave everything. Fantasy and reality were not matching up today. Garvey left.

CHAPTER TWENTY-SEVEN: NEW ALLIANCE

To rid themselves of outsider influence, both literally and figuratively, the Varcolac burned Lavario's finery. As Lavario's stuff burned, Garvey remembered dying.

He was under a branch right as it fell, toppling his skull with a loud, crackling thump. Dazed, he'd stared up at the sky with the type of resignation he'd felt since being brought to Lavario, part of the first bloodservant cohort. He knew he was going to die with a title like that, the tales of destiny they tried to sell be damned. But he never expected it to be so soon, not after he'd made it through all those terror-filled nights to emerge out the other side with a lover instead of a master.

Life didn't flash before his eyes as everyone said it would, just a series of regrets. He'd spent his entire existence strolling through small moment—a collection of kisses, hand holding, and walks in the rain that he promised himself would add up to something meaningful in the end.

Tonight, his promise to himself came true. Those small moments burned. The bed where they first made love, the dresser Lavario protected until, one night, Garvey's socks made their way inside a drawer, the curtains they picked out together, the books they'd read, the chairs they'd sat on. Lavario had kept everything from their life together. Except him.

It was fitting, Garvey told himself, to force this on Lavario the way he'd forced a new life on him. Forever a walking cautionary tale. His very name was shorthand for a colossal fuckup committed by a powerful wolf. He could forgive that. Sometimes Garvey admitted to himself that he'd forgiven it a long time ago. Occasionally, on the right day, he'd even admit he loved Lavario. Right now, he'd at least admit he was glad Lavario was alive. But he couldn't forgive the end to their tale. Not yet. Lavario, his lover, too proud to be a Moondog. Too special to live outside the great packs with his creation.

"It wasn't always bad between you two," Kijo said.

It jolted him out of his memories. Mazgan had asked him to stand behind Kijo. *Place of honor for all your hard work,* he'd said with that self-satisfied sly smile of his. He didn't think Garvey knew that placing him next to the triumphant daughter would twist the knife as deep as it could go. Everything Lavario had ever lost in one location.

Garvey shook his head. He wasn't going to talk about their relationship with Kijo. "He gave up everything for you."

"We need to talk after this."

Garvey could only imagine what she wanted to say to her least favorite relative. "I'll look forward to that."

He was dying again. The lover looked down at him. Tears the master never would have cried mixed with the blood on his head. He could only tell the difference as they fell.

* * *

"What's the scheme?" Kijo came right to the point, as she normally did.

Since everything had changed, Garvey did his best to act as though nothing had changed. He kept his tone and mannerisms light, mockingly cheerful. "Hold up a tick, let me go get my white cat and swivel chair."

She probably didn't understand the reference, but she understood the tone well enough. She clamped her glare on him. Those eyes of hers were death thoughts. Lingering on them made him uneasy. You didn't know or want to know what was beyond. Troubled, Garvey relented and looked away.

"Whatever it is he promised you, you're not going to get it. He will betray you."

"Probably," Garvey responded. He didn't bother lying.

"I can make promises, too."

Unexpected. Inconvenient. Garvey twisted around on the uncomfortable chair not-so-graciously provided for him. Her entire room was an affront to good taste now that Garvey could get a look at it. He'd never been here before. Grays, browns, shades of gray and brown. And what was a maybe an ashtray. Even the chair she sat in looked like something a child made. He wondered how she'd feel if he told her about Mazgan's apartment with its Lavario-level frills and Boo Hag folly. He'd test those waters later. Right now he had to think of a response.

Garvey's options for dealing with her were limited. Refusing to share information could only end badly for him. Out of respect for Lavario, she'd always kept her hands anchored to her sides. Those protections no longer existed for obvious reasons. Challenging him and killing him were options now that would effectively make his schemes and plans a moot point. Kijo was the type of wolf to do exactly that without much prompting. It was better to fess up while he could. Unfortunately, he'd have to be mostly honest with her.

Garvey bolted a smile to his face and began an exchange that he hoped would end with him intact. "Good news, sis. You don't need me to tell you anything. Mazgan will do that. He thinks you two will rule over the new world order together as lovers. He is going to save your pack from a life in second place."

"He is not my lover," she said with disgust, crossing her legs. "The plan is to kill the guardians?"

The idiot actually told her that? He suppressed an eye roll and a sigh. "Among other things."

"And what's your role in all of this?"

"Promises first."

Her lip curled, exposing teeth. A low growl rumbled in her throat. Eyes, now golden with a dark circle of black in the center, narrowed. For a moment, Garvey thought he'd made the last mistake of his life. Kijo was not the type to fuck around with anyone's nonsense on a good day, and today had not been a good day. He was ready to make a run for it, hoping he could perhaps get to Mazgan before she finished him off, when she relaxed and spoke to him in an emotionless voice. "What did he offer you?"

Surprised, and with confidence building, Garvey leaned back in his chair. His darling sister had a plan of some sort, and she thought she needed him for it. Best of all, the circumstances clawed at her. "He'd make me true wolf."

Something like pity rippled across her features. "That is impossible, Garvey. No one can do that for you."

He knew it was true—had known it all along—but he did his best to work his features into something resembling crestfallen disappointment. Being a true wolf was never his goal. He wanted his pack safe. And yeah, revenge. Suspicious as he was of Kijo's motivations, he had to concede that she was at least being honest with him, a courtesy Mazgan never extended. "What will you offer me, then?"

"Lavario." Garvey was about to start his objection when she cut him off. "I will make him a False Moon. And I won't kill you."

"Moondog," Garvey corrected her.

She raised the tips of her fingernails from the chair in a dismissive gesture. "Moondog, as you say. Isn't that what you've always wanted?"

As far as deals went, it fell under the *good enough* category. Truthfully, the won't-kill clause was the best part of it. He'd like to prompt her for an extended warranty. He gave her a quick nod of the head and said a few words he hoped conveyed how happy he was with her offer.

"Good. Tell me the plan. Tell me your role in it."

Quickly as he could, knowing her patience for exposition waned after a few minutes, Garvey gave her a rundown—the botched extraction of Tovin, the subsequent fallout, the release of vampires, and the destruction of the Boo Hag system of bloodservant distribution. Afterward, a world Mazgan envisioned where guardians no longer existed and werewolves did as they pleased, took as they pleased, killed as they pleased. Ruling through force, the Varcolac way.

Kijo said nothing for a very long time. Muscles in her cheek and eyelids spasmed as she struggled to maintain the outward appearance of calm. Garvey never understood why she bothered. Anyone in her presence felt the anger beneath the surface. It was a near constant rolling wave of energy. Finally, after what seemed like forever as Garvey twisted around on the hard chair, she spoke again. "And that is why you're here? There is a portal *here?*"

"Yes," he confirmed.

Those black eyes turned golden. "That fool!"

"Would you like me to stall?" Garvey came in afterward, every so sweetly.

She was in a bind. Garvey knew it. She knew Garvey knew it. Eventually, she caved with a sneer and a forceful wave of her hand. "For now, do as planned. Only," she amended, "be less discreet. Leave. I'll be in contact."

For an instant, Garvey almost felt bad for poor Mazgan, who was most likely giddy levels of happy right now as visions of his life with Kijo danced around in his empty head. Kijo had promised to make Lavario a Moondog. To deliver, she'd either have to cozy up to Mazgan—who had refused to exile Lavario, preferring full view of the constant humiliation—or take his place. Garvey was already betting on the track his pony would take.

CHAPTER TWENTY-EIGHT: WHAT THEY GOT TO KEEP

Submissives walked by to ogle them, pausing to jeer at Lavario in a way he normally would have responded to with a quick show of violence, a love tap to remind them of their rank. Today, they were here to remind him of his. After the fight with Kijo, he'd gone from beta to omega, from a wolf who made important decisions to a wolf who guarded over the redundancies, chauffeured, and did menial tasks. Forbidden to challenge to reclaim any lost ground, Lavario could only sit in his cage while his packmates taunted him.

Square one. Lavario's least favorite of all the squares.

"This is insufferable," he said after being ordered to sweep.

"At least you have your fancy robe. That's something." Amber plucked at the edges of it as she trailed behind him. She'd recovered some of her former impudence once she realized horrible death wasn't immediate. She did keep her voice to a whisper, lobbing her taunts in a muted hiss to the side or back of his head.

"I got to keep you as well." Lucky him. "And this." He gestured to her and to the elaborate chair that looked so out of place amongst the filth. He swatted her hand away from his robe. It was a trial to keep it clean. He didn't need her pawing at it.

"Lucky you." He had to smile at her parrot of his thoughts. "So what now?"

"What do you mean?"

"Now that the other guy is gone, we should think of a plan."

Lavario chuckled with no real humor. Dip—the other guy—was out today. Hunting or doing whatever it is the stupid creature did in its spare time. The girl was bold again. "If you wished to plot, there was no need to wait for our companion's absence."

"Then why haven't we been plotting?"

She was looking down at him again, her fists on her hips. Lavario was growing somewhat fond of her outrage, the endearing and ever-present crease between her eyebrows. But less fond of her young, optimistic belief in half-formed plots and schemes. There were no what-could-go-wrong moments of self-realization where she winked at her reflection. He loved it in her and hated it in her.

"Because there is no point. I cannot advance in rank."

"So, you're just going to push around dirt," she stopped to criticize his sweeping, "and then sit around on your fancy chair wearing your fancy robe?"

Lavario raised an eyebrow, now far less refined in structure. He was naturally very hirsute, as were most of his kind. Keeping himself groomed to standard was a fuss in which he could no longer indulge. Left to its own devices, his hair had a sense of manifest destiny, stretching east to west across his body. He worried over whether or not arching his eyebrow was more comical than derisive at this point. "I am accepting my situation. It is not going to change anytime soon."

"Whatever you say, archmage butthurt." Amber kicked at the plates that littered the cell floor. Dip brought them their food but never bothered to clean up afterward. Stomping and flinging the plates didn't seem to actually serve to calm her down. She was more frenzied than ever before. She whirled on him. "Do you know what I think?"

The answer to that question was always the same. He had long since stopped asking *what* and simply responded. "That I am the worst werewolf ever."

She tilted a thumb-gun at him again. *Got it.*

His patience snapped. He tossed the broom to the side where it landed with a clap, rattle, clank. "You were living a similar life when I was the pack's second. By choice. Pretend that you're not being forced to wear that horrible sweatshirt or eat this terrible food. Pretend I offered you a comfortable bed and you spat in my face and slept on the floor. Pretend I offered you things much better, but you decided to reject each one because I'm a soulless killer whom you will never forgive."

Instead of a response, she picked up one of the plate shards and heaved it at him. She tossed as many of the broken fragments as she could before collapsing into a corner of the cell to weep. Lavario remained silent, allowing his companion to grieve. Dirt on her face had turned to mud and the jinxed sweatshirt became a makeshift tissue before she was finished. "Why don't you just kill me? I push you and push you and push you, and you just sit there with that smug expression on your face."

Lavario disrobed, transformed, and felt the same thrill he always felt as he became wolf, the same joy as whatever being before him gazed on with a mixture of fear, reverence, envy, and loathing. "Tell me again you want to die." She gasped when he spoke. "Tell me to kill you, and it will be done."

He did his best not to loom menacingly although he was too tall, too furry, too toothy to do much else. Fear, confusion, horror: her emotions were so different from the persona she presented, the one of a brave woman who could challenge the monster without fear or hesitation. Maybe one day. "I don't want to live like this." She whispered it, her eyes wide.

"Command me to end your life, then."

He sat down beside her, hating the thought of the filth on the floor touching him, and extended his paw. All she had to do was reach out, and he'd pull her to him. Quick and as painless as anyone could ever want. He offered her death on this dirty floor, swaddled in her filthy clothes.

Her lip trembled as she looked at the invitation. It wasn't what she wanted—Lavario could feel it inside of her, the I-want-to-live undersong of her entire being, so out of sync with everything she'd tried to cultivate—but she reached at out for him, too proud to back down from her folly. Tips of fingers brushed his before she withdrew. One more look at him and she shrugged off all assumed mannerisms and let herself be afraid.

Knees to her chin, eyes puffy and swollen from crying, she gulped out, "I don't want to die like this either." She looked directly at him, not something many people did when he was in wolf form. "I'm so scared."

"I know." He pulled her to him, using a little more force when she hiccupped before contact. "And I know that I am a monster to you. And I know I do not deserve your forgiveness." He stroked her cheek with the back of his paw while her mucus coiled through his perfect black fur. Grief gumbo. He heard her call it that before—something her mother had called it. Lavario did his best to not to notice the dirt, the goo, the mess. This was not the way a guardian was meant to live.

"What's up with this?" Amber picked up the picture of Tovin, which fell to the ground when he took off his robe. Another thing he got to keep. Lucky, lucky him. "You keeping this around is kind of creepy, stalker wolf."

Were there any other types of wolves other than stalker wolves? Lavario didn't think so. "It is a missed opportunity at the moment."

"An opportunity for what exactly?"

"To feel happiness again, however briefly."

For once, she didn't say anything. Hatred was there, percolating brain to heart. Pity and compassion worked their way through, too. Upon mixing, both turned to guilt. To honor the memory of those she lost, she didn't want to feel complex emotions toward their killer. He rubbed the ridge of her brow with his thumb, careful with his claw. She'd be a fine hypocrite yet.

Chapter Twenty-Nine: What They Didn't Get To Keep

A muted scream from an unknown source woke Lavario. It wasn't Amber, so he paid it little mind. Always tormented by their horrible living conditions, the redundancies moaned and wailed through the night. They were the humans the Vercolac kept in case they needed another. By now Lavario could grit his teeth and sleep through their torment. Another scream. And another. At this point, his companion should be on edge—her brain waves an onslaught—but none of her emotions came to him. She had to be too far away, dead, or sleeping peacefully through the commotion.

Lavario's eyes swooped open. His other senses took over when he only saw broken plates scattered the floor of the cell, no Amber. Ears rotated. Rats skittered around him, the redundancies a few cells over moaned, but he didn't hear the sound of Amber's voice. He inhaled deeply, catching her scent. And Mazgan's. Despite the fact he knew that the Alpha Guardian wanted him to get angry at this point, a low growl escaped from his throat and he felt his hackles rise, claws extend, and ears flatten so that the tips overlapped on the back of his skull. Success. He was livid.

Not totally knowing what he was going to do, Lavario flung open the gate to his cell and marched toward the scent of his young companion.

"Lavario," Amber's voice, tight and strained, cut through the fog of anger.

Mazgan held her by the arm, twisting her entire body upward so that she had to stand on her tiptoes. Her sweatshirt was gone, tossed to the floor beside her. Her short, curly hair was matted down with sweat. Blood seeped out of welts where claws penetrated her flesh. She must have been standing there for a bit now. Some of the blood was dry, new branches veined from the wounds, trickling down to her elbow where the blood pooled and dripped to the floor below. Her undershirt was soaked.

Mazgan beamed. "Welcome. I was about to show your young slave what she has to look forward to." He twisted her arm again. The woman gritted her teeth but made no sound. "Dip tells me you two had a moment last night."

He felt his hackles rise even farther. Of course Mazgan would put an end to any peace between him and his servant. Her emotions were bound up with his. Her peace was his peace.

"This is against the rules, Alpha Guardian." Lavario kept his voice flat.

"I did not think you would mind. You do not care for rules," Mazgan cheerfully retorted. "But do not worry, I am not going to hurt her. I respect our traditions. She is yours by right. She is only here for a show."

Dip brought up one of the redundancies—the source of the screams from earlier—which kicked, wailed, and babbled nonsensically as the stupid half-breed pawed haphazardly at its flesh. Whatever language it had before was forgotten. It was a thing with skin too dirty to have a discernible race, a frame too emaciated to have a discernible gender. It only had enough dangling self-awareness to understand that being brought out of the cage was never good.

"Human, this is what will happen to you when Lavario falls, and he will fall. Dip," Mazgan commanded, "get on with it."

Stunted, more doglike than human or wolf, Dip was the monstrous result of a first desperate attempt to keep humans from going extinct. Ugly, vicious, stupid, careless, and impatient, the experiment made a rather lackluster Adam to be sure. Even Dip's wolf form, something seen as a gift, was an affront. Transformed, he crawled around on all fours like a common dog, not by choice or as camouflage as some of them did to avoid detection but because he had no other option. Worse, he limped. The sight of him gangling along was loathsome.

The creature opened its jaws.

Amber looked from the ugly wolf and to the thing huddled on the floor. Experience, combined with an intuitive understanding of context, told her what was going to happen next. The monster holding her arm twisted it again when she tried to close her eyes or look away. Pain, intense, unyielding, tore through her. As always, she forced down the cries. But she looked. It would only get worse for her if she didn't.

Dip started at the legs, taking large bites with his canine teeth.

The first screams tore through her. The first spurts of blood made her vomit. The noises the thing made as it ate caused her to empty her bladder. The humiliation she felt as the waste trickled down her leg finally made her cry out in a low, agonized whimper. She couldn't take anymore. She was sure of it. After this, she'd take Lavario's hand, he'd pull her to him, and she'd leave this world and its monsters behind. All these conflicted feelings would stop. Simplicity. Death was simplicity.

She moaned again as Dip bit into the human's stomach. It—no he, Amber could see the penis now that the tattered pants were torn off—twisted on the floor weakly. Blood gurgled from his mouth, caking the outline of it in a way that reminded her of the first time she'd put on her mother's red lipstick. Her mother. She wanted her mother. She'd give anything to smell her again, to feel her hands gently twist her hair into little braids.

The human's eyes went wide. He stopped moving. Alive, he panted and his muscles flexed. Fingers, raw and broken from his frantic attempts to escape, seized violently from time to time. Trauma, combined with severe blood loss, wouldn't allow him to live too much longer. Amber was sure of it.

Ten minutes later, the man finally died. Tossed back in the cage, the body no doubt stayed there until it rotted.

* * *

She'd stopped talking to him, so he read her thoughts.

Strange how looking up at the sky calmed her. She'd forgotten about it locked inside their cell, and now here it was—just the same as she left it. When the cold water hit her skin, she didn't flinch, cover her breasts, or squeal. Half-aware of what was going on, she only thought, *Werewolves have garden hoses?* It seemed like something they shouldn't have. Just the same, she was grateful when the smell of her own waste washed away from her.

But she was cold. Hazily, she looked down at her trembling limbs and snorted at them. Her knees were so funny! Look at them thudding together. She turned to Lavario and laughed. He didn't. "Serious face," she giggled at him and pulled down her lips into an exaggerated scowl, forced her voice to a lower register. "I'm a serious werewolf. I told you not to leave the cell and you did. Look what happened, young lady."

Lavario wrapped her up in his frilly robe, the regal yellow garment he'd worn before his fight. Paws rubbed up and down her body, using the delicate fabric to dry her skin like it was some type of cheap rag. It angered her a bit. Secretly, she'd always dreamed of wearing the robe after she killed him. She was going to strut around in it as she looked down over his dead body, she was going to wrap herself up in it every day afterward to remind herself of what she'd done. Disgraced, she was wearing it now.

He took her back to their prison. Amber wanted to feel the same pulsing energy she felt whenever she thought about her revenge against him. Anger tried to well up inside her, but she was too tired for it, and each time she looked—the green eyes in her night terrors were so tired, defeated—all she could muster was a quick burst of *his fault* before she went numb again and started laughing.

CHAPTER THIRTY: LAST TIME HE GOT TOLD TO DO SOMETHING

Kids playing in water. Blood. The laughter of the dead coming out of the mouth of a monster. The same dream came to her again, as familiar to her as the beat of her own heart. Variations were rare—same old, same old until she woke up with a scream or jolt or whimper. Tonight, it was her father instead of Lavario. He shouted, *Your fault! Whore!* as he held the body of his dead son, her brother.

It was as he said it would be before she left his home. God was punishing her. She'd put on her college sweater, her makeup, her weave, and then spread her legs. No one laughed in His face, especially not a little girl. This was the price her family paid. She should be dead instead of them, instead of the man who got eaten alive. Tears bubbled over and she choked on a sob.

"Amber," a voice cut through.

Wildly throwing her hands in any direction she could, Amber struck out in blind fear. When she connected with something furry, she realized it was probably Lavario. Unnerved by his wolf form at first, it was now a normal part of her everyday life. Vain and particular as he was, she was almost certain he stayed transformed because he looked better that way now that his fancy clothes were gone and his eyebrows looked like something someone might draw on Wooly Willy.

"It is not your fault, Amber," Lavario said softly. "You are not being punished by the universe."

She hated how he knew her feelings. She suppressed another cry, her body shook with the effort to keep the noises to herself. Carefully, he slid over and pulled her to him. Guilt ripped through her, telling her she shouldn't take comfort from her family's killer, but his fur was warm and she was so cold. There was no one else to offer her any solace.

"I am!" she blurted at him.

"No, no one chose your family because you are wicked. The thought is ridiculous."

Why then? She wanted to shout it at him but didn't. She suspected he'd heard it just the same, though. She wasn't sure how extensive his abilities were, but he was right more often than not. "My father told me—"

He cut her off. "Yes, and I told Kijo she'd be carried off by goblins if she didn't cease her frenzies. During her teething period, there were a lot of goblins, and they all yearned for the flesh of noisy children with black hair, black eyes, and no manners."

"She believed that?" Amber tried to picture the wolf woman as a frightened child, worrying about being whisked away in the night.

He laughed but stopped for a moment when he saw her face, which was probably a mess, and then did it again. "Oh, yes," he finally said. "She believed it."

She gave him a light slap. "It isn't funny."

"You are right. It isn't." His rested a paw on each shoulder and gently pushed her away so she was looking directly into his eyes. "Amber, it would serve my interests to allow your guilt. Believe me when I say I alone am to blame for the death of your family. Hate me. Give yourself some peace."

Some of the old fire came back to her, the sense of self-righteous anger followed by the feeling that hurting him would make it all go away. It would right the wrong done to her and her family. As quickly as it came, it left her again. She wasn't any closer to liking him, but she wasn't any closer to killing him either. Needing him was another matter.

"We should to do *something*," she told him.

It almost looked like he cocked his eyebrow. Facial expressions were hard to see since his fur was so black, but his eyes remained expressive. Frustration blazed through them, followed by the patient look she hated so much. His tone was fatherly when he finally decided to respond, "Anything I do now will most likely cause trouble for you, Amber."

She stopped herself before she puffed out her cheeks. "There has got to be *something*."

Lavario flopped down on the floor with a great sigh. Dirt shot up around him. Without thinking about it, she tapped at his back leg with the tip of her toe the way she'd done to her stubborn collie when it didn't want to go outside at night to pee. "I am not a collie," he reminded her.

"No, you're a goddamn awful werewolf. Get up off your ass. Come on." She whistled at him and tapped him with her foot again. "Come on, boy. Come on." With a growl, he stood up with his hackles raised and his ears folded back on his head. Instead of going meekly back to her corner, the way he no doubt thought she would since it had worked for him in the past, she congratulated him. "That's it. Who's a good boy?"

He shrunk back down to his human form, no doubt with a lecture ready on his lips. He always went human to give her advice. She didn't give him the chance. "You look *terrible*," she told him.

Whatever it was he was going to say, he forgot it in an instant.

"Grab my chair," he pointed to it.

"It's heavy." The damn thing had to weight over a hundred pounds.

"Be strong. Carry or fight. Your choice."

She grabbed his chair.

* * *

Tempted to tell her that the last time someone told him to do something, he ate her family, Lavario settled for a series of agitated hand gestures.

The iron bars of their prison cell were simply salt-in-the-wounds decorations. One tug and the gate collapsed. Lavario walked through, Amber walked along with him. "Where are we going?" She was somewhat hesitant but followed him down the hall, keeping pace the best she could while dragging his chair. The sound of the carved wood hitting the ground with indelicate, stuttering thuds made him grit his teeth. The last beautiful item he owned and she was lugging it around like it was a plank.

"We are doing *something*." He emphasized the words the same way she always did and then smiled despite himself when her face lit up in response. If nothing else, the young woman was a fellow rule breaker.

Even when he kicked down the first door, the only thought that crossed her mind was a quick: *Whose room is this?* She wanted it to be Geri's or Freki's. Lavario could perhaps accommodate that later. For now, they were in Lora's room. With Lora. Her expression was his favorite cocktail of outrage, hatred, and fear. He did owe her an explanation. "My companion needs new clothes," he explained. "Pick out what you like," he sad to Amber.

Seriously? very quickly turned into *Well, okay then.* Lavario did adore her willingness to roll with it. If they were here to get clothes, she'd go get herself some clothes. Lora made some small attempt to stop

Amber, but Lavario showed the other wolf his teeth until she slunk back down to a sitting position. He couldn't challenge her for rank, yet it was well within his rights to take from weaker wolves. She could challenge him or accept it. She opted for acceptance.

Soon afterward, Amber reappeared with a suitcase, a bag of cosmetics, and a brush. Lavario gave her a quick too-much look when she shoved all the items into his hands. "In for a penny, in for a pound. Yes?" *Why not?* Lavario thought and shrugged. On their way out, Amber made one last-minute impulse theft: a dinner roll. The absurdities of her whims. Lavario loved them. Sometimes.

They shut the door behind them and moved down the hall. Just as Amber was becoming impatient—which didn't take too long—they reached their destination. Lavario knocked this time, giving himself some time to place Amber's suitcase at his feet. Oscar, false guardian, answered with a rebuke that turned very quickly to concern once he saw who stood on the other side. "Lavario? What do you want?"

He didn't bother to respond. He grabbed the wolf's collar and yanked him out the door without any ceremony, though there was some type of ritual for appropriation that he couldn't quite recall. Something, something blood rite. Probably. "Bye, Felicia!" Amber chimed in. As far as Lavario was concerned, that was close enough. Both walked into the room together. Amber shut the door behind them using the legs of his chair. The room was sparse, Varcolac sparse. Amber put her hands on her hips and stuck her jaw out. "This shit is depressing."

"We will see to décor later. And to some better attire." Lavario would not wear khaki. Ever.

She brought some clothes out of the suitcase for inspection, holding up a few of Lora's shirts, colorless polo blouses, to make faces at them. "Immortal beings who can turn into giant wolves and kick ass shouldn't wear this shit." She folded them up nicely and put them in drawer. Once all the items were in their place, she turned to him once again. "How long do we have here? I thought you couldn't challenge anyone?"

"I didn't challenge anyone. I took their stuff."

"So?"

"So, pack rules allow taking items through force. Here, you must be strong enough to keep your possessions. If you're not, then you do not deserve them. To get their belongings back, they'll either have to challenge me or use force. Either of those scenarios ends with me winning. We will be fine here." He was at least eighty-five percent sure of this. Technically, they could go to Kijo, the pack's second. Lavario doubted his daughter would make much time for tattletale werewolves.

Sarcastic nodding followed. "Makes sense. I guess."

Her scorn amused Lavario. It didn't make much sense, but it was the way of his kind. "They will follow rules."

"What does that mean?"

Lavario got the gist of what she was asking. Basically, *how long are we safe?* He did not know the answer to that question. It was possible his daughter would intervene—perhaps Mazgan would put pressure on her to do something about him. He did not want to get into the complexities of wolf politics with the girl. It was better to be brief, reassuring, confident. "It means I am now runner-up for worst werewolf. Go congratulate Oscar on his promotion."

To his surprise and delight, she did.

CHAPTER THIRTY-ONE: NEW RULES

As Mazgan paced the room that once belonged to her father, Kijo looked down sourly at his "gift," a sword she had absolutely no use for. Like most of her pack, she used her teeth and claws to fight. She wasn't a damn ninja. She also wasn't an "it's-the-thought-that-counts" sort of wolf, so she tossed the blade to the side with a careless snap of her wrist.

What she was or wasn't didn't concern Mazgan. His head didn't even turn when the metal went *clank!* and echoed across the empty chamber. He was too wrapped up in his anger over Lavario taking over Oscar's room. The last ten minutes had been a solid rant punctuated by violence, occasionally directed toward random objects, other times her. She was accustomed to it by now.

According to Mazgan, there had to be some legitimate way supported by law to remove Lavario from Oscar's chamber. There were none. Pack rules were clear on matters of property rights—can't defend it, can't keep it. Oscar's weakness was his own concern. Mazgan wouldn't accept that as the answer. He was enraged when his perfect punishment, one that allowed him to gawk at Lavario's misfortune from a safe distance, had such a glaring loophole.

The only thing that surprised Kijo was that her father stayed with the redundancies for as long as he did. Patiently, she waited as her superior stormed around the mostly empty room.

Today was the day he came to tell her about the plan. Mazgan started to share it before a lower-ranking wolf came in with the news about Oscar. Mazgan had taken it with his normal aplomb. A quick smack to the side of the other wolf's head, a roar, and a never-ending tirade.

She wasn't sure what else Mazgan expected now. At some point, her alpha had to go back to what he came here for. He couldn't tell her he wanted to destroy the entire system of distribution for bloodservants and walk away.

"Oscar can have one of my rooms, Alpha Guardian," she offered. "There is not much else to be done."

She sighed when he didn't respond. Getting him to talk had never been this difficult before.

"Alpha Guardian," she started again, heavy-handed this time, "perhaps we should discuss the bloodservant matter you brought up earlier."

"Yes, of course, my love."

Her teeth wanted to pop out at the term of endearments he'd been addressing her with ever since her father's demotion. Rage wasn't something she could afford right now; this game required finesse, so she sucked her teeth back down along with her pride. "You said you wanted to change the system of distribution, Alpha Guardian. What would this entail?"

Mazgan nodded, as if snapping himself out of a dream. "Yes. I am here to discuss the future. We can deal with Lavario later."

She gave him a gracious, subservient nod of her head, urging him to continue.

Typical of him, he said a bunch of stuff before he finally got to the point. Kijo half listened to all of it, nodding her head at times she felt was appropriate. Occasionally, to give the illusion she was paying attention, she'd say a quick affirmation followed by his title. At last, Mazgan said, "It is time for you and I to lead this pack into the future. We will destroy the Boo Hag system. We will create our own, you and I. Together."

"How, Alpha Guardian?" She asked it as though she hadn't already been told.

He puffed himself up, ready for the big revelation. "Vampires."

"Vampires are gone, Alpha Guardian."

Stories of vampire kind were old, far older than she was; fraught with death, destruction, and near extinction, the tales were not good. Before Garvey told her about Mazgan's plan, she simply assumed vampires were extinct. There were accounts of them living outside their world, beyond the Door, but no one had used the portals for many years. Vampires became children's tales. Myths. Fodder for human pop culture. Bringing them back seemed like impossible madness. But Garvey said that's what Mazgan had ordered him to do. Now Kijo had her confirmation.

His dull brown eyes finally had some type of spark in them. Mazgan was excited, renewed. "No, my love. They exist. I will use them to destroy our enemies. This will be *our* world."

"It is already our world, Alpha Guardian."

Her statement had enough Varcolac pride in it to make Mazgan reward her with a benign smile. "Yes, but everyone will know it. No more hiding our true forms. Humans will see. They will bow. We will have absolute control over everything."

Kijo wanted to laugh at him. Humans were in their place regardless of whether or not they knew it. Seeking to subjugate them in the open was the course of a new wolf or a hot-headed, lower-ranking wolf eager to establish dominance. Guardians existed to prevent such folly, to champion the pack's best interests over personal glory. There was very little Mazgan could say to convince her releasing vampires to destroy a large chunk of their food source was an idea born from anything but a need to posture.

But Kijo was in no position to laugh. Her fight against Lavario, while hailed as a win, was still criticized by many of her peers. Forfeit—in this context—was her disgrace as well as her father's. He didn't forfeit to avoid his own death but to let her live. She was surprised when no other challenges were issued. Mazgan probably had something to do with that. Going against him now would almost ensure the next few years of her life would be challenge after challenge. Confident in her abilities, Kijo had to concede that the process was tiresome and lower-ranking wolves got lucky from time to time. Knowing that, she continued, "I will not help you with this, Alpha Guardian. It is foolish and underhanded. Absolute control often very quickly turns to no control."

"You sound like your father," he sneered at her.

I am his daughter. She wanted to say it, but kept silence as her official response.

It was hardly a surprise when he struck her. Blood leaked from the corner of her mouth and began its descent to her chin, down her throat, and then into the itchy fabric of the shirt that she now hated. She would not frenzy. Doing so, flinging herself at him with rage, would only give him cause to punish her. So she gestured to the door, a polite request to leave.

He was half-transformed, fuming. "I came here to offer you my love."

"Alpha Guardian," she was cold, logical, "I do not want your love. I want power."

* * *

To Kijo, the situation with Oscar sounded more like a flashback than a revelation. This would be the second time Lavario took a room away from the guardian. He'd done the same to two others way back when she was a new wolf. *This is now mine*, he'd said and shut the door on their faces. Once three separate living spaces but now one, Kijo's new apartment was her father's admonishment that the might-makes-right mentality of the pack had its unintended consequences. Instead of getting the message, the displaced inhabitants spent the next century trying to get the rooms back using force, something which never ceased to amuse Lavario.

Kijo worried endlessly about the ramifications. He'd always told her they'd never wise up and attack as a group because rules, rules, rules. She wondered how he'd feel knowing his daughter gave up everything without a fight.

Purging him from their memory began with the bonfire. Weeks ago, Kijo's brothers and sisters took all of her father's lavish furnishings and dumped them into a big pile in the courtyard and then set it all ablaze. As a community, they said good-bye to an era of outsider rule.

Conflicted and distant as she was, Kijo had been a part of that moment.

Her pack continued on without her. The first wall between her chamber and Oscar's new living quarters was being erected. Buzzing saws and the steady thud, thud, thud of power tools cut through her reflections on her current situation. Not good. After seven hours of contemplation that was the only conclusion the constant noise would let her come to.

None of her old friends would meet her in the eye after her chat with Mazgan. Even Geri and Freki, long-time belly-crawling sycophants, avoided her, ducking their heads with apologetic licks to their wormy mouths. Last time she felt so alone, she'd been left in the forest to die. Being separated from her pack was like that.

Kijo wanted to bend. She wanted to visit her father.

Dusty outlines she couldn't quite bring herself to clean marked where Lavario's furniture once dominated her space. Kijo's sparse furnishings only managed to halfway obfuscate the remains. It made her feel like a child dressing up in grownup clothes. Nothing fit, all she could do was stand there and look at her ridiculous reflection. Each time her eye caught movement—a branch or a curtain in the breeze—she turned her head to it to seek its counsel. "Father…" she began. And ended. There were many shadows amid so much negative space. Kijo spent a lot of time talking to nothing.

It was still Lavario's.

After days of waiting for him to walk out of his bedroom to chide her or to offer her some frilly silk garment he bought on a trip, Kijo just had to admit it. It had his smell. His memories. Even the chair she sat in—the chair she brought from her old apartments—betrayed her in this space. Her father was right. Cheaply made furniture sucked. Functional chairs. Functional bed. Functional clothes. How it itched. How uncomfortable it all was. Odd she never noticed it until she brought her spine-bending chair to a space where a lovely custom-built mahogany chair once stood, its cushion deep and welcoming.

Stiffly, she got up to pace around the room. *Why didn't I just stick with my initial plan?* Moondog life couldn't be that bad. If she'd done that, she would be lecturing him about the dangers of his idiosyncrasies while he sipped away at some fancy wine he had imported from who-knows-the-fuck-where. Instead, she was sifting through his wreckage. Unwelcome nostalgia jolted through her when she came across the bear he'd taken out of the keepsake box. Before he left, he tucked the worn stuffed animal under a floorboard. No doubt for her to find.

She found it. She'd tried to throw it away.

Time was not on her side. She couldn't afford to sit around feeling sorry for herself for too long. Duty snapped her back to the present. Mazgan would no doubt continue his plan without her. Without Lavario by her side and minus the support of the pack, she would be too weak to stop him. A difficult road lay ahead of her.

Challenges would come. But let them. Kijo was guardian. Kijo was Varcolac. She would fight for what was hers. She thought back to the apartments. Lavario staked his claim to the space, to every space he had ever inhabited. *This is mine*, he had said. Then, he had turned to her, *Now, go find your own.*

PART THREE

DEVIL WITH A BLUE DRESS

CHAPTER THIRTY-TWO: THE BROWN DOG

Time for another pep talk. Tovin took a deep breath.

Yes, he would say the right things. He would *not* try to run away. Bloodservants were companions. Companions were destined for great things. Great things included being a werewolf one day. No, he would not laugh or mock any of that. It made perfect sense. *Now smile. Bigger. Bigger. No, more natural. Good. Right, now don't piss anyone off today.*

Tovin splashed some water up in his face.

Months ago, the deadbolt of his new home clicked in its place, and Tovin's position within Eresna's life took a different road. No less luxurious than his previous dwelling, the villa-like enclosure she moved him to had the amenities of an expensive resort and the privacy of a maximum-security prison.

Eresna tried. Grudgingly, Tovin admitted it to himself. Preparing him for his new life simply proved a larger task than she was willing to undertake. The more he bungled the role she wanted him to play, the less tolerant she became. He'd been demoted from mistake to liability.

Never alone, whatever werewolf assigned to him followed to make sure he didn't encounter any of the other companions. Sometimes it was Kurt, a human who knew what the werewolves did and worked with them regardless. Usually it was Nadine.

Yuri was with him today. "Hello, Tovin."

Werewolves did not knock. Beyond embarrassment now, Tovin didn't bother covering himself anymore. A bit sleepy, he blinked at her. Water trickled down his chin. "Hello, Yuri."

"Get dressed. Breakfast. Eggs and crepes sound good?"

He nodded.

A few minutes later, he joined her at the table. The garden are of his new home was his favorite part. Today, the lilacs were in bloom, pleasant company for the new morning. The moment his rump hit the chair, Yuri asked him the same question she always did. "Are you going to see Guardian Eresna today?"

Same answer. "No."

Atypical of her, she didn't press the issue. No follow up, just a half hour of silence as she watched him eat. The moment he was done, she spoke again. "Guardian Eresna has a new companion. He's here today."

Food lurched in Tovin's stomach. "Oh," he stammered. "Oh. Okay. Good."

"She wanted me to tell you you're fine here. She wanted me to tell you she feels bonded with you, and she wants to know if you're happy here in your new home."

"Happy meal! That's me!" He meant it as a lighthearted joke at his situation.

The sides of Yuri's face pinched together. Tovin braced himself for a lecture about avoiding dark humor. Instead, her look softened. Her mouth opened and shut a few times as though she were searching for the right words. "Tovin, do you remember the dog in the alleyway? The brown one you'd play with when your mother went to work?"

He did. Quietly, his voice constrained by emotion, he told her so. He'd come to think of his life before werewolves simply as *then*. Often he told himself the opposite should be true since an aggregate of *thens* made him who he was today. But the sum total of first kisses, broken hearts, broken bones, garbage disposal disasters, walking home in the rain, and book clubs seemed woefully inadequate, everything within his new life outside of their respective realms of expertise.

Life demanded he leave his younger self behind. Painfully, Yuri brought him back. "That was me," she told him.

Animals never worried about things the way people did. Tovin depended on that in his younger days. Discouraged from being too outwardly affectionate or emotional, he'd lavished all his hugs, all his tears, all his secrets, and all his heartache on that dog. And doughnuts. Many, many doughnuts. Now Yuri was claiming to be her. "Did you even like doughnuts?"

She shook her head. A moment of humor overtook her somber attitude. "I was even less fond of being tied to hydrants."

Embarrassment combined with outrage. Tovin's emotions were a convoluted mix, and he couldn't separate the individual strands. A thought occurred to him. "Did you... Are you why I'm *here*?"

"Yes, I brought you here." Her tone was not even a bit contrite. She must have seen his facial muscles twitch. "Would you rather I'd left you out in the street when your mother kicked you out for being gay?

Perhaps you'd rather have taken your chances with your abusive father?"

Tovin bristled. "I got my own life sorted out. I'm not your sad story to fix."

"Yes. I kept you alive to do it."

"You don't feel bad about any of this?"

She gave him a small, indignant sigh. "No, I don't. You were to be the pampered companion of a *very* attractive Guardian. Amazing sex, unlimited money..." she trailed off. "Obviously that didn't happen. Now that my plan has gone wrong, you need to listen. Tovin, Kurt is going to teach you what you need to know. Obey him. I was your friend back then. I am your friend now. I have watched over you your entire life. Do this."

Reeling, Tovin gave her a few awkward head gestures to indicate he heard and understood. He probably looked like a bobblehead.

"Good. Now go get dressed in some of your finer clothes. I'm going to take you to socialize with a few other werewolves. The more you're seen, the better. Be charming. Make them adore you."

He went to do as she instructed. On his way to the bedroom, he stopped by his desk. Items were scattered about—some on the floor, some tipped over—as though someone had rifled through his possessions while he and Yuri ate. Yuri was his immediate suspect. Friend or foe, she'd been the one distracting him for the last hour. "Maybe it was the wind," he told himself.

Paranoia felt unwarranted. Caution felt necessary. He took a moment to glance back at Yuri, who was sipping tea. Behind her, a woman in blue emerged then vanished behind a tall shrub. His self-described friend didn't seem to notice, her eyes remained fixed forward. Either Yuri didn't see the woman, or she knew she'd be there.

It hurt Tovin to acknowledge which was more likely.

CHAPTER THIRTY-THREE: THE WOMAN IN BLUE

Socializing with other werewolves turned out about as bad as Tovin expected, especially since Garvey was one of them. Put Tovin on a couch and he could tell you the exact moment his life went to total shit. Online dating. Adventure. He shook his head at his former reckless self. At least he hadn't tried sushi.

Daydreaming offered some escape.

Today, he went parasailing. Rainbows ballooned above him, arching in a flawless blue sky with a few smatterings of small, white clouds. The wind cut through his clothes. His hair whipped around his face in a way that made him look awesome and feel free spirited. Below, a handsome man drove the boat. He was single. And into trivia, meatloaf, and unfiltered tap water. No, wait. He came with a new filter, one of those high-end ones.

That was nice. Tovin smiled.

"What is he doing?" Nadine asked Garvey.

Garvey shrugged. "Sweet treat." He poked Tovin in the side. "You almost done with the paperwork?"

Ah, yes. The paperwork. Tovin looked down at it. What he thought was one of Garvey's nonsensical lies turned out to be a nonsensical truth. Life had become layers of unbelievable: werewolves, werewolves who drank human blood, werewolves who drank human blood and kept humans around as pets, and now werewolves who drank human blood, kept human pets, and made their human pets do paperwork no one even seemed to care about.

It was all as insulting as it was surreal the more Tovin thought about it. "What should I put for outcome of event?" Tovin asked, allowing his voice to hint at irritation.

"Disappointing," Garvey responded and spared him a slight glance.

Nadine chuckled and pressed her tongue up to the point of her tooth. "You're only disappointed because you didn't get his pants off."

"True," Garvey responded. "But I'm not sure I could even get to his tree anymore through all the tinsel."

Nadine snorted at the mention of the clothes.

Yuri had suggested a more elaborate outfit, something fitting for Eresna's companion. Afterward, Tovin dressed himself in what looked like a *traje de luces*. When he looked at himself in the mirror, he saw a car littered with bumper stickers—tacky, tasteless. Everyone probably wondered what type of schmuck was at the wheel. *Just me*, Tovin thought. *Just me.*

True to her claim she was his friend, Yuri came to his defense. "He looks fine. And you should have done the paperwork yourself, Garvey. It's been *months*."

"Quiet, underling," Garvey boomed at her, simultaneously humorous and serious.

"Garv," Nadine warned him. "Don't be a suckbucket."

Bickering, the three of them went at it the way they always seemed to whenever they were in the same room together. Tovin tuned them out until they started to hash out Tovin's chase and capture. Garvey imitated Yuri's reactions. "Oh no!" he shouted, "My poor stupid cub!"

Apparently Nadine didn't want to laugh at her friend, so it came out as a snort-fart noise hybrid.

The lady from the garden earlier, the one in the blue dress, also chuckled a bit. Tovin glanced her direction. Like him, no one paid any real attention to what she did. Listless, she drifted back and forth across the room without receiving so much as a friendly nod from any of the werewolves. "Hi," Tovin said to her. She seemed like a good start-up for the whole socializing thing since she was the only other human in the room.

She didn't say anything back.

"Hello..." the werewolf sitting next to her responded, eyebrow raised.

Tovin didn't know the werewolf who addressed him. He managed a weak, unconvincing smile. Rickety as its foundation was, it collapsed within seconds. The werewolf went right back to watching the squabble.

Tovin tried again to get the attention of the woman sitting next the werewolf. He stared straight at her, hoping she'd eventually turn her head his way. When she did at last, there was no welcoming smile on her face. Assessing him, her head cocked to the side, she took her measure then got up from her chair and walked out of the room.

"You charmer, you," Tovin mumbled to himself.

At least he was finally done with the paperwork. "Done," he announced. As usual, no one acknowledged him. Garvey and Nadine were too busy talking about which member of *NSYNC was the most fuckable. Yuri was off to the side, licking her wounded pride. "The paperwork is complete," Tovin repeated himself. He wasn't sure what else to do.

From out of nowhere, Eresna responded, "Excellent. Good job, my pet. How useful you are to me." It made Tovin jump. He didn't even know she was there. Almost as a reflex, he tried to hand her the file. Eresna curled her lip, tilted her head, and then turned away from him. Another *faux pas* to add to the list.

Gracelessly, Tovin flopped the document back on the desk. "Oh. Sorry."

She rolled her eyes. "Catalogue it. Nadine, go with him."

As the two of them made their way down the hall, Tovin swore he caught small glimpses of the woman. Smatterings of cool blue here and there against the brown of the walls, flashes of a hand knuckled around where walls became ninety-degree angles. Shadows beside him. There was no sound. Heels like hers would have clicked, tiny little drumrolls building up to what amounted to nothing.

CHAPTER THIRTY-FOUR: BREAD

Nadine abandoned him. She pointed to the double doors at the end of the hall, gave him an encouraging pat on the shoulder and said, "Library is there. You've got this. You were born for this."

"Thanks," Tovin responded.

Their filing system was straightforward. There was a place to scan the barcode on the form; the machine beeped and then told him where he should go in the vast library. Row 700, section 300b. That's where Tovin's story would reside. Anyone who stopped to read it would know his basic details, such as his age, gender, height, and weight and would read a trace outline of the events that brought him here.

None of it was too terrible. Tovin left out the parts where he tripped and fell. His injuries were attributed to unforeseen problems during capture. Vague enough to save face—one of the few perks of filling out your own account of events. The ending of it all troubled him a bit. Disappointing. The story of his life. Tovin thought about rewriting it. No one would ever check.

"Maybe I'll get away on a jet ski." That would be cool. "Or I'll find a machine gun loaded with silver and kill them all." Even cooler. Imagination was fun. Tovin lost himself in the fantasy of it, letting his brain indulge in every whimsical solution to his current problem it could think of.

Way too soon, he felt someone at his shoulder. Assuming it was Nadine there to drag him back to the gathering, Tovin didn't turn around. He begged for a few more minutes. He took no response as a good sign. Eventually, the lingering feeling of unease he associated with the presence of others evaporated back to a nice, stagnant calm.

Nearby, a book fell to the floor. Immediately, his malfunctioning brain told him he *had* to pick it up and put it back on the shelf. *Super important*, it assured him.

"Fuck you, limbic system." He obeyed the impulse's command.

He turned. It was curious at first sight.

Janitor's closet. Seductive locks lined the length of the entry, including an electronic one off to the side. To Tovin, they were a tantalizing peek of glistening abs, or a leg lifted up at the edge of the road. *Are you going my way? Well, are you?*

He was. Or at least he would have been.

"Hello, hi, sweet treat."

Tovin nearly jumped to the top shelf. His bowels were up in his throat when he said, "Garvey, what the fuck are you doing here?"

"What are *you* doing?" he countered.

"Paperwork."

Garvey gave the janitor's closet an amused glance. "Umhm."

"Go away," Tovin told him.

"Look at you. Getting all bossy." Garvey crinkled his nose to suggest how cute he thought that was. "To answer your earlier question...well, I told Eresna I was going to have sex with you."

Unwillingly, Tovin thought back to the woods, to Garvey's mouth on his own, and to the way the other man's hands felt on his body. He wanted to say so much. Shouting obscenities until his voice broke was the brave thing to do, courageous and certainly smarter, but not as appealing as saying yes until his voice broke. Typical of himself, he decided to say nothing.

He started to leave.

"Hold up a tick, sweet treat." Garvey grabbed Tovin's arm to prevent him from walking away. "Listen for a second. Eresna has a new boy, if you haven't heard."

"Yuri already told me." Tovin pulled away from Garvey.

When Garvey continued, his tone was biting. Whatever he wanted to say, he was hell-bent on saying it, whether Tovin wanted to listen or not. "You're always in your head. Get out. Eresna doesn't give a shit about the complexities of your emotions or what you're going through. She doesn't want some sensitive soul off on wild fantasies. She wants the guy who was taken away from her—the guy who looked like he was carved from obsidian, had life breathed into him by the gods, and then sent by the angels for her to fuck every night. She wants a delicacy, the type of servant only a guardian could command. You could belong to any of our kind. Even me. Even a False Moon."

Common. Anyone with a van and a whim could pick him off the street without much consequence. Someone might look for a day or two, maybe a week if he were lucky. Then he'd be discarded into the pile of missing people whose pictures muddled the walls of post offices, community notice boards, and benches. The other guy mattered. No one was going to slap his photo on a bench where flatulent hobos slept or on community notice boards where unruly teens with magic markers lurked, ready to scribble away the remaining evidence he ever existed. Tovin was probably a one-eyed pirate with a dick on his head by now.

"I can't be that guy. I'm bread. You know, bland and basic."

Garvey chuckled a bit and once again touched the side of Tovin's face lightly with two fingers. "Bread is great. There is nothing more comforting than the smell of it. Can't have a sandwich without it. Bread is the building block for a lot of great things. Basic. Sure. But sometimes the basics, even if a little boring, are the best."

Tovin saw Eresna in his head, her fantastic colorful clothing and the elegant rooms in which she dwelt. He had to do better if he were to survive. Eresna's impatience with his lack of progress was noticeable. "Yeah, but how do I make bread more interesting?"

"Slather some butter on yourself."

"Meaning?"

"I was being literal. I took the bread thing as far as I can go, given you all the advice I can give. Now we're back to sex. Or I'm thinking about eating you. Also literal." It didn't help when Garvey cocked his head to the side as if contemplating exactly which one he meant. "Make your decision fast. I have errands to run."

"You have errands?"

"Yes, sweet treat. I have errands." It was tired, frustrated.

"Oh. Like the bank?" Tovin was bewildered.

"Yes, to the bank. To the bank where my money is." Garvey snorted and shook his head in disbelief. "You are too much sometimes. You want this or not?"

Despite everything, and there was a lot of everything, Tovin did want Garvey. He knew it was a horrible mistake now—a hellacious, atrocious mistake—as he knew it was in the woods earlier. The more reckless part of his brain simply didn't care anymore. He might be dead soon. Garvey didn't say that exactly, but Tovin knew that's what he was trying to say. "I want to have sex with you. But," Tovin amended, "I don't like you."

Dry, exasperated, Garvey responded, "Well, I'll put away the pocket knife I was going to use to carve our names into the tree outside with little hearts around it."

"What about your errands?" Tovin hated to think that someone would come looking for Garvey in the middle of them having sex. Tovin was enough of a joke as it was.

Garvey placed both hands to his own face, dragging the tips of his fingers temple to chin, exasperated. "They can wait. So, yes? No?"

"Yes."

Triumph looked good on Garvey. Gone was the man Tovin remembered from the woods with the humor-filled brown eyes, cautious fingers, and coaxing lips. It was a demanding mouth that closed over his, pressing open his lips; strong hands that pulled him closer until they were torso to torso; purposeful fingers that found the claps and buttons of his elaborate outfit and undid them one by one until Tovin felt the cool air on his exposed skin. No more wasting time. Both of them were naked in what seemed like mere moments. Garvey's hands—far more confident than Tovin's own—explored audaciously, cupping and stroking at random while Tovin relegated himself to the shoulders, the torso, the mouth, licking, biting, tasting where he could.

Garvey put his hand on Tovin's shaft and stroked it, softly at first, then with more force. "I love it when I can feel the blood respond. Makes me want to taste it."

"What?" Tovin shot up.

"Only a sample," Garvey assured him with a harmless puppy dog tilt of his head.

He didn't look harmless. Golden eyes, wolf eyes, stared down at Tovin. Fangs protruded. Excited, terrified, Tovin kissed one of the incisors, letting it puncture his lower lip. A taste. Garvey licked at the small wound.

"Yum," Garvey said. Tovin could tell he was pleased with himself. Pleased with the noises Tovin made. Pleased with the way hips moved in time with the new rhythm Garvey's hand created. Even more pleased when Tovin released himself. The smug look on his face the entire time told Tovin as much. "There we go. Nicely done, sweet treat."

Garvey did not finish. He was up and moving after planting one last kiss on Tovin's forehead. Quickly, with a saturated grin, he grabbed a few papers from Tovin's file and used them to wipe his stomach.

"Seriously?" Tovin hoped he wasn't going to have to redo that. It was torturous enough to begin with without having to approach Eresna to ask for a new form, especially if it occurred to her to ask why he needed one.

Garvey chuckled in response. "I put these papers to some actual use."

Irritated, Tovin finally found his voice. "Are you going to—"

"Nah, I owed you this one. Denying myself today gives me something to look forward to later when I'll get more than a taste." The eyes were golden again when he said it. This time, Tovin found it a little less titillating. "We're going to finish this someday, sweet treat. Unless you die. Try not to die."

There wasn't much Tovin could think of to say to that.

Worried, he watched Garvey leave. Whatever the werewolf was up to, it couldn't be good. Garvey was an id-filled comet wobbling in its orbit. He was shoemaker levy 9. "What's Jupiter?" Tovin asked himself.

CHAPTER THIRTY-FIVE: OTHERS LIKE US

Smells of land and sea merged, crashing and rolling along a deserted shore until the silhouette of a man emerged in the distance. Tovin put him on a white horse and then dressed him up in a pirate outfit. At some point he'd get off that horse and swashbuckle the hell out of—

"Are you with me?" Kurt's voice was clipped. His face was a misplaced comma, full of awkward stops and starts that couldn't possibly be deliberate. One of the few people Tovin could interact with, Kurt already knew everything Tovin knew about the werewolves and then some. He just didn't seem to care. More than that, he seemed to admire what they were doing. He actively worked with Eresna and the others to perpetuate the myth the bloodservants were the beneficiaries of destiny.

"What? Yes." Reality sucked. Tovin only popped in briefly to answer the few scattered questions Kurt would occasionally snap his way. Lucky for him, clipped, noncommittal responses worked just fine for the other man. He wasn't much of a conversationalist.

Kurt moved on without him, gesturing to the television in front of them. "Amazing, isn't it?" The end result of the brainwashing process showed movielike on a big screen within Tovin's very posh, extremely comfortable dungeon. Jerald's face—the face of the man Eresna would take as her public bloodservant—had loomed on the big screen, a hovering hypermasculine reminder that Tovin was not what Eresna wanted.

"Yes. It sure is," Tovin agreed pleasantly enough.

Jerald reacted as Tovin expected at first. Obscenities, first shouted in Spanish, then translated into English a second later for either clarification or effect; violence, blows that probably would have been devastating to any human adversary landed like swats on an immobile Eresna, who would occasionally blink at the man as though she simply couldn't fathom what it was he hoped to accomplish; grief, loud moans that escalated to caterwauling only to devolve to small whimpers and croaked requests to call his wife and daughter. All of it cycling right in front of Tovin for reasons only Eresna and Kurt knew.

You're special. You're destined for something much more than what you were before. Other people in your life didn't understand you. Everyone was holding you back. Become what you were meant to be. She repeated variations of the same song until the man got it stuck in his head.

It started slow. One day he didn't scream, run, swat, or ask for his family. Soon after he was wearing the clothes Eresna gave him with great pomp while spouting snippets of the tune in what was actually a singsong voice. Then it was full on delusional—great destinies, the burden of being chosen, good-bye to cargo pants. Today he and Eresna were having a friendly chat about what he'd do once he was a werewolf like her.

"Amazing." Tovin repeated again with what he hoped would pass as sufficient awe before switching to what was on his mind. "But why am I watching it?"

"Feeling more comfortable here?" Kurt had a habit of ignoring the current line of conversation in favor of useless small talk.

"Yes, I'm fine." Tovin learned not to re-ask questions. Kurt would answer them in his own sweet time, or he wouldn't at all.

"Good. Your room is to your liking?"

"Yes, it's fine." Tovin was at least free to wear what he wanted as he was free to move about the rather large villa-like enclosure she gave him. He had all the books he could want, an outdoor patio and garden, and Kurt for whenever he wanted to feel the presence of another human being. Not a horrible deal all in all. Comfortable as it was there was no purpose to any of it. Tovin woke up, showered, read, and lounged in his pool all with ennui that he oddly never felt during his petty little life as a salesman.

"Good. Good."

"Yes. Good."

And the stimulating conversations didn't help much.

It felt like they'd almost reached their cap for the day. Kurt pushed one of Tovin's books around a table with the ridge of his thumb, sending a clear signal that he was now disinterested in whatever Tovin would do next. Nothing about that bothered Tovin much. The beach—where his comforting yet cliché daydream waited—called to him.

"Hello, Tovin. Kurt." Tovin jumped a little bit, once again startled out of fantasy. It was the first time he'd heard Eresna's voice since he'd found the janitor's closet. Panic tasted like copper. He was so sure she'd know he wanted to investigate, that he was planning on breaking in there. If she did, she didn't give any indication of it. As usual, she only gave him the briefest of glances before directing her attention elsewhere.

"Guardian," Kurt greeted her.

Eresna gave Kurt a small peck on the cheek as a response, which he accepted with a very businesslike head nod. No one reciprocated affection quite the way Kurt did. He probably gave her a firm handshake after fucking. And boy did they fuck.

"Good afternoon, Guardian," Tovin echoed, trying to keep his voice light but respectful.

Eresna didn't touch Tovin. She didn't even move toward him as though she considered it an option. She went directly to whatever business brought her here. "What do you think?"

"About?"

Unlike Kurt, Eresna had precious little patience for one-word responses. She wanted Tovin to tell her all he knew at once, not half an hour's worth of yes-no exchanges. "About what you've seen these last few months. About Jerald." She made a hand gesture that said: *I've told you what I want, now get to it.*

Everything that immediately hopped into his mind—crazy, creepy, mad, stupid—was all wrong and he knew it. Eresna may have known that's how he felt, but Tovin knew better by now than to flat-out say it. Though he knew it would annoy her, he kept his responses clipped, direct. He was safer that way. "It was fascinating. Jerald seems nice."

"You need to get better at lying." Her eyes narrowed; her nostrils flared. Tovin—his collection of mannerisms, especially the way he drifted in and then out of his present-day situation—was a constant source of irritation to her. He just wasn't sure why in this particular case. "Work on it." She directed that to Tovin. Afterward, she turned to Kurt. "Help him work on it."

Kurt gave the table a grimace and an eye roll before he stopped to answer. "I'm trying."

She didn't exactly say try harder. Like everything else, Kurt was just supposed to know that's what she wanted and then act accordingly. She left with no other word—just a terse peck on Kurt's cheek and a small nod for Tovin.

"What was that about?" Tovin asked as soon as he heard the door click, the lock snap in place. Normally Eresna at least stayed with them for a few hours in order to put up the front—for whose benefit Tovin could never quite tell—that she liked him or was at least interested in his comings and goings. He wasn't exactly sad to see her go and miss out on those precious moments of forced, awkward conversation, but her rapid departure was atypical. Atypical bothered Tovin.

"She wants you to be ready," Kurt answered.

"Ready for what?"

"To mingle."

"Oh." Tovin blinked. "I thought I was never going to see anyone other than you." He assumed he'd remain in his little prison forever, reading books and passing time as Eresna said he would. Social interaction wasn't something he craved. He didn't recall ever asking her or Kurt for the chance to meet all of the other human slaves. "This seems to be working just fine." Tovin pointed to the room around him.

Kurt's face was mired in agitation. "You'll have to join the other companions."

"You mean the cult?"

"Careful." Kurt's eyes snapped to his. "She'd be very displeased to hear you call it that."

"It's not a cult. I'll do better."

An honest spy, a spy nevertheless, Tovin often thought of the other man as the tinfoil hat perched on top of a paranoid head, a pseudo-filtration system that only worked because Eresna believed in it.

"She's right. You are a terrible liar." Slight as it might have been and as quickly as it was gone, the smile Kurt gave him was one of the first Tovin had ever seen on the other man's face. Before it could possibly be misconstrued as a moment between them, he rushed into his next point. "She's also right that you need to get better at it if you're not going to be a liability."

Liability...Tovin knew what that meant. "Why now? I'm perfectly happy like this."

"Things changed."

"What changed exactly?" Tovin snapped back, losing patience with the other man's terseness.

Kurt took a deep, calming breath. "The other companions found out about you."

"How?" Tovin took a step backward.

"All I know is someone told them there was someone living in Eresna's quarters. They think you're more special than them now, which is causing quite a stir. There's been a lot of infighting."

Fantastic. Tovin forced himself to sound calm. To his ear, his voice sounded panicked when he spoke. "When do I have to meet them?"

Kurt shrugged. "You should be ready now. You've had plenty of time to adapt to your situation."

"I have adapted." Rough start, though. Attempts at escape were numerous and shamefully ineffective. On more than one occasion, Kurt remarked that Tovin was lucky Eresna had bonded with him already, as killing him would have been the standard response otherwise. Tovin felt about as fortunate as being held captive by a mad, blood-sucking werewolf queen allowed him to feel.

"You really haven't. You don't get it." Kurt gave him a cross look.

Reflexively, Tovin began to defend himself, "I get—" but then stopped. Maybe that was true. Kurt might have been a tinfoil hat, but Tovin was the sick puppy no one wanted to get too attached to. Previous signs—the lack of eye contact, interaction, or even slight acknowledgements from the werewolves who brought him his food and various comfort items—were ignored simply because Tovin preferred it that way. It was like being allowed to stay in during recess all over again. "Okay. Right. I'm probably missing a few things here or there."

"A few," Kurt agreed.

For once, and grudgingly, Tovin prompted him further, rolling his arm to propel the man beyond their typical one-liner, mandatory-interaction responses.

The other man was in no mood. "I'm going to give you this one bit of advice. This one little bit and that's all. Others like us—those who know the real deal—are either dead, useful, or compliant. Decide where you fall."

CHAPTER THIRTY-SIX: HE'S BEING COMPLAINT

Dead, useful, or compliant. Tovin settled on the last, deciding very firmly that he didn't want to be dead while accepting the fact that he was most likely never going to be useful to the powerful queen. Compliant by default. That was him.

"You are bread." He said it to himself and then sighed, before knocking on the ornate door that separated him from Eresna. She didn't answer it herself. Tovin was ushered into the shewolf's chambers by Nadine, who smiled broadly when she saw him on the other side of the door. The bright green jumper gave her red hair the sheen of dying embers.

"Terrible Tovie. How are you, little love? Got your running shoes on today?" Nadine was always the one who fetched him whenever he tried to escape. Rather than being annoyed by it, the shewolf seemed to see it as a fun game they were playing, a sort of higher stakes hide-and-seek wherein Tovin—once caught—had to spend a few months in a naughty-boy cell. She gave him a big grin and exaggerated wink. Unlike most of the others, she didn't bother to hide her incisors, which came to sharp points right above her lower lip, and would actually run her tongue up and down the point when she was especially amused.

Tovin hated her most of all. "I'm fine. Thank you."

"I bet. Finally dropping by to say hello are we?"

"Yes, I thought it was time."

"Past—" She rolled her hand for dramatic effect, then continued. "—some might say."

Tovin gave her a tight smile. He felt the edges of it stamp into his face. "I've been—"

"Busy?" She licked the tip of her fang, pressing the tip of her tongue against the point so that the flesh puckered slightly. She was having a great time.

Tovin swallowed and shifted his weight slightly. All tongue and tooth, Nadine showed no mercy and continued to look down on him with amused eyes. Tovin reminded himself why he was there and continued, "No. I've been afraid."

When Tovin rehearsed the line—in his head, to the mirror, with a potted plant in the hall—it was said to Eresna, and her demeanor instantly changed from somewhat hostile to motherly within seconds. At least one part of his fantasy came true—for once. Nadine's mouth rolled up shop and her eyes lost their mocking glint. It wasn't quite motherly, but at least it wasn't wolfish either.

"Oh, Tovie, you silly thing. You'll be fine. Come on now." The rest of walk down the hall was wordless, just the way Tovin liked it. Occasionally, Nadine would glance over her shoulder to encourage him with a big smile, which Tovin acknowledged with as much grace as he could muster. "And here we are. Guardian, Tovin is here to see you."

"Thank you, Nadine." Colorful, nearly translucent fabric swirled around Eresna as she stood to greet him. She must have heard he was here to make amends. Eresna planted one small kiss on his cheek before she offered him a light gesture that was an invitation to sit. "Tovin, it's good to see you."

"Thank you, Guardian." He'd already lost his I-was-too-scared-to-visit line to Nadine, who was standing right behind him. Recycling the exact thing wasn't an option if he wanted to come across as genuine. He needed some other type of excuse that hit on the same concept. "I'm sorry I have not been here before. I was worried you might be upset with me. Kurt assured me that wasn't the case."

"Not at all. You are always welcome." While she was going through the motions with him, it was clear she wasn't taken in by any of what he said. By now, Tovin knew the lip quirks and head bobs associated with politician mode. Tovin was grateful for the first part at least. It was encouraging to know even if she didn't believe him, she'd at least play pretend with him.

"Thank you. I'm here to—"

"I know why you are here."

"Okay, I just want to—"

"Look, I'm going to save us both a lot of time." Eresna cut him off again, giving him a knowing, yet not unkind look in the process. "This is what I want from you. You are going to toe the line, you are going to act as though you believe in your great destiny, and you are going to act as though you believe others here have the same great destiny. You will mingle. You will host."

The rapid change in demeanor startled Tovin into silence. Once again, he wondered what she knew and what it meant for him. "Why did you even bring Jerald?" It was always a mistake to question her, he knew this by now, but he couldn't help himself. As far as Tovin knew, she brought the other man specifically to avoid having Tovin do any of those things.

"Things change. Plans change with them." Vagaries annoyed Tovin, and Eresna hardly seemed prone to engage in improvised decision making. Whatever their other grievances, Tovin had to acknowledge that the shewolf was, like him, a planner. Something happened, but as was the case with Kurt, Eresna wasn't forthcoming with the details. Tovin remained quiet in the hope she would offer up some type of reason as the silence stretched on awkwardly, but she only favored him with a slight smile as she idly twisted the edges of her skirt with one long, graceful finger.

Tovin gave up. At least she wasn't treating him like he was stupid anymore. Her honesty about the process was the first time she'd ever acknowledged that something more sinister lurked under the fine clothes and lavish accommodations. Tovin would take that as a small win. "What do I need to say to them?"

"Do you need a script?" There was no menace to her voice, just a slight change in her body language that told Tovin to proceed with caution. Truthfully, a script wouldn't hurt. It wasn't like he had a lot of experience telling brainwashed human slaves that their delusions were true. The closest thing he had was when he told a woman that a shitty, low-budget fridge would last for at least ten years and not do anything to her power bill. Even that he couldn't say with a straight face.

"Maybe some talking points?" Introduced first as a joke, the notion suddenly grew on Tovin. "Those would actually be *great.*"

It wasn't. She rolled her eyes slightly and looked behind her to Nadine, who simply shrugged in response. "You are quite the bother."

"Why am I alive then?" The question had always been part of his plan. Beyond fear at this point, Tovin only wanted to know what he needed to know.

"Lavario wants you."

Something told him that this was the real answer, not some made-up shit to pacify him. Tovin didn't expect her to be honest. For a moment, he didn't know how to respond. Everything he'd gone through in his head before their encounter prepared him to respond to lies or carefully placed half-truths. After he'd thought about his response for as long as the awkwardness level in the room would allow, he gave up. "Oh," he said.

Eresna's lip quirked upward. "Think of yourself as a chip whose value is unknown as of yet. Lavario sees you as his. This works to my advantage. Getting rid of you would remove an advantage, create an enemy I don't want."

"Who is he?" It was a name that had been tossed around, and Tovin vaguely remembered his face from before—the tall well-dressed man with almost transparent green eyes and olive skin.

"He is like me, a Guardian. He belongs to another pack, and he's quite desperate now. He'll probably come for you at some point."

She sounded so sure. Tovin nervously twisted at the fabric of his own clothing. "And when he does?"

"He can have you."

CHAPTER THIRTY-SEVEN: BUILT-IN MAP

"Tovin is dangerous," Eresna said the moment Tovin was out the door.

Yuri's worry for Tovin chafed under Eresna's words. Already demoted due to the debacle with the extraction, she didn't dare vocalize how she felt. Being Garvey's subordinate was bad enough; she didn't want to test whether or not she could sink any further.

Eventually, her queen would forgive her for the bungled extraction. For now, she was left on her own to fret.

As if sensing her dilemma, Garvey gave her a one of his grins, that mocking tooth of his jutted out idiotically. Superior to her only in rank, an actual fight between them, minus Eresna's protection, would end very poorly for him. She showed him all her canines as a reminder. "Yes, I see your point," he chomped at her.

Posturing was all she could do. Wolves like him always knew the length of the lead, and he had a lot of slack left whereas hers was noticeably restrictive. Happily for Yuri, she didn't have too long to stew in indignation.

"Harsh." Nadine snuck in a reproachful glance at Eresna as she came back into the room. "And him with his wee tail tucked between his legs."

Affronted, Eresna raised her chin at the tone. Her upper incisors protruded. "It wasn't that long ago you told me to bury him in the rose garden."

Nadine licked her tooth. "The li'l goof would be useful that way."

Tough talk about rose gardens, mulch, and live burial was exactly that—talk. Though Yuri knew Nadine would not let it interfere with her work, her friend had grown fond of Tovin during their chases. Nothing like hunting someone down to stir Nadine's wild affections.

Eresna knew it, too. She looked at the shewolf with sympathetic eyes. "I will only act if necessary, Nadine. The punishment will be as light as I can make it. But he's up to something. He's always going to the library. Trouble."

Brash as always, Garvey snorted a bit at their queen's claim. "The barely-in-his-twenties guy on a mission to uncover the entire truth of werewolf kind with his plucky gumshoe attitude and a little help from the Dewey decimal system? He's dangerous?"

Far more humble than most guardians, Eresna didn't require constant subjection—no titles, no bowing, no endless "no, ma'ams" and "yes, ma'ams." There were lines, however. Wise wolves did not cross them. "Garvey, I am no Moondog. Do not forget it."

It pleased Yuri to see the False Moon sag in his seat, but she was too concerned by the conversation to gloat.

"How are his lessons with Kurt going?" Cautious, Yuri waded into the conversation.

Nadine guffawed. Even Eresna cracked a small smile.

Garvey responded. "How do you think? Never mind. Here, let me show you." He prepped himself like a stage actor. Suddenly, his eyes were wide, his face glowing with innocence. "Hey, everyone! Werewolves drink blood! Did you know that? Also, I'm pretty sure you're all slaves."

Nadine took up the role of a human. "But, Tovin. You can't be serious. We're all so awesome and important!"

Somehow, Garvey's eyes got wider, more childlike. "No, I'm earnest. I'm earnest as fuck."

Yuri chuckled. She couldn't help herself.

"And that's why he's dangerous," Eresna reminded them all, cutting the meat away from the funny bone.

Garvey waved at her worries. "Stall until he learns the script. Make Kurt earn his keep."

Optimism wasn't on Eresna's to-do list. She chatted with Garvey and Nadine about how to best address Tovin's issues. The three of them formed a circle. Cut off, Yuri made the situation less awkward for herself by sinking down into one of the chairs.

Yuri followed their conversation, making her own notations as she went along.

Any number of things could go wrong. On the obvious side, there was the storage room in the library. Already curious about it, Tovin spent a lot of time simply watching werewolves enter and leave. He'd pretend to read a book, but artifice wasn't his strong suit. Everyone knew.

"He may as well put it on a T-shirt," Nadine summarized. "Or announce it on a bullhorn."

Far more worrisome was the portal. Werewolves of all stripes knew exactly what it was. Despite its drab appearance, it thrummed with an almost sexual rhythm—a slow, methodical back and forth to ferment the blood. Hidden in the open, it was harmless to most humans, nothing more than an odd-looking door in the middle of a makeshift gallery of sorts. But it called to certain people. Those who felt the tug almost inevitably ended up seduced by it.

Tovin ventured near it a few times, turning his head to the side as though he heard something. Bad sign, bad start.

"Take him to it. See how it goes," Garvey suggested.

Nadine shook her head. "Yes, let's take our pyromaniacs to the firework stand next. See how that goes."

"It actually makes sense," Yuri ventured back to the conversation.

The three of them turned to look at her. Garvey's mouth was open in a big grin. For once, she—the sour killjoy—agreed with him. While she had their attention, Yuri volunteered her reasoning. "We've always taken a wait-and-see approach, but perhaps we should find out what we're dealing with before we decide what to do. Be preventative instead of reactive. The portal is kept out in the open so we can see when it calls out to humans. We would only be hastening the result if Tovin is drawn."

"There you go," Garvey said. "Rationalized like a pro."

Nadine gave her a dark look. Protective, her solution was to herd Tovin away from the library altogether. "Taking him to it puts him right on the path of danger."

"Oh, he'll eventually find the road himself," Garvey reiterated. "Sweet treat's got a built-in map."

Wasn't that the truth?

Red-faced, Nadine tantrumed more objections. Each of them road the wave differently.

One of Yuri's favorite things about Nadine was her rowdy, gentle love. It was like being held by a T. rex wearing combat boots. Sure its arms were short and stumpy, but you were super close to its heart as it stomped through the forest, trampling anything that got in both your paths.

Pragmatic at the start, driven only by the most advantageous outcome, Nadine eventually shifted alliances to passionate, fierce love for a few select. Yuri wasn't quite sure how, but it seemed Tovin made the cut.

"This is what's best for Tovin," Yuri assured her friend. "To keep him safe."

"This kid is Sookie-ing us," Garvey quipped. "He's so lovably prone to disaster."

No one understood the reference.

Nadine finally agreed after a few minutes of soul searching.

"Yes, fine." Eresna capitulated as well. "But I'm taking him. I don't trust any of you to be objective."

So it was agreed. They would bring Tovin to the portal connecting to the Door.

CHAPTER THIRTY-EIGHT: THE PORTAL

Seemingly weightless—even though two massive brackets held it in place—the door dominated the room. *Touch,* it seemed to say. The wood's dark grain was threaded with red veins, which spiraled in a dodgy, inconsistent pattern of loops and bends from top to bottom. Aside from the color of the wood, which Tovin had never seen before and thought looked otherworldly, it was unremarkable. The texture was coarse, the frame splintered. Worst of all, it stank like rotten potatoes. Tovin wrinkled his nose.

So why was he drawn to it? This was the third time today he'd circled back around. His hand twitched at his side, moving upward. A superstitious inkling pulled it away and told him touching would be very bad. Little hairs on the back of his neck, erect and pulsing, agreed there was something else, something ineffable, about the experience. Tovin brushed away those thoughts. Even as his hand slumped to his side and relief immediately followed, he scolded his superstitious self. There was nothing remarkable about this door.

Other explanations nagged at him. "What is it?"

He wasn't talking to himself. As always, there was someone with him. "Only a door."

Eresna. He was only moderately surprised to hear her voice. Sending him here felt like a test at the start, a preliminary run of some sort. Tovin, safely facing away, rolled his eyes. Something about her made him want to push a button. Through her, he was meant to feel invincible, powerful, untouchable. Knowing she was trying to cultivate these feelings, he suggested, "Maybe it's dangerous."

The energy in the room changed. She never called him out on it, but there was no doubt in Tovin's mind she knew he wanted to provoke her. Just as there was no doubt in his mind he'd succeeded.

Normally serene, smooth, the lines of her face were clunky. Tovin was unsure what emotion they were being told to represent. Instead of responding, she came and stood beside him, placing a reassuring—or warning—hand on top of his shoulder.

Beautiful. Confident. Eresna played the part of a queen very well. Standing next to her made him feel like a gauche joke. After all this time, he didn't wear his clothes any better. Unlike her. No matter what she wore—no matter how over-the-top it would have looked on anyone else—she looked fantastic. Today, she had on a taupe tulle number embroidered with a vibrant blue floral pattern.

Minutes passed. She didn't collect him or try to move him away from sculpture. Finally, the lines of her face relaxed until she was the polished queen there to guide him once again. When she spoke, her voice was soft, musical. The words fell out effortlessly. "This door was crafted a very long time ago. Looking at it makes me feel things I don't know how to express. Sometimes it feels as though it's asking me to touch it."

Hearing her echo his own concerns surprised him. Bonded. He didn't fully understand what it meant since nothing changed for him, but she had an uncanny ability to guess his feelings. Sooner or later, Tovin knew he was going to have to confront the notion she wasn't guessing. For now, he was willing to stay stuck in there's-a-reasonable-explanation mode.

"Only a door. As you said." He forced himself to sound unimpressed.

"But you said danger." Her lip quirked upward with some humor as it did when she found his lies amusing. Never nasty, those quick flashes gave him a glimpse of who she might be underneath the persona she cultivated. From time to time, he saw it when she interacted with her subjects. With them, she was open and generous. With the humans, she was closed, calculated. Tovin knew the difference. Seeing behind polite façades was his life before all of this. It was the only useful survival skill he brought with him.

"Time to go back, Tovin."

Once again, he got the feeling this was a test of some sort. Did he pass? Only Eresna knew.

She spun on her heel. Her steps made very little noise as she walked down the hall, a tiny click-clack as heel followed toe. To his ears, his own feet sounded like they belonged to a five-hundred pound, tap-shoe-wearing donkey as he clumped after her. Everything he did felt equally awkward. His speech was clunky—full of stops, false starts, filler words—his mannerisms were jittery, and he could never decide if he should or shouldn't look someone in the eye. Inept as she was flawless, he tumbled from one moment to the next.

She expected him to follow wherever. Obedient, like a dog.

He gave the door one last look.

Touch, it said.

Later, he promised himself.

He wasn't sure how he knew, but he got the sense the door heard him, and it was waiting.

* * *

Tovin was special in all the wrong ways. Yuri could tell from her Alpha Guardian's expression that she was sure the portal had indeed reached out to Tovin. Bad. Very bad. Humans who heard its call almost always went insane and had to be put down.

Yuri watched him leave with Eresna.

Grudgingly obedient, he followed her while thinking, *Wrong, wrong, wrong, wrong* about everything he did along the way. His feet were too loud. His breathing was too heavy. He'd said something improper, gave her a hand gesture he was sure she'd misinterpreted. Unwanted protectiveness tunneled its way through her, pushing practicality off to the side like upshot dirt. Goofy as the boy was, Yuri'd come to care about him all the same.

Yes, the Portal reached out to him, which was bad...but... "Tovin," Eresna said gently, "do not visit the gallery again without an escort. Understood?"

He gave her a small, confused nod. Yuri's heart swelled with love for both of them.

Yuri watched her Alpha Guardian shut the door to Tovin's room, sealing him inside using good, old-fashioned locks and a tiny bit of magic. At least Yuri knew he was safe through the night.

CHAPTER THIRTY-NINE: NOT SO SAFE

Come! a female voice urged Tovin out of bed.

"Not now," he said to it, pulling his blanket tighter around his body. Every waking hour was spent obeying—yes this, yes that, I'll get it—he'd be damned if he was going to be as subservient and useless in his sleep. No. He was going to go back to fighting the giant killer robot on a rampage throughout the city. For whatever reason, the shotgun that was also his hand was effective against the metallic menace. Blue and white sparks flew from its left shoulder as it tumbled to the ground, ready for the kill shot. Nearby, the man of his dreams—literally, Tovin supposed—clapped his hands to cheer him on. If previous iterations of the delusion were anything to go by, the two of them were going to do it regardless of what Tovin said next, even if it was something bad like, *Now the real sparks will fly.* Free from the pressure of being even slightly charming or original, Tovin raised his shotgun arm to finish his kill and—

It felt like someone had a carjack under his eyelids. A series of commands ticked them up ever so slightly with each iteration: *Now. Quickly. Now, now, now. TOVIN. NOW.*

"Later!" he snapped back.

His room surged up before him as the smoking cityscape with its nearly dead robot overlord fizzled away. Fluttering curtains made a whapping sound as the breeze blew them side to side, up and down. Hair scurried along his scalp ever so slightly, pulling a little bit on flesh that was suddenly hyperaware of any sign of contact. His bedroom door, the one leading out of his prison, was open. Light from the hall, a morphed cut-out rectangle, touched him all the way up to his groin.

Determined, he walked up to the door and shut it. "No. A whole lot of no," he said to whatever it was that opened it.

Tovin rolled back over on the bed and shut his eyes. Pitch black, the room didn't lend itself to shadows anymore. When a light moved across his face, it was the moon, it was his imagination, it was a werewolf there to check on him, it was... He opened his eyes briefly. A ghost. A motherfucking ghost. And she was the mysterious woman in blue. Great. Fucking fantastic.

Later, it said and settled down next to him.

* * *

Eventually, he followed it. Or her. He didn't know what ghosts wanted to be called. Perhaps there was some sort of PC ghost-specific pronoun floating out in the netherworld somewhere. He wasn't about to ask. Bad enough he was where he was, doing whatever it was he was doing. *A whole lot of no* turned into a terse *Okay* and then a *Fine, fine. I'm coming. Let me put some clothes on* as the young woman hummed an eerie, impossible to explain away waltz in his ear.

This way, she told him, waving her hand cheerfully.

Fear wasn't something Tovin could allow himself to feel at the moment. Since he was already being held captive by blood-sucking werewolves, he didn't think a ghost would add all that much to the danger equation. Besides, she seemed nice enough for someone dead. Their initial encounter aside—he supposed he could forgive her for the open door, the singing, and the not-quite-touching but touching—she had been reasonably polite, not at all prone to boos, chain clanks, or jump scares. Although Tovin could not make out many of her features, she seemed like she might be rather lovely; her long gown and spectrally wispy hair flowed behind her, ripples in a pond. Best of all, she didn't talk very much except to offer very succinct directions. There were no questions, no "tell me about yourself," no games, no periods of awkward silence. He was expected to follow, nothing more. More of the usual, Tovin supposed.

They ended up in the gallery. Very bad. He stopped to turn around. "Uh, why are we here?"

Come, she told him. It was less cheerful this time. Her brow furrowed in agitation. *Hurry!*

Well, he'd gone this far. Although he knew she was leading him to the strange door in the library, he supposed he may as well put one foot in front of the other and get down to it. The dead woman was dead set on getting her way. *Haha,* Tovin thought to himself.

And here he was. It looked the same as when he saw it last time. Again, he felt the same energy behind it, the overwhelming feeling that he should not, under any circumstances—

Touch it, she told him. Of course. When he didn't move, she repeated the command in the same agitated way from before. Tovin took a few tentative steps forward and ran his hand along the frame of the door. His face scrunched up as he concentrated on what he was doing rather than his companion, who had lost most of her good cheer and was now downright furious. *Here*, she told him while she tapped the middle of the door. *Touch it here. Now!*

Her tone was fierce. He obeyed in a rush, no longer thinking about anything beyond pleasing the entity so he could get back to the relative safety of his room. An electric shock went straight through him with a jolt. Tovin stepped back, grasping his left arm at the wrist as though he'd been bitten by something venomous and was trying to stop a toxin from going straight to his heart. Panting, he scrambled backward to gape, open-mouthed, at the door from a distance. It hadn't changed. Or had it? Though it was standing, Tovin got the sense it was in motion.

"Happy?" he asked the woman.

Her eyes, nothing more than bright lights in the darkness, gleamed.

CHAPTER FORTY: DEVIL WITH A BLUE DRESS

The portal in front of him was one of the hubs to the Door itself. Behind it, a whole other world waited. There were at least three humans there—Rigby, Lance, and Ace—who were about to have a bad day. They deserved it. Not that it mattered much to Garvey. Good or evil, they guarded the last two remaining vampires and were therefore in the way. Sure, he could take the vamps from them easily enough. But then they'd be alive to tell stories.

He had other problems right now.

Less discreet, Kijo's mandate could translate into almost anything. Garvey decided it meant he globetrotted using the portal in the Boo Hag rather than the one Mazgan had acquired. Garvey wondered if it would be enough for Kijo. Subtlety wasn't his defining trait, and this had a whiff of caution Kijo might detect.

Garvey puzzled over his options.

In front of him, the portal called out its steady, never ending mandate. *Touch.* "Hold up a tick," he told it. "I'm thinking."

As if it understood, the portal ramped up its efforts, sending out a wave of energy that twisted itself up along his spine.

Thinking became impossible. He wasn't clearheaded enough to plot any further mischief.

Garvey surrendered to its will. "All right, all right. Time to go pay a visit to Rigby and the gang."

* * *

Meanwhile, on the other side of the door...

"Come on." The girl giggled again as Rigby pulled her forward. "Best seat in the house." This was a sure thing. Women loved this shit. The danger, the thrill, the taboo of fucking while the floor beneath pulsated as the monster below unleashed its fury on whatever fool was this week's fodder. It was a scene that had played out for Rigby a hundred times before.

He knew what to say. "I'll let you push the button."

And she was in. It was the button. Chicks loved it. Rigby's friends looked at them both as he pulled her farther into the control room. They smiled wider when he shot them a quick wink and a thumbs up. Melinda pretended she didn't notice the exchange—the quick manspeak for *I'm totally getting this tonight. Give me your praise and approval. Rock on, Rigby. Rock on.*

"Where is it?" she asked shyly. Affectation or not, Rigby didn't care. The coy looks, the way she stroked his muscles, her rapt interest in his job...it all made him hard.

"It's right over here, doll." Rigby cool-walked to the panel and presented the button as though he was one of those game-show girls presenting a prize. "It's even red. Like blood." Ghoulish, he drew the word out while sticking his fingers up to his incisors to simulate fangs. His boys laughed. Obligingly, Melinda shrieked attractively and drew into a scared ball, even placing her hands to her reddened cheeks. Nice.

Then, again. "No. It," she whispered, as though she thought she would be overheard. Reverence, almost delight, touched her voice.

"Oh! Ho! Right for the jugular, huh, doll? Molly, it..." He whispered the word in the same hushed tone. "...is right below us. She's sleeping. Hungry." His buddies—more props as far as Rigby was concerned—all oohed in unison, the usual pre-sex soundtrack. A hundred times. A million times. A billion. Rigby was red-button deep in pussy that wanted into this room. The girl shivered in response but smiled at the same time.

"When does it...she...come out?"

"Her door opens on a timer. Right at midnight. You'll know when it's time. You'll hear her favorite song."

"Her song?" Melinda acted surprised that he would do such a thing.

"Yeah, me and the boys gave her a theme. Let us know when the show is about to start. You'll hear it, doll." With that, he turned, dismissing her for the moment. He had man stuff to do. She had man stuff to watch him do. "All right, down to business. How's our guy doing?"

"About how you would expect." Lance beamed his toothy, crooked grin. No girl, no matter how desperate she was to see this show, would fuck that boy. He got one to jerk him off once. Everyone watched through the blinds while the girl turned her grimaced-yet-determined face away as Lance huffed and wheezed his way to completion. She didn't even get to push the button. Rigby was sure she felt cheated through the whole process. "He's about to shit himself."

"Let's see what we've got, boys. Open 'er up."

On his command, the metal support beneath the planked wood floor slid away. Light creaked between the slats, barely illuminating the face of a young man, probably midtwenties, tied up with ropes in the room below. When the metal door clanked into its casement, the sound made him jerk his head quickly toward the noise. "Hello?" Desperate. Tired. It never failed to get Rigby started.

"Hiya! Comfortable?" His friends chuckled. Some fake poor-thing noise came from Melinda. She grabbed at his shoulder as if to stop him from teasing the man any further. But there was a glow—her eyes, her cheeks—urging him to continue.

"Please," the man began as each one always did. "I haven't done anything. Let me out."

It was hard to see tonight's special. What little light went to the lower level reflected off dust particles, making the facial features of those trapped below appear warped and grainy. The person who built the facility no doubt did it by design. In the old days, this was a horrible but necessary task only given to those deemed suitable. No one wanted to see the victim or think about him back then. Hell, they probably knew the person. Today, it was the job of any tech who could push a button and withstand a few minutes of screaming and then body disposal. Rigby was self-aware enough to realize he was exactly the type of person who would want this job, even going so far as to ask his superior for a high-powered lamp. Riffraff-ish, or so he was told. "We know, man. We know. It'll be over soon, though."

All smiles, he and the boys continued the prep while the man begged for his life and the girl looked down at him with feigned discomfort. She was trying hard to make out his features without looking like that's exactly what she was doing. It was enough to make Rigby think about a second date. Of course, then he'd have to figure out some way to get Molly back into the other room without pushing Melinda down into the pit. Hardly seemed worth the effort. "That about does it. Let's run the security lock."

A hundred times. A million times. A billion times. The system was always flawless—locking and unlocking, then resetting itself as it was designed to do. System checks were supposed to be done daily every five hours, but Rigby only did them the night of the event and only for the pageantry of it. Decisions you reflect on when the door jams at 11:57 PM.

"What's wrong?" The girl furrowed her brow as the gear clanked and clanked, not catching. "The door is going to shut, isn't it?"

"Yes, of course." Nonplussed, Rigby pushed the lock button over and over. "What's going on, Ace?" The tech guy, another guy exactly like Rigby but with a longer title, gave him a wild look that said, *I dunno. I don't fucking know.* He swatted Rigby's hand away to push and re-push the same button.

"The door is going to close, right? It's going to close before twelve?" At 11:59 PM, the girl stared at him and shrieked. "It's closing now. Tell me it's closing."

"It's closing." Everyone looked beneath them. The man below peered back up, a smile on his face, a long incisor poking out on his bottom lip. No longer begging or crying, the man looked more amused than anything else.

Twelve AM. Devil with a Blue Dress, the song Rigby heard a hundred, a million, a billion times before started to play.

Beneath them, another door slid open and out came Molly. Not wearing a wig or shades to match, she skipped the man below and went straight for the hatch. There was a crash at the door. One of the planks buckled with the force of the impact. Rigby glanced down to see one pale white esurient eye, as glassy and clear as a child's marble, glowering up at him before the next impact. This one dislodged one of the planks, enough for one hand—clawed and grasping. Molly hissed each time her arm retracted with nothing.

Everyone had his own way. Ace cried while he pawed at a door that was layers upon layers of steel. That door locked like it should have. No one was grateful. Lance took over button-pushing duties. Melinda stared dumbly down at the man below, who looked back up with some half-apologetic grimace. Rigby regressed to a childlike state where sensory deprivation made everything better. He covered his ears, trying to block out the song. Frustrated, he fled to the back room to hide in the hammock, rolling himself up in the fabric so he at least blocked most of his vision. Melinda snapped out of whatever state she was in as she watched him leave. She started to scream. And scream. And scream. It felt like a hundred times, a million times, a billion times before she was done.

Little other motivation was needed on Molly's part. One more charge at the door was all it took. The planks snapped as the song once again hit its refrain. Up came Molly. Her tattered blue dress hung in threads at her waist so that her breasts were exposed. Claw marks branched out across her chest; deep veins ran from her throat to a once-pert left breast. Both the dress and the girl were lovely at some point. Rigby always liked to picture her as a high-class debutant on her way to a spring dance—a matching blue flower corsage on her wrist—when she was attacked. At some point, he was told she was actually the daughter of a whore, and she had stolen the dress from the daughter of an affluent businessman. They let her wear the dress when she met Timothy, the vampire in the holding facility adjacent to hers. Rigby always maintained the first image.

Unlike Timothy, Molly did not procrastinate—a quick killer. After a few moments of screaming, gurgling, and pleas that started off as frantic and then yielded to half-hearted, Rigby's coworkers and his date were all dead. Sucking and slurping noises followed, almost worse than the screaming.

Rigby did his best to suppress his whimpers as he listened to her feed, hoping Molly would simply forget about him and retreat to the basement once her hunger slackened. Often times, his discarded date waited for her there. Even creatures had simple memories and routines. She would leave, expecting more food to be waiting for her below and this would be an awesome story he'd tell to his next date the next hundred, million, billion times he brought girls here.

The song ended. Rigby doubled his efforts to remain silent, relying on Molly's inability to count—three humans being the same as four to her. Sniffing. Then, "Rigby."

The few times he heard her speak before were always remembered with a thrill. He loved hearing soft murmurs exchanged with whatever man or woman was on that week's menu. He loved it even more when the captive tried to talk back, when Molly's food tried to reason with her. This time each syllable of his name pulled something out of him.

"Rigby." Dainty feet clad in torn-up blue slippers traced a path to him until he could hear the hem of the dress rustle across floorboards, nearer and nearer until it finally dawned on Rigby that she must be very close for that type of detail.

"Rigby." Above him, Molly scrutinized him—part curiosity, part recognition. Denial never had time to work its way to acceptance. He was still telling himself, *I'm going to be fine, just fine* when Molly cut his brain's connection to the rest of his body.

Molly did go back to her cell, Rigby's head clutched to her chest. Lounging in what passed as her sleeping area was the man she was meant to kill that night. She sniffed the air again. No, no man. A monster like her. She lifted her trophy to show him. "Rigby," she explained.

"Good Golly, Miss Molly," Garvey said with a chuckle.

CHAPTER FORTY-ONE: THE DOOR

Garvey stood before an ancient doorway between worlds, created and sustained by powerful magic far beyond what any of his kind possessed. Dragon magic. No one knew where the dragons had gone. If they were dead, alive, sleeping, or exploring other worlds, it was anyone's guess. But they left behind the Door and its portals, which connected other worlds to the Door.

Over the course of its history, it had been called by many names—some reverent, some irreverent, some practical, some scornful, some holy. Now it was called Vukojebina, a cheeky nod to its role in the creation of new wolves, who looked upon its threshold their first time after passing their test. It was one disrespect Garvey took exception to.

Half-breeds like him never stood here as triumphant new wolves. He was the first False Moon wolf to ever stand before it at all. Now, at last, he was here as some type of victor. The moment was undermined by his two vampire companions. Molly, who kept saying "Rigby" over and over as if it were the only word she knew—for all Garvey knew, it was—and Timothy, who kept talking about how hungry he was in only the most consistent and simplistic of terms.

They were poor company for a moment as magical as this one could have been. Garvey found himself wishing they were, at the very least, the suave vampires from television shows and movies. Realistically, the undead were stupid. And they stank. Decomposing bodies tended to do that, even those repurposed by powerful magic. Garvey always found himself resenting humanity's romantic notions to the contrary. Still, the pompous aristocratic bloodsuckers going on about ancient rights and species superiority or even lovelorn ancient teenagers moping after some human whose stupidity seemed statistically improbable would have been preferable. Mostly, he wished they were Moondogs like himself who would understand everything he was feeling.

"Hungry." Timothy said it at least once every five seconds it seemed. The word was usually followed by, *eat now, blood,* or *human,* each stressed with more force as if Garvey did not understand Tim's needs and further explanation was needed.

"Rigby." Molly always followed after Timothy with a sneer. She had lost some of her good humor from before—the toothy smiles and the gurgled chuckles all replaced with a persistent scowl. Though it seemed unlikely, Garvey got the sense she actually remembered Timothy—remembered and hated—but that was impossible for a vampire. Goldfish monsters. She was probably hungry, impatient for another kill.

"Hold up several ticks. We'll eat soon." He'd been reassuring them of that for the last hour, at least. Neither seemed impressed by this point.

Molly made what sounded oddly like a disappointed sigh, a low clucking deep within her chest followed afterward. Timothy stressed, "Human," once more. After another grumble and a sideways glance at her companion that looked an awful lot like she was denouncing him as an idiot, Molly moved forward and placed her hands on the door. Synapses were required. The passage only functioned if the person using it could select criteria. Garvey smiled at the long-dead woman. "You have to have this many," he held up one finger, "brain waves to use this ride, Molly."

Under her fingers, the door shimmered. Magic sought out what the user wanted, cycling through all of the various possibilities until only a few scattered worlds remained. Molly wanted human blood. Unfortunately for Earth, it had the most options. Most of humanity was destroyed on the other planets during the population booms of his kind and the subsequent wars that erupted. Earth was meant to be a new start where they could correct the mistakes of the past and maintain a constant and well-regulated food source. With hungry eyes, Molly looked at the new world—a fresh start for her and her kind. "Yes." It was the first thing she had said other than Rigby.

Any other wolf might have been alarmed—wolves and the unexpected did not get along. Consistent, predictable, dull: his kind liked the world to function according to rules and structure. Yet here they were with Molly's rapt face pressed into the frame of time while Timothy stood behind panting out frantic words, *Human, blood, human, blood, eat, eat, eat.* A more sophisticated wolf would have at least been curious about how something like this happened. Garvey wasn't sophisticated or typical. He didn't care how it worked, nor was he bothered by the fact it did. Unexpected and him got along perfectly fine.

He shrugged and laughed a little bit. "Whelp, time to go make a few people have a very bad day." He pushed Molly out of the way gently. If she did have the ability to remember, he hardly wanted to be on her bad side. Stupid and fetid notwithstanding, vampires had fangs.

"This part requires a bit more finesse." Once the user selected a world, a corresponding portal had to be found to connect the two worlds. Garvey knew exactly where to look for one. The Door shimmered again until a room appeared. Inside the room, a blond-haired man looked back at them without seeing. Extreme focus scrunched all his features together so that his eyes and nose pinched in the center as a fleshy concentric mess. Garvey could make out the green of the eyes— unmistakably his sweet treat.

Of course, Tovin would be there. What a nerd. Garvey felt a moment's pinch of envy that the portal had called out to Tovin.

Surprised, irritated, Garvey held on to the leashes as both vampires rushed at the image. Luckily, whatever allowed Molly to sort through worlds did not allow her or Timothy to travel. The two vampires remained pressed against the frame, clawing and licking at the surface while Tovin continued to inspect the passage on the other side.

"Yes," Molly repeated whenever Tovin stepped closer.

"Hungry." Timothy again.

Molly looked at Tovin, a yearning not so dissimilar from Garvey's own and reached her fingers toward the door as Tovin did the same on the other side with a timidity that Garvey remembered all too well. Sweet treat couldn't even commit to deviancy with vigor. And he was being very naughty. Eventually, his hand found its way to the surface. The muscles in his face relaxed as he stroked the boundary, and Garvey found himself remembering close to the same transformation in the woods when Tovin's mouth finally opened to Garvey's.

For a moment, Molly's hand lined up with his. She jerked back on contact and then looked to her hand quizzically. "Felt him."

"Oh, yeah?" Surprises abound tonight. She hadn't done any of this during their test run.

"Yes. Felt him." Looking at her hand, she traced her palm where Tovin supposedly made contact. A new emotion slowly nudged out the dull animal hunger in Molly's face until she almost looked like she was back on track for the dance. She stole a dress. She could steal the handsome young man on another world, too.

"Dibs," Garvey said. Molly jerked her head in Garvey's direction with a scowl. "He likes men, and you're dead. It wouldn't work out."

"Mine." She wasn't having any of it.

"We'll sort it out when we get there. For now, let's agree we're not going to eat him, right?"

"Eat." The animal was back. She lunged at the door again, pushing Timothy aside.

"No. Don't eat."

"No eat."

"There you go. You got it." He watched her grin and prance eagerly. "That's not making me feel super optimistic, Molly."

CHAPTER FORTY-TWO: FORM AND FUNCTION

Relief irritated Garvey. Watching Tovin's backside as he hustled out the room shouldn't make him feel anything other than vague lust, perhaps some annoyance with the young man for putting him in a position where he had to stand around and wait while two hungry vampires tugged at their leashes. Instead, he let go of all the dread he'd been holding onto on the other side of the portal. Tovin was safe.

Maybe. Sort of. Garvey gritted his teeth at the ideas nagging him.

Be less discreet.

Again. This was the last order Kijo gave him before turning him loose, a direct contradiction to Mazgan's orders to keep everything low-key for now. Fretting over how to compromise between the two orders became Garvey's new pastime ever since Kijo pulled him aside and spelled out his options—obey her or die.

At least she was always straightforward. Mazgan was more of an artist about the whole thing, waiting for perfect moments to unleash a master plan, which would paint the world with broad strokes. Everyone needed to know who did it, why he did it, and how it was going to change everything. Kijo only wanted the world to function. She didn't especially care how that was accomplished or who accomplished it. *Art v. science,* Garvey supposed.

Here he had both. Predators understood opportunity—it had a smell, a feel, an electrical current akin to sexual awareness that teased at possibilities. The two vampires at his side sensed it the same way he did. Watching Tovin was akin to watching a vulnerable animal swim to shore.

Leashes snapped, snapped, snapped at the force of the two creatures jerking themselves toward what instinct said would be an easy meal, trying to close that all important gap before it was too late. Garvey felt his teeth protrude from his gumline as he watched Tovin, who was now nearly outside of his reach, almost too far away to be of use, with a strange mixture of arousal and hunger.

"We did agree we're not going to eat him?" Garvey asked Molly. He didn't bother with Timothy, lost cause.

"Eat him," Molly said.

"No, don't eat him."

"Ummm," she responded.

Garvey told himself he was doing this to prevent the death of his pack. One human boy is worth that. Garvey dropped the leashes.

* * *

Supernatural creatures were such assholes, Tovin thought. The ghost left without so much as a "Thanks" or "Good-bye" after she'd made him follow her.

Minus an explanation, he was left to assume business here was concluded and he was free to go, so off he went quickly as he possibly could. His footsteps sounded like shotgun blasts in the empty room. Under the constant, heavy-handed thudding reminder he wasn't supposed to be there, Tovin thought he heard a leather whip crack. *Only imagination*, he decided, although he simultaneously made up a very long list of other things it could be.

Then the whipping noises stopped and the heavy thuds began, staggered like out-of-time drumbeats. Tovin hurried his pace, gradually at first, but soon he was running without knowing what the danger was, only that previous history suggested it wasn't likely to be anything good.

Something slammed into Tovin's back with enough force to launch him to the floor. He hit it with his shoulder, sliding a few feet before righting himself to face forward. What looked like an old man was on him an instant later, reaching with water-parched hands cracked like dry earth. Facial skin drew up in a feral snarl and puckered up around his eyes. The dull brown of the irises were covered with layers of cataracts. Not an attractive package. And then there was the smell. Jesus. It was rotting potato levels of earthy-yet-sour. Tovin scrunched up his nose and held his breath.

Not human, Tovin realized. "Get off!" he yelled, more of a reflex than a serious command.

The thing hissed in response. Saliva dripped between teeth gaps; pointed yellow canines mired in a glossy-white gumline rushed forward, snapping.

Tovin grappled with wrinkled flesh that slid jellylike around bone. He kept trying to push the creature away as it lunged again and again and again, but his hands only sunk into flesh or slid around it. Punches made it hiss louder. Insults made no difference. Tovin refused to plead.

"Off!" he repeated. This time he planted his left leg in the thing's stomach and pushed outward. The creature staggered backward but, relentless, it quickly regained balance and charged before Tovin could pick himself off the ground to either run away or put himself in a better fighting position. Once again on top, the creature snapped and clawed. Burning pain launched itself through Tovin's arm and into his shoulder as nails grated his flesh, twisting up chunks of flesh with each swipe.

Tovin assumed it couldn't get any worse. After thinking that, the sky didn't open up to rain exactly, but he heard the same out-of-time thuds he heard before—louder and louder—until a shape emerged. Tovin was pretty sure that meant he was going to be dinner for two. The other creature, this one female, looked every bit as hungry, a single-minded animal gleam in the eye, and moved toward him with as much purpose as her male counterpart.

Instead, she sank her teeth into the collarbone of Tovin's assailant, shaking herself once her teeth pierced through flesh. The male howled in fury. Claws that had been ripping at Tovin's flesh windmilled up above its head in long arcs as it tried to dislodge its attacker. The female bit in deeper, this time on the side of the other creature's throat, and twisted upward. Black ooze the consistency of river-bottom silt dribbled out of the puncture wounds at the neck. A large bubble of it pushed past tightly clenched lips. Without much ceremony beyond that, the thing's eyes closed, its legs stopped twitching, and it looked...deader. Tovin guessed.

The theoretically female ate at it. She stopped briefly to look up at Tovin as he slouched away from the scene. "No eat," she said, mouth full of dribbling flesh. "No eat Ovin."

"Thanks," Tovin said without much certainty.

"Good girl, Molly. No eat Tovin." Garvey looked down at their topic of conversation, who was panting and clutching at the long gash in his arm. Almost absentmindedly, the werewolf bent down and healed him. Afterward, his expression darkened, his voice deepened. "You're not supposed to be here. Were those bites or claw marks?"

In shock, all Tovin could manage was a weak "I know. And, uh, claws."

Brown eyes veered further away from mirth. "It would be best if you didn't say anything about this to anyone, sweet treat."

"Treat." Molly, the creature, said to them both.

"Stop that." Garvey glared at the creature, who said it again between mouthfuls. Bewildered, the werewolf shook his head at it.

Getting out words was a struggle for Tovin, especially since Molly was at his feet happily eating away. Every so often she'd lift up her head to smile at him, her mouth covered in corpse gunk. Bile worked its way to his mouth. He swallowed it back down and forced himself to look away from the scene and back up to Garvey. "What is that thing?"

"A vampire."

"Oh." Tovin sighed at himself and tried to start again. Foggy, he shook his head and stumbled out, "A what?"

Garvey repeated himself with less patience. "Vampire."

"Okay, but—"

"No more questions. And what did I say to you about trying not to die?"

"Just that. Try not to die."

"Right." Garvey quirked his eyebrow at the response. "Well, you're doing a shit job of it. What are you doing here?"

"My bedroom door was open." Tovin did not mention the ghost or anything else.

"Ah," Garvey chuckled, the brown eyes lit up with glee. "I know how that goes. All right, you seized the day. Did forbidden stuff. Fun, fun. Time to go back upstairs, get in your jammies, and then go back to bed."

"Wait. What are you doing—"

Garvey cut him off again. "Bed."

"Bed," Molly agreed.

"That's right, Molly. Say good-bye."

The thing jolted up quickly and stretched out toward Tovin. "Feel him," it said and then did exactly that. Ick-covered hands found their way to Tovin's face, to his hair, then to the line of his neck. Like the dead male, her pale blue eyes were covered in cataracts. Questions sort of flew out the window the longer the thing kept stroking him. Why Garvey was there, why he had two vampires—well, one now—or what he planned to do with them. None of it seemed especially pressing anymore. All that mattered was getting out of there.

Garvey's face matched Tovin's in disgust. The line of his mouth was drawn and twisted so that one half went up and the other down. "Very, very weird," he said. Then, just like that, he shrugged it off. "Oh well. Like I said...go. And, uh, keep this to yourself."

"Go," Molly echoed.

Tovin went.

CHAPTER FORTY-THREE: THE CLOSET

Gunk from the vampire's touch puckered his skin. Where it dried, it pulled. The glue-like substance was a pungent reminder of his recent brush with death. Tovin wiped it off using his sleeve. Flakes of it lazed down to the ground, falling like snow.

Shaking, hands gripping his knees, he slouched over to regain his breath. Stopping only made the burning in his lungs worse, the pain in his side more acute.

He straightened himself up to move forward but stopped in his tracks.

Try not to die was generally good advice.

Tovin knew he wasn't following it when he pressed the pause button on fleeing to gawk at the now open janitor's closet. Tedious instinct asserted exploring the closet defied common sense. It tweaked his unwilling limbs toward safety, but idiocy would not be denied once the woman in blue appeared right next to it.

Tovin, she said, *I opened the door for you. They don't know you're out yet.*

"No," he told her, "I've been dumb enough for one day, thanks."

Not nearly, she responded. *More than happy to haunt you until you agree.*

Given one could be worse than the other, Tovin felt this was a situation where clarification necessary. "What do you mean by haunt exactly?"

Unlock your door over and over. Bet they'll be mad when they wake up.

Well played, ghost.

Tovin staggered toward danger. Grave-like, the black rectangle of the door appeared to slouch into nothing. No light came in or went out. The only sound was his own heavy breathing, the concerning pulse of his frantic heart.

Tovin fiddled with the edges of the wall for a switch.

No lights, the ghost informed him.

"What good is it to me open it, then?"

Keep going, she ordered without further explanation. *Faster.*

He followed her down the stairs, pausing every so often to feel out the lay of the land with his feet, to search for the end of the wall with his hand. Eventually the ground became even. Tovin stumbled into what felt like a vast room. Stagnant air laced with the smell of mold tickled his nose. Sneezing, Tovin looked around for some sign of the ghost.

"Okay, I'm here. Why?"

She appeared in front of him. In the darkness, she was two pale eyes, the vague outline of a head—more ghostlike than she'd ever been before. Tovin gasped.

Sorry, she apologized.

"No problem," Tovin assured her. "You can't help that you're dead."

He thought she smiled as she lifted up her arm to point toward what looked like nothing but more darkness. Staggering, Tovin put his hands out in front of himself, moving forward zombielike. When his outstretched hands hit something solid, he stopped.

"Now what?"

Read.

A soft light came from the dead woman's body.

In front of him were rows and rows of files that appeared to be death records.

"Whelp, you can't say they're not meticulous," Tovin commented.

Read. Hurry.

Tovin grabbed three or four at first. And then he grabbed more and more.

Each one he pulled down had the same thing written down for cause of death. *The Door. The Door. The Door.*

ABOUT THE AUTHOR

Jacqueline Rohrbach is a thirty-six-year-old creative writer living in windy central Washington. When she isn't writing strange books about bloodsucking magical werewolves, she's baking sweets, or walking her two dogs, Nibbler and Mulder. She also loves cheesy ghost shows, especially when the hosts call out the ghost out like he wants to brawl with it in a bar. You know, "Come out here, you coward! You like to haunt little kids. Haunt me!" Jackee laughs at this EVERY time.

She's also a hopeless World of Warcraft addict. In her heyday, she was a top parsing disc priest. She became a paladin to fight Deathwing, she went back to a priest to cuddle pandas, and then she went to a shaman because I guess she thought it would be fun to spend an entire expansion underpowered and frustrated. Boomchicken for Legion!

Twitter: https://www.twitter.com/ImmutableMoon

NineStar Press, LLC

www.ninestarpress.com